Also by Kimberly Mullins

Notebook Mysteries Series
Divided Lives (aka K.R. Mullins)
1897 A Mark Sutherland Adventure

LIGHTS, CAMERA, Murder!!!

LIGHTS, CAMERA, Murder!!!

KIMBERLY MULLINS

Lights, Camera, Murder!!!

Copyright © JKJ books, LLC 2024

First edition: November 2024

All rights reserved.

No part of this book may be reproduced in any form or by any electronic or mechanical means, including information storage and retrieval systems, without written permission from the author, except for the use of brief quotations in a book review.

Mailing address for JKJ books, LLC; 17350 State Highway 249, STE 220 #3515 Houston, Texas 77064

Library of Congress Control Number: 2024921894

ISBN (paperback) 979-8-9916865-2-5

ISBN (hardback) 979-8-9916865-1-8

ISBN (ebook) 979-8-9916865-0-1

This is a work of fiction. It is based on historical events within the New York and California 1913.

Edited by Kaitlyn Katsoupis, Strictly Textual

Cover Art by More Visual, Ltd

*To Jonathan and Joshua-my favorite boys who eat ice cream when I have a bad day.
To Claudia, your visits mean so much to me.*

Chapter One

The heroine jumped from the out-of-control train, hitting the ground hard, and rolled away as it sped by.

The audience gasped, waiting to see what adventure she would move on to next.

The piano rang out, punctuating the movie's action.

"The audience is full tonight," whispered Merle Cooper into her sister's ear.

Jean kept playing the piano. "I know," she said, casting a furtive glance to her left.

Her sister's gaze followed Jean's. "Well, well," Merle said as she looked at the man who'd snagged Jean's interest.

"Hush, the movie's playing," Jean whispered, pulling her gaze from the tall red-headed man. "The end is coming up." She watched the screen and gave the final scenes a loud clang on the piano. The audience clapped as the film ran out.

The lights came up and the people started to move to the aisles that led to the small lobby of the theater.

The man who held the two sister's interest, Patrick Flannigan, sat with his sister Lottie and her girlfriend Elise.

"Ready to go?" asked Elise.

Lottie and Patrick nodded an affirmative; their small group

stood and walked with the crowds toward the lobby. Patrick stopped and studied the theater entrance. Without turning, he said, "You can go on ahead without me."

Lottie looked at Patrick's retreating figure then at Elise. Elise shrugged. Lottie had an idea of why he wanted to go back into the theater. He'd brought them to watch the same film multiple times over the past week. "Forget something in there?"

He looked toward her. "Yeah, I think I did." They watched as he headed back in.

Elise walked up to Lottie. "Home?"

Lottie placed her hat on her head and pinned it in place. "Maybe a stop at the tearoom first?" she suggested.

Elise nodded and they strolled hand in hand out of the lobby entrance onto the crowded streets.

Patrick walked determinedly toward the theater. The curtain had been moved to cover the entrance. He pushed it aside and was surprised to see the movie running again. This time without sound. The piano player was up on the stage, acting out parts of the movie!

Patrick watched the woman mimic the actor's wide gestures and fear of the villain. When the actress went to jump off the train, the woman tucked her hair behind her ear and then jumped as well. He started forward in surprise to catch her. He needn't have worried; she somersaulted off the stage and landed on her feet almost directly in front of him.

When she saw him, she jumped back and shouted, "Hey! You're not supposed to be here!"

Patrick silently studied her and answered, "I, uh, I came back for something."

"What?" she asked suspiciously and tapped her foot on the wood floor. The sound could be heard echoing in the empty room.

He moved past her to his seat and picked up his hat. He flipped it in his hand, and it landed on his head in one neat move.

She nodded. "Cute. Now that you have it, you can leave."

He walked toward the entrance. He stopped at the curtain and turned toward her. "How did you do that?"

"What?"

"That jump from the stage. Isn't it dangerous?"

"It can be," she admitted, "but I know what I'm doing."

"How..." he started when a voice interrupted him.

"Jean! Jean!"

"In here, Merle," the woman in front of him called out.

The woman appeared in the doorway. Patrick's eyes widened. The woman had light blonde hair, that fell in short waves to her neck. Her dress was silver and much shorter than most women wore. He couldn't help but stare at her.

Jean and Merle were used to the attention Merle attracted. They both ignored him. "Are you headed out?" Jean asked her sister.

"Yeah, the party's started. Wanna come?"

This was a familiar question and Jean answered as she always did. "No, I don't think so. Don't stay out too late. I'll lock the door behind me."

"Don't wait up," Merle admonished, her wrap dropping off her shoulder and revealing her arm.

Patrick frowned at the scar he saw there.

"Bye." Merle adjusted her wrap to cover her arm; she noticed his attention, smiled broadly, and winked at him before she turned and sauntered off.

Jean just shook her head and watched her leave. Once the curtain fell back, she turned to Patrick. The movie continued to play behind her, illuminating her figure. "On your way now," she said to Patrick, waving him away.

Instead of moving, he asked, "Need any help cleaning up?"

She tilted her head at him. "Know how to use a broom?"

"I think I can manage it."

Jean went to the small room beside the stage and reappeared with two brooms. She tossed one at him, which he caught deftly. "Start at the front and work your way back," she directed.

They began sweeping and the room was completed in short order. "What's your name?" she asked as she took the broom from him and returned them to the closet.

"Patrick Flannigan."

She turned back to him. "Thanks for helping, Patrick. I'm Jean Cooper."

"It's nice to meet you."

They stared at each other for a long moment. She pulled her eyes away from him and walked toward the lobby, Patrick following her. She walked to the small ticket booth and got her jacket. They walked out and she turned to lock the door behind them.

The sidewalk was empty. The crowd that had been at the movie had moved on to other destinations.

"Would you like to go for a walk?" he asked.

"You know, I think I would."

"Which way?" Patrick didn't mention he had a car. He wanted to spend as much time with Jean as possible.

"I live that way," she said, pointing to her right.

He nodded and they started toward her home.

Jean cast a glance toward him. "So, what do you do, Patrick?"

"I'm a policeman. I moved here this year from Chicago."

"Was that your girlfriend you were sitting with earlier?" Jean asked bluntly.

He smiled at that. "You noticed me?"

She stayed silent and he couldn't read her expression in the limited light.

"It was my sister and her girlfriend," he supplied.

"Hmm."

"What about you?"

She understood the question. "I'm not seeing anyone."

He mulled that over as they continued to walk. She stopped suddenly in front of an apartment building. "This is my home." She turned to go into the building.

He put out his hand to stop her. "Jean, would you like to go out with me sometime?"

"I would," she answered. "There's a phone in the hallway." She pulled out a pencil and paper, scribbling on it before handing it to him. "Or you can reach me at the theater after 3 pm each day."

"I'll see you soon," he promised.

Jean nodded and smiled slightly. "I'm looking forward to it." She entered and turned back to wave. He was still there and nodded toward her. He turned and walked away.

She shook her head and walked up the stairs to hers and Merle's apartment. It was located on the fifth floor, and she was careful not to step too hard. In the past, she'd run up the stairs for exercise and had gotten yelled at on all five of the floors. At her door, she put the key in the lock and opened it. The lights were on, and the room was brightly lit. "Why are the lights on?" she muttered as she pulled off her sweater. At that moment, her sister sauntered out of the bathroom in her nightgown.

That's why. "You're home early," Jean remarked as she folded up her sweater.

"The party was boring," Merle said, playing with the ribbon that was wrapped around her short hair.

"Hmm. That's probably a good thing. You never seem to get enough rest."

Merle dropped the ribbon and put her hands on her hips. "Jean, what did that man want tonight?"

"What man?" Jean asked coyly.

"You know, the large good-looking redhead," her sister said in exasperation.

"Oh, that man," Jean replied drolly.

"Jean," Merle said threateningly, raising her fist.

Jean held up her hands. "Hey, now. There's no need for violence. He was just a nice man who walked me home."

"Why?" Merle asked, dropping her fist to her side.

"Why? He just wanted to walk me home."

"Yeah, I know that. What did he talk about?"

Instead of answering, Jean asked, "How about you tell me why you're asking about him."

Merle dropped her hand from her hips and walked to the couch. She dropped down and put a pillow over her face. She lowered it and said, "Jean, he's a copper."

"I know," Jean said and sat in a chair in front of the couch.

"You know!"

"Yeah, he told me. How did you know?"

"I recognized the woman with him, Lottie Flannigan. She was involved in that Becker mess. I mentioned her and a tall redhead to a man at the party. He said he's seen him around her before and that he's a copper." She laid her head back. "Did he mention me?"

Jean frowned. "Why would he?"

Her sister glared at her, and she responded. "The answer is no."

"Then what did you talk about?" Merle asked, leaning toward her.

"You know, there's other topics than you. We just talked about normal things."

"Good. Maybe that's the extent of it," Merle said and moved the pillow to the end of the couch and laid down.

"Until tomorrow."

Merle sat up quickly, holding her head. The ups and downs were making her dizzy. "What's this about tomorrow?"

"He wants to see me again."

"Why?"

Jean sighed. "Merle, I know you're the pretty one, but occasionally men do like to talk to me."

Merle grimaced. "Full of myself, aren't I?"

"Just a little bit." Jean grinned, holding her hand up with her thumb and forefinger a small distance apart. "Anyway, I think he just wants to get to know me."

Merle was still dubious. "You'll let me know if he starts asking questions about me?"

"You have my word."

Chapter Two

Patrick's apartment

Patrick opened his door still thinking about Jean. *The lights were on!* He stopped, reached for his gun, and looked for the intruder.

Lottie came out of the kitchen with a drink in her hand. "Whoa there, cowboy. I'm not armed."

"I thought you were a burglar." He walked toward the kitchen came back with a bottle of beer and took a long drink.

"One that turned on all your lights and helped himself to a drink?" Lottie asked, sitting on the couch.

"Well, you know. What're you doing here, anyway?"

"I had to know If you talked to her."

"I did."

"You did?"

He grinned and sat next to her on the couch. "You don't have to sound so amazed. I have had other dates."

"Not since you moved here."

He shrugged. "Just busy with other stuff."

She hit him. "Well, tell me. What's she like?"

He took another drink. "Her name is Jean. She plays the piano."

"I know she plays the piano, goober. What else?"

"She is... She's unexpected," he said and explained the summersault she did off the stage that exactly matched the one the actress did in the movie.

"Well, you should be used to women who surprise you," Lottie teased again.

"This is true. Aunt Emma and you keep me on my toes. Speaking of surprises, when is his appeal?"

"You mean Becker?"

"Yes."

"It's scheduled for November."

"Does he have a chance? Will he survive all of this?" Charles Becker had been a lieutenant caught up in the corruption that had infiltrated the New York Police Department. The authorities were using him to take the fall for the murder of local businessman, Herman Rosenthal. He'd been found guilty once, but the courts determined an appeal was necessary due to irregularities in the first trial.

"I think there's enough to get a new trial and from there... I'm not sure of the outcome. This will at least provide him a chance."

"But you're not involved this time?"

"No, we finished that when Chris and I sent our letter of appeal. This time, we'll be spectators." Chris and Emma had worked on the Becker case as associates for Justice John Goff. They had documented the mistakes made throughout and communicated those to the proper officials.

Lottie stood. "Elise'll be waiting up and I need to go."

"Movie tomorrow night?"

"Again? The movie hasn't changed yet," she pointed out.

He rested his head on the seat. "Yeah, I don't think it has."

She smiled slightly. "Of course I'll be there, but I don't think Elise will be joining us." She leaned down and kissed him on the head. "Get some rest, big brother. I'll meet you there tomorrow night."

"See you," Patrick murmured, still thinking of Jean.

Chapter Three

The next night Patrick ran up to the ticket booth. He was late.

"I already have them," Lottie called from the entrance, waving the tickets at him.

"Thanks!" he said and ran over to her.

Merle was taking tickets and called out, "Last call! The movie's starting!"

Lottie grabbed Patrick's hand, and they ran into the theater. The piano keys could be heard throughout the small lobby. They hurried through the curtain and into the darkly lit room.

"What was that glare about?" Lottie asked as they sat in the crowded room.

"What glare?" he asked and looked around them.

"Not in here. It was the ticket taker. She was not happy about something."

He glanced down at their still clasped hands. "Probably this."

"It's none of her business if I hold my brother's hand or not."

"She's Jean's sister."

"Ohhh, so she's being protective."

"Shhh!" The sound came from their right side.

Patrick smirked at his sister. "Yeah, shhhh."

Lottie huffed a bit, let go of his hand, and sat back in her chair with her arms crossed. She moved her attention from the movie to the piano player, whose features were alternately lit by the bright lights of the movie. *Who's this girl who's caught my brother's eye?*

Jean didn't look toward the audience; her attention was on the picture and her cues for the music. She enjoyed playing the piano for the movies, but she wanted to jump up on stage and perform the stunts. *No, I can't. I have to do my job.* She turned her concentration back to the music.

Patrick found the movie as exciting as it was the other times he'd seen it, but his eyes kept moving back to Jean.

When the movie ended, the audience clapped and stood to leave. Lottie and Patrick stayed seated as the others left the theater. "What now?" she asked.

"We wait."

They watched Jean close her piano and waved up to the small window where the film still flashed out. The room went black, and Jean flipped the switch by the stage. The area was illuminated as she moved from the light switch toward them. "Hello, Patrick," she said. Jean looked at Lottie and then at him questioningly.

"Going to tell her who I am?" teased Lottie.

"Stop." Patrick glared at his sister. "Jean, this is Lottie, my *sister*."

Jean smiled more easily and held out her hand. "It's nice to meet you. I understand you're a lawyer?"

Lottie looked over at her brother.

"Not me, didn't say a thing."

"My sister mentioned she recognized you from the newspapers," Jean said, changing the story to simplify it.

Lottie gave her a guarded smile. "Yeah, I try to stay out of the spotlight now. It's nice to meet you also." She turned to Patrick. "I'm headed home now, big brother."

"All right, thanks for coming with me."

"No problem." Lottie nodded toward them and headed for the exit. Merle passed her in the narrow entranceway and bumped her shoulder 'accidentally'. Lottie was never one to let it go and asked her, "Did you do that deliberately?"

"Who me? Why would I do that?" Merle asked innocently with wide eyes.

Lottie looked her in the eye. "You wanna try that again and we can see what happens."

Merle started to lean in to do just that when Jean ran over. "Merle, please don't cause any trouble."

Patrick had seen the deliberate hit and watched to see how this would play out.

When Merle wouldn't move, Jean grabbed her sister by the arm and pulled her away from Lottie. "What're you doing?" she whispered gruffly.

"They came in together holding hands," her sister said, turning her focus to Patrick. He returned her gaze with uplifted brows.

"She's his *sister*," Jean whispered back fiercely.

Instantly, Merle's eyes dropped. "I didn't know." She turned back to Lottie. "Sorry."

Lottie just stared at the woman and then turned to Patrick. "See you soon."

"Wait," Jean said. Lottie turned toward her, her exasperation showing with her tapping foot. "I have to let you out." Lottie nodded and gestured for the other woman to go ahead. Jean hurried to the door and put her key into the lock. She turned it and opened the door. As Lottie walked out, Jean said, "I'm sorry. She's protective; it's just the two of us."

Lottie turned to her and said, "I feel the same about Patrick. But she needs to watch herself. A move like that could get her a belt in the mouth."

"Yeah, I get that."

Lottie nodded and strolled out. Jean shut the door behind her.

"Well, I think that's my cue," Merle said, suddenly at her side.

Jean turned and saw that Merle had her coat and hat. "Where are you going? We still have to clean up."

"I have a party to get to get to. People are waiting," she said and handed her sister the coat. Jean absently helped her put it on.

"I told her I'd help clean up," Patrick said from the theater doorway.

"But..." started Jean.

"No buts," Merle commented and kissed her cheek before she headed out the door.

Jean called after her, "Don't stay out too late!"

She just laughed and waved without turning around.

Jean closed the door and turned the lock. "Time to clean up," she said, and she turned toward him and started to go back into the theater. Patrick blocked her path. "It looks like we both have overprotective sisters."

"Looks like." She waited for him to move.

He backed out of her way and then followed her to the stage to retrieve the brooms. They silently cleaned the theater.

"Jean," Patrick called.

"Yes," she replied as she continued to sweep.

"Is this where you want to be?"

"What, piano player-slash-janitor isn't exciting enough for me?"

He paused and turned to her. "No, it isn't that. I think you want more."

"I do." Jean stopped sweeping to lean on the broom. "I'd like to go to California."

"To do what?"

She nodded towards the screen.

"Movies?"

"Yeah, I'm not sure when or if that will happen."

"What's holding you here?"

Jean bent to scoop the debris into the dustpan and walked over to the garbage cans. Patrick came over and removed the top for her. "Thanks." He didn't ask his question again, waiting patiently. "A lot of things, I guess. My sister's here."

"She doesn't want to move?"

"She seems happy." She frowned.

"What's wrong?"

She shook her head. "It's nothing." Her eyes moved to the doorway and her thoughts turned to her sister. She changed the subject. "What about you? Are you doing what you want with your life?"

"I'm doing what I like."

"As a policeman?"

"Yeah. It kinda runs in the family. My aunt is a private detective back in Chicago. Her friend is the head of the Pinkerton Detective Agency there, as his father was the head before him," he explained.

"It must be nice, being where you want to be." She met his eyes and held there. She broke contact first and said, "We need to finish up." They both went back to their task and met at the trashcan. Once the debris was cleared away, they moved to the lobby. Merle had cleaned up the area before she left. "We can leave now."

"Jean," Patrick said. She turned to him and was folded into his arms. She leaned in and his head lowered. The kiss was soft and tentative. Once he felt her response, he pressed down, and her lips parted. It went on until he stepped back.

She put a shaky hand to her hair. "Wow."

He rubbed his hand through his also. "Yeah, wow."

"Do you want to walk me home?" she asked with a small smile.

He returned it. "I would." Jean opened the door, and Patrick went through and waited while she locked the door. They started out together. She put out her hand and he took it. "When can we have a proper date?" he asked, letting his hand swing with hers.

"You mean with food and no work," she teased.

"And a place to sit."

"The theater has early matinees on Sunday. I should be done by three if you want to meet here."

He thought about that and asked, "Sunday would be wonderful."

"What're you thinking?"

"Walk around Central Park and an early dinner?"

"I'd like that."

He stopped her and put his hands on her shoulders. "Jean, I like you."

"My but you're a forward one."

"I like to keep things above board."

"We'll have to play cards one day," she said cryptically. "I like you, too."

He grinned. "Shall we continue?"

"Yes, please." They walked slowly, enjoying each other's company.

"Patrick Flannigan. Are you Irish?" she asked.

"What gave me away?" he teased.

She reached up and tugged his hair. "Well, it could be all the red."

"I am. My parents were from there."

"Have you been there?" She couldn't detect an accent.

"I'd like to go one day and meet my extended family."

"Have your parents been back?"

He sighed. "No, they passed a long time ago. I was taken in by Tim and Dora Flannigan. They adopted me. I don't remember my real parents as well as I'd like."

"I'm sorry."

"Don't be. I have wonderful parents. What about you?"

"Merle and I are from Texas."

"I didn't detect an accent."

"My sister," she explained. "She thought we should blend in."

Hmm. Merle seems to be a contradiction. She wants to blend in, but her personality does the opposite. "Your parents?"

"The same as yours, unfortunately. They got sick and passed."

"Why not stay there? You had a home?"

"I would've liked to," she admitted. "We were working on a ranch."

"A ranch? With horses and cows?" he asked with a laugh. Patrick couldn't imagine Jean, or Merle for that matter, living on a ranch in Texas of all places.

Jean's laughter echoed his. "Oh yeah, we didn't own any land, but we did lease some. We had horses, cows, chickens, the whole works!"

"Can you ride?"

"Some," she replied with a small smile.

"You sounded like you liked the work. Why did you leave?"

"Merle, she wanted more. Life in the big city and all that. But I miss the land and sky. You don't get that here."

"And you wanted to be with her?"

"Of course. She's my family. I want to stay close to her."

"She's protective of you."

"That she is. Your sister appears to be protective of you, too."

"Lottie? Yeah, she's great. She moved here first. I followed later, to help with some police work. It was a big to-do."

"The Becker trial?"

He looked surprised. "You followed it."

"Yeah, it had as much drama as the movies we show."

"It did at that."

"What did Lottie have to do with it?"

"She's a lawyer and worked as a clerk at the judge's office that was involved in the prosecution."

"Is she going to be involved in the appeal?"

"No, she and her partner left the justice's office and started their own firm."

"You both have a handle on where and what you want to be."

"We're getting there."

They stopped in front of her building, and they had another slow kiss. When they parted, he put his hand up to brush her hair off her shoulder. "I'll see you here on Sunday, after the matinee?"

"You're not coming by the theater the next few nights?"

"I can't," he said regretfully. "I have a case that I need to work on, and it'll be long hours. I'm going to try to wrap it up before Sunday."

She nodded. They'd only been seeing each other for two nights, but she knew she'd miss him. "I'm looking forward to Sunday."

He gave her hand a final squeeze and said, "Go on, I'll wait for you to go up."

"Bye," she said and walked through the door he held open for her. She started up the stairs and turned to confirm he was still there. He was. She smiled widely and turned to head inside. The door closed behind her as she walked up the stairs.

Once she was out of his sight, Patrick walked back to the car he'd left at the theater. It was a long walk, but it gave him some time to think about the next few days. The area was less crowded, and he easily retrieved his car and headed home to Greenwich Village.

He whistled, thinking about Jean.

Chapter Four

Jean put her key into the door and entered the small apartment. She and Merle could only afford a place that was basically a large room. Their beds were in the corner of the room and the furniture they had was provided for by the landlord.

She undressed and got ready for bed. Once she laid down, she couldn't sleep. Her mind was on Patrick. "Sunday," she murmured happily and drifted off to sleep.

"Jean! Jean! You have to get up!"

Jean's eyes opened slowly. "Are you finally home?" she asked with a wide yawn. A quick glance at the clock showed it was 4 am. "Why did you wake me up? I was dreaming about Patrick and Sunday."

Merle ignored her and ran to the dresser. "Something awful has happened."

"Tell me!" Jean demanded, suddenly wide awake.

"We have to leave now!" Her sister's one purpose was to pack. Merle ran to the closet and pulled out their suitcases. Clothes were yanked out of the closet and dresser, thrown into the open bags without being folded. "Jean! Get up!"

Jean got up and pulled on her skirt and blouse. She went over and took the clothes Merle was pushing into the suitcases and organized them. She folded each item and helped to empty the drawers. "Are we coming back?"

"No!"

"But..." she said, thinking of Patrick.

Merle grabbed her sister's hands. "Listen to me, we have to leave now! I saw something I shouldn't have."

Merle started to pull away, but Jean gripped her hand and held her. "We can go to Patrick. He's a policeman; he can help us."

"That's exactly why we can't tell him. The police are after me!" Merle went back to throwing things into her and her sisters' bags. She slammed them shut. "It's time to leave." With a bag in each hand, she went to the door. She turned and saw Jean standing there, unsure of what to do. "You always wanted to go to California, didn't you?"

"Yes," Jean said slowly, looking around. "Not coming back," she muttered and started to grab items she didn't want to leave behind: pictures, books, and other items.

"Leave those!" Merle demanded.

Jean whirled on her sister; hands full. "No! This is all we have. I will NOT leave everything behind!"

It wasn't often that Jean put her foot down and Merle said, "Oh for God's sake. Fine." She dropped the suitcases by the door, and she and Jean started to fill boxes from the closet with items around the room.

Once done, they stood at the door. "Can we go now?" Merle asked, exasperated.

Jean stood with her hands full of boxes that covered part of her face. She mumbled, "Yes."

Merle opened the door, and they moved out and started down the stairs. At the first step, Merle looked back. "Remove your shoes," she said. They quickly took them off and continued down the stairs saying nothing. They didn't want to be seen or heard.

Exiting onto the empty street, Merle and Jean stopped to

put their shoes back on. Merle strode off determinedly. "Wait," said Jean as she yanked on her shoes with one hand and balanced the boxes with the other. Shoes on, she raced to catch up with her sister. "How are we going there and what'll we pay for it with?"

Merle didn't answer; she just continued walking quickly, her high heels clicking on the sidewalk. They had walked a few blocks when Merle stopped abruptly, causing Jean to smash into her.

"Ow!"

"Sorry," mumbled Jean, trying to see over her boxes. "Are we walking to the train?" If they were, it would be a long walk. The station was nowhere near their apartment.

"No, we're taking an automobile," Merle replied.

"A car?" Jean asked, shocked.

"This one," said her sister, touching the car that stood next to them on the street.

"What?" Jean got a good look at the vehicle. It was a long car with four doors and tufted leather seats that could fit five people. There was also a black canvas top, folded down. She leaned toward her sister to whisper, "Are we going to steal it? Merle, this is an expensive car. What if we get caught?"

"We're not stealing it. I have these." Merle held up a set of keys and jingled them. "Now shut up and climb in."

Jean did as she was told. They stored the items in the back seat and Merle climbed in behind the wheel. Jean walked to the front of the car.

"Jean! What're you doing? Get into the car!"

"But what about the crank?" Jean asked, looking around the front of the car for the device.

"This is a new car. It doesn't require a crank. Get in!"

"Oh, okay," said Jean, shaking her head. She jumped into the passenger seat and watched as Merle started the car with a turn of a switch on the dashboard.

"How does this work?" Jean asked. She was fascinated by the contraption.

"Maybe we discuss this at a more opportune time?" her sister asked wryly.

"Of course. Let's go."

Merle punched the gas, and they lurched forward. Jean grabbed the dash. "Do you know how to drive this thing?"

Merle didn't respond. She pumped the hand pump, and they lurched forward again until finally, the car started moving steadily down the road. "Sure, I can drive! See!" she cried triumphantly, banging her hands on the steering wheel.

"Stop!"

"But we just got going," complained Merle.

"We have to stop at the theater and leave a note for the owner."

Merle slowed the car. "Are you kidding?"

"No, he gave us jobs when no one else would," said Jean.

"That old man dropped everything on us. We don't owe him anything."

"Us?" Jean commented.

Merle sighed. "I know, I didn't help as much as I should have." She banged the steering wheel and said, "Fine!" She turned the car around and drove down the familiar path to the theater. They eased to a stop and Merle watched as Jean wrote the note. "What'd you tell him?"

"I thanked him for giving us jobs when we needed it."

"Nothing about why we're leaving or where we're headed?"

"No, I just said we're homesick and wanted to go back home.
"

Merle nodded. "That's good, some misdirection."

Jean jumped out of the car and went to slide the note under the door. She hurried back to the car.

"Anything else before we leave town?" asked Merle dryly.

Jean sighed. "No, that should be it." *Patrick.*

Merle pulled the car onto the empty road, and they were once again on their way. The buildings blended together as they drove by. Jean stared forward and asked tentatively, "Do you know where we're going?"

"West."

"Okay, are you sure?" Jean asked. "We could just stay here... things might work out."

"Jean, baby, there's no going back. We're heading toward our future," Merle replied, staring determinedly forward.

Jean sat back and continued to watch the scenery fly by as they drove quickly out of the city. There was very little traffic to slow their getaway.

After a while, Jean took a deep breath and said in a rush, "Merle."

"Yes?" Merle responded absently. The roads were empty, but she didn't want to take any chances. They couldn't afford an accident or a flat tire.

"Where did you get the car?" Jean asked, keeping her voice light.

Merle's hands gripped the steering wheel tightly. She didn't want to discuss it.

"Merle, please."

Her fingers loosened and she admitted, "From the house I was at tonight."

"So, it is stolen," Jean accused.

"No, it was given to me."

"This CAR is worth at least five thousand dollars. Maybe more. Who do you know that can give gifts like this?" Jean asked, banging her hand on the dash. "Dammit, Merle! Who?" Her patience was at an end.

"The same one who can give me these." She used her right hand to upright her purse onto the seat, spilling out jewels.

Jean didn't say anything, her eyes wide as she struggled to understand what she saw. Even in the low light, the jewels sparkled.

"They're mine," Merle said defensively.

"From tonight? Or from other times?" Jean asked. She reached out to pick up a diamond necklace.

Merle's mouth was drawn tight. She didn't respond to Jean's question.

"Was this some sort of payment?" she asked. Her eyes darted to her sister's face.

Merle bit her lip and didn't answer.

"Merle, tell me! *I won't judge you.*"

"Oh no? You just did," Merle said, wiping a hand across her face.

She's crying! thought Jean. "Can you tell me? Please?"

Merle continued to drive; she had no choice.

"Was it the parties?"

"Yeah, that's where I met them."

"Them?" Jean asked with a frown.

"Bob Strathmore and his wife Catherine," Merle said shortly.

Strathmore? That's a famous name, one that reflects money and prestige, thought Jean. *How is Merle involved with them?* "Go on," Jean encouraged.

"At first, it was just the parties, lots of free food and booze. I was having a great time, so I kept going back. By the time I'd been to five of them, Bob asked to see me. *Alone.*"

"What was he like?" Jean asked, her curiosity getting the better of her.

"Rich. Very rich. He reeked of it," Merle muttered. She remembered that first meeting: he was wearing a tailored suit she could've saved for a year and never had enough money to purchase.

"Were you attracted to him?"

Merle gripped the wheel again and tried to answer honestly. "I was attracted to his money, initially."

Jean bit her lip. "Did you sleep with him?"

"Yeah. I did."

When Jean didn't say anything, the silence settled around them. Finally, Jean asked, "How long did it go on?"

"For a few months. Then it changed."

"Was it his wife?" asked Jean.

"Yeah. I didn't know who she was, and I didn't care. I loved my plush bubble where I had a rich man who wanted me." She sighed; the next part would be hard to admit.

"Merle?" Jean asked when the silence dragged on.

"I found myself in a sexual relationship with Bob and Catherine. The first time it happened, I was drunk, barely aware of where I was."

"After that, you still went back?" Jean kept her voice level, not wanting to stop the explanation.

Merle closed her eyes briefly and said, "I don't know why. I just wasn't thinking. I didn't want to think. I liked what I was experiencing. I knew it was wrong, but I couldn't seem to stop myself."

"They forced you; you weren't aware of what you were doing," stuttered Jean.

"No. After that first time, I was a full participant. I enjoyed the perks, and it was fun." She glanced over at Jean. "You don't appear to be shocked."

"No, maybe if we still lived in Wyoming, but not here." The city had exposed the sisters to all kinds of new things and behaviors and Jean had stopped being shocked long ago.

Merle smiled slightly and said with some sarcasm, "So, you have all of the experience now. You can handle anything."

Jean grimaced. "Well, not personally, but we've seen all kinds of things since we moved here. I'm not all that shocked."

"You aren't?" she asked hopefully.

"For now, I'm just protective of you."

"Thanks, sis."

Jean laid her head on Merle's shoulder. She was curious and had to ask, "What happened that led us to leave our home?"

"It was me. I started to put pressure on Bob and Catherine."

"Both of them?" Jean asked in surprise and raised her head to look at Merle's profile.

"Oh yeah. I had a plan, see? I knew this type of relationship couldn't last. I wanted some insurance for when things went sideways. I approached each one of them separately. I knew that neither of them would want our relationship made public."

Blackmail. "What were you expecting to happen?"

"Exactly what happened. They gave me jewels and money to keep my mouth shut and to keep coming back to them."

"And you kept pushing," Jean guessed and sat back with arms folded over her chest.

"You know me well. Yeah, I kept pushing. The first payments were great. But I wanted more."

"Did you have an amount in mind?"

"No, not really. I felt so free, parties every night and all the money and jewels I wanted."

"Until..."

"Until tonight. Catherine came into the bedroom and found me with Bob. She had a gun."

"You could've been killed!"

"Oh, believe me, that thought ran through my head. She was furious," Merle murmured, thinking of earlier. Bob had been on top and inside her when they'd been interrupted. "She screamed at him."

"How did he react?"

"He didn't take her seriously at all. He told her to get out and turned back to me." He'd started to move his hips again, ignoring his screaming wife. Merle followed his lead and moved with his body. "She walked to the bed and tried to hit him with the gun."

"I don't understand. She knew that you were sleeping with him."

"She thought it was only ever the three of us together. He hid the fact that he and I had started having an affair first. Or she knew that and ignored it. It could be either."

"What happened after she hit him?"

"He backhanded to the ground." Merle had watched Catherine as she'd lay bleeding from the mouth on the floor. She didn't feel any emotion for the woman. They'd had sex together, but Merle felt no love for the woman; she was in it for the money. "Bob had gotten up from the bed when the gun went off. It was so loud! Then Bob fell backward on me. I felt like I was suffocating trying to get him off me. Finally, I was able to push him off. I crawled off the bed, grabbing my clothes, praying I wouldn't be next."

"Did she go after you?" Jean asked and reached out to grip her sister's arm.

Jean stared straight ahead. "I didn't want to wait to find out. I was at the door when she turned the gun on herself."

"Oh, Merle!"

"I stood there for a long time, staring at that door. I couldn't turn around to face that scene."

"Didn't anyone hear the two shots?"

"The party was still going on and it was loud. Those sounds could've been champagne bottles being opened. I could hear some being opened downstairs."

"What did you do next?"

"I did the one thing I didn't want to do; I went back to see if they were dead." Jean stayed quiet as she watched Merle relive the horrible act. "They were both dead and it was a damn mess. I calmly dressed and left the room."

"You didn't climb out a window?"

"No, that wouldn't have worked. We were on the third floor in their private wing."

"Oh."

"And I wanted to be seen. I was there every night. They would've known something was wrong if I just disappeared. I went out through the main room. I danced some, drank some, and then left with the car. And here we are."

"Will you be, okay?"

That statement, from someone who cared about her, caused Merle to start crying again. Jean reached out and steered the car to the side of the road. The car came to a slow stop. Merle laid her head on the steering wheel and cried. Jean pulled her over to her and patted her back. The storm of tears wound down and Merle said into Jean's shoulder, "We have to keep going."

"Can you?" she asked, stroking Merle's hair.

"Yes." Merle took a deep breath and let it out. She pulled away from Jean and put the car back on the road. They drove into the night.

Patrick, Jean thought fleetingly.

Chapter Five

"Patrick!" He stirred but didn't get up. The bed was warm and the room dark. "Patrick!" A fist pounding on the door, followed by his name.

Patrick pulled himself out of the bed and stumbled through the living room to the door. He opened it and found his neighbor standing there with a heavy frown.

"You have a call."

Patrick rubbed his face, moved to the phone hanging on the wall, and picked up the receiver.

"Just once could you answer it?" his neighbor complained as he walked back to his apartment down the hall.

"Yeah sure, next time," Patrick muttered. He spoke into the transmitter. "Flannigan here."

"Patrick?" It was his captain, Frank Griffin. "We need you to come in."

He straightened quickly. "Did our suspect move early?" They'd had word that a violent confrontation was going to happen.

"No, it isn't that. It's another case, a double murder at the Strathmore house."

Patrick whistled and said in a low voice, "That's an expensive area."

"And political, which is problematic. We need someone over here to help manage the scene."

"I'll be on my way in a few minutes. You're there?"

"I am, and I have half the police force on site, taking statements. I need your input on what happened here."

"See you there," Patrick said briskly and hung up the phone. He moved quickly back to his apartment. His pants were on the chair, and he grabbed a clean shirt from the closet. He put his shoes on, grabbed his jacket, and walked out of the apartment. The door slammed shut behind him and the neighbor stepped out in the hallway to glare at him. "Sorry," he commented as he passed to the staircase. He started down, taking the stairs two at a time.

"Yeah, whatever," the man muttered at Patrick's back and went back inside.

Patrick shrugged and moved quickly down the rest of the stairs and out the door. His car was parked at the curb; he walked to the front, bent forward, and turned the crank to start the motor. He jumped over the door into the driver's seat and steered it into the empty streets, making his way to Strathmore's house.

The roads started to fill with cars and people the closer he got to his destination. He found a spot to park, pulled the car to a stop, and got out. The house stood tall in front of him. It was brightly lit, light shining from every window. Officers lined the streets, trying to both keep the people out and others in. Patrick shook his head and headed toward the door. At the doorway, Frank called from inside. "Patrick!"

He continued in and saw his captain. "Frank." He walked over to him. "A lot of people here," he muttered.

"Lots of people to interview," Frank responded.

"Want me to start over there?" he asked and motioned to the groups of well-dressed people.

"Not that way, I need you upstairs." Frank turned and started toward the stairs. Patrick followed him. Frank stopped abruptly and said over his shoulder, "It's bad up there. You okay with that?"

Patrick said, "I'll have to be."

Frank nodded and started walking up the stairs again.

Patrick had been to murder scenes many times, but he took a moment to breathe in and out as they got to the door. Frank waved at the officer standing at the door. "We're going in."

"Yes, sir," the officer said and stepped aside.

They entered. The bodies hadn't been moved and the smell hit them at the door.

"Whew!" Patrick gagged at the smell.

"Yeah, we'll have to move them soon."

"Can I speak with you?" The coroner came up to Frank.

"Over here." Frank and the mortician moved to the body of the man near the bed.

Patrick spotted the photographer. "Okay if I take a look around?"

He lowered the camera and said, "Yeah, I'm done. It's a mess."

Patrick nodded. He went over and studied the man first. "Looks like a bullet to the neck. There's a flood of blood forming a path from the bed to the floor." *There are blood smears on the bed. Was there someone else here?*

"That's right," said the coroner.

"And the wife?" Frank asked.

The three moved to her prone body. The gun was on the floor by her hand. "The gun must have been put into her mouth and the bullet came out the back," Patrick said.

The coroner confirmed it by moving her head to show the wound.

Patrick had seen this type of wound before, but nevertheless, he had to control the queasiness that it inspired. "She put the gun to her head. Desperate move," Frank commented. He reached up to loosen his tie. He'd much rather be at home with his family, but he had a job to do. "The bullets all appear to be from the same gun."

Patrick stood and drew an imaginary line from the woman to the man. "She shot him and then turned the gun on herself?" He returned to the bed and studied it for a long moment.

Frank turned to the coroner and photographer. "Give us some time."

The coroner nodded and said, "I'll have the wagon ready to move the bodies."

They left the room and Frank moved to where Patrick stood by the bed. "What do you think?"

"He's naked and she," Patrick glanced over at the woman again and said, "is fully dressed, stockings and shoes."

"Yeah, the stockings would definitely have to go." Patrick glanced his way with raised eyebrows. "What? They don't match the outfit."

Patrick smiled slightly. "Geez, Frank. Really?" Frank liked to add levity to crime scenes. It helped people to pull back from being too personally involved. He turned back to the bed. "Something happened here, sex. Look at that smear; the blood stain drags past him onto the other side of the bed."

Frank stepped back. "Wife enters, husband is having some fun and gets caught."

"She has the gun with her," Patrick supplied.

"Husband gets up to confront her..."

"And BANG. She shoots him in the neck."

"He falls back and bleeds out on whoever is in the bed."

"And the blood, was the other woman shot?"

Frank mulled this over. "No. I don't think so."

"The wife would've blamed the husband. What we have here is ..."

"A witness," supplied Frank.

"Looks like."

"Well, shit," Frank said, all levity gone from his voice. It was going to be a long night.

"What? What's up?"

Frank dragged his hands through his hair. "That means all of those empty-headed drunk's statements will have to be read."

"I can help with that," offered Patrick.

"Yeah, I'll need you here until they're compiled. When do you need to be on your case?"

"Not until tomorrow. Correction," Patrick said, looking at his watch, "tonight."

Frank glanced down at his watch. "Yeah, the bodies will be transported, and we need to move downstairs and help with the statements." They moved to the door and opened it. Frank yelled to the men waiting with stretchers. "Okay, let's go. Get this area cleaned up."

Patrick sidled down the stairs, trying to give the men room. He moved to observe the officers taking statements at the bottom of the stairs.

When Frank joined him, Patrick asked, "Who found them?"

"The maid. She went in at a specified time each evening to help Mrs. Strathmore undress for the evening."

"She couldn't do that on her own?" Patrick asked in surprise.

"The rich don't do anything on their own."

"Is she still here?"

"Let's find out. Officer Park," Frank called. The uniformed officer spoke to the man he was taking a statement from and walked over to the duo.

"Yes, Captain?"

"The maid you interviewed earlier, where is she now?"

"Over there." Park gestured to the hallway. They turned to see a tall, sturdy woman with her head down in her hands. Patrick and Frank moved over to her.

Patrick asked, "Ma'am, can I ask you some questions?"

Her shoulders shook and she didn't raise her head when she said, "I just want to leave. Can I leave?"

"In just a moment," Frank told the woman. "Would you like something to drink?"

She raised her red face and sniffed loudly. "Yes, please."

Frank turned and yelled, "Bring this woman some water!"

A man in a tuxedo ran over quickly with a glass; she smiled wanly at him as she took it. She looked at the glass and, when they started to ask her questions again, she raised the glass and swallowed the contents in one gulp. She took a deep breath and gasped out with a wheeze, "That wasn't water!"

"What was it?" Patrick asked and grabbed the glass from her. He ran his finger along the edge and tasted it. "Vodka."

"Why the hell did you bring her vodka?" Frank demanded, exasperation clear in his voice. It'd been a long night.

The man lurched to one side. "You said she needed a drink." He must have been a guest and not staff.

"Well, not that kind!" Frank shouted, "Someone get the idiot away from me!" Officer Park approached and took the man's elbow to guide him away.

The maid slumped on the wall and her chin dropped to her chest. Patrick jostled her. "Ma'am, wake up. Wake up."

Officer Park walked back over to them and observed the woman. "What happened? She was fine when I took her statement earlier. She was a little emotional but nothing like this."

"That nimrod," said Frank, referencing the young man still weaving around the room. "He brought vodka to her, and now she's passed out."

Patrick tapped her face lightly. "Yep, she's out."

"It might be the stress and the late hour that contributed to this," Frank said. "We need to move her to a room and have an officer wait with her." He called over to a young officer who was trying to take a statement from an obviously inebriated woman. She kept putting her hand on the man's leg. He pushed it off and rushed over to Frank.

"Yes, sir?"

Frank put his hand on the man's shoulder and asked in a low voice, "Kelly, would you like another assignment?"

Kelly glanced nervously at the woman behind him. "I would,

please. And hurry," he said as the woman approached the trio with a determined gait.

"You get this woman to her room; we will have to interview her later."

One of the house staff came over to them and said, "I'll show you where it's located." Kelly lifted the maid and followed quickly.

The woman was getting closer, and Frank stepped into her path. "The officer is rather busy. Let me get you someone else to talk to."

"But I want to talk to him. He's cute," she said drunkenly through the hair on her face. She blew out a breath and reached up to push her wig further back on her head.

Frank smothered a laugh and said, "Madam, we want to talk to you." He looked around for the one person who could get this statement. His eyes settled on Jack, a large man that appeared to be made of granite. "Jack, come over here." The officer nodded and excused himself from talking to the house staff.

"But I want the other one," the woman complained.

"Madam, I think I can help you," came a deep voice. She looked up and up again at Jack. When she landed on his face, she smiled and reached up to straighten her wig again. "This one'll do," she said.

He offered her his elbow and asked, "Will you come with me?"

"I'd love to."

Patrick and Frank watched him guide her into another room. Patrick asked, "Are all of them like that?"

"Mostly. The party was in full swing when we arrived. We had to stop the band from playing to make the announcements."

"Okay, let's get this over with." They each took a waiting guest and began taking their statements.

By the time they were finished, the sun streamed through the windows and the room was finally empty. The last guest had been escorted home, and the remaining officers happily followed them out.

"Do you think she was in this last group?" Patrick asked.

Frank cut him a look. "It could be a man."

"Yeah, we are in New York," Patrick replied with no judgment in his tone.

"So, a man or a woman. We need to review all the statements to find him or her." Frank placed his hand on the very tall pile of papers that sat between them. "How do you want to do this?"

"We each take half?"

Frank nodded and split the pile, handing half to his friend. Patrick stood, taking his share with him.

"Patrick, want to join me at home for some breakfast?"

"Will Annabeth mind?" Patrick asked, looking at his watch. It was barely seven in the morning.

"She won't mind. She loves to feed everyone. Give me a lift back?"

Patrick smiled broadly. "Well, I guess I have to, since you built the car for me." Frank's hobby was fixing up cars and reselling them.

"It's the least you can do," retorted Frank and accompanied Patrick to the door. It was a relief to be leaving and going home.

"Sir," called a voice from behind them.

They turned to see a member of staff in a dark suit. Frank rubbed a hand through his hair. "Forgot about you. You're the house manager?"

"Yes, sir."

When the man didn't continue, Frank asked rather brusquely, "Did you need something?"

The house manager wrung his hands and looked behind him. The rest of the staff stood there with similar expressions of worry. "What should we do now?"

Frank understood his question. The owners were dead; did they still have a job? "Get some rest and return like normal tomorrow."

"Today," muttered Patrick.

"Today," confirmed Frank. "We'll notify the next of kin and they'll give you direction."

"And what about Mabel?" the manager asked again, delaying their exit.

"Mabel? Is she the maid?"

"Yes, sir."

"Is she still asleep?"

"Yes, your man is still with her."

"Tim!" Frank called to an officer at the door. "Tell Kelly to check on the maid and, if she's still out, he can head home." He turned back to the manager. "I'll have an officer at the front and back exits. We'll want to interview her again later today."

"Thank you."

"We'll be in contact with you," he promised. With that, Patrick and Frank finally headed out the door. The scene outside was completely different from when Patrick had arrived. There had been numerous cars parked in the driveway and the grass. Now, Patrick's car was the only one remaining.

Patrick climbed in and tossed the crank to Frank. He caught it deftly and cranked the engine. Once it started, he jumped into the passenger seat. Patrick moved it out onto the road.

"Running well," Frank commented.

"Like a top." The car made a sputtering sound. Frank hit the dash with his fist, and it stopped.

"Smooth," laughed Frank. Patrick joined him.

They were quiet until they got to Frank and Annabeth's apartment. It was early yet, with only delivery people out—milk trucks, bread, and others. Patrick parked the car at the curb directly in front of the entryway. They went into the apartment on the second floor and entered quietly. They needn't have, as the household was awake and moving about their morning activities.

A young man ran up to them and hugged Frank. "Long night out?" He didn't wait for an answer and called to Patrick, "Hey!"

"Hey, Jojo," Patrick returned the greeting.

Jojo turned and called, "Ma, Frank's home."

"Well, tell him to get in here. We have breakfast waiting," called his mom.

"He brought company."

"The more the merrier," she called back.

They entered the kitchen and found the large table full of food.

Annabeth paused her stirring of the large pot on the stove. "Patrick, good to see you."

"Got enough for me to join you?" he asked. He'd been a frequent guest but didn't want to impose.

"Of course. We have plenty. Go sit."

"Do you need help with that?" asked Frank. She was about to move a large pot and pour it into molds.

"Please."

Frank knew what was expected and moved quickly to the hot pot. Annabeth handed him potholders and he poured the material into the molds. The room smelled of food and candles. Annabeth's business was selling candles and lately, she'd branched out into face cream.

"It smells good," Patrick commented.

"Always does," said Frank as he moved to set down the still hot pot.

"Sit down and eat," Annabeth directed. They joined Jojo, who'd already filled a plate and was stuffing his mouth. He grinned and grabbed another biscuit.

"Better be quick," Frank warned Patrick.

Patrick took him at his word and filled his plate quickly. They ate and, when their appetites were sated, Jojo looked at the duo. "Who died?" he asked.

"Jojo!" scolded his mother.

Frank smiled slightly and said, "Catherine and Bob Strathmore."

Annabeth's eyes widened. "Both of them?" she asked. "What happened?"

Jojo was silent as he waited for their answer.

"We aren't sure yet," Patrick replied.

"Yeah," said Frank. "It's still early in the investigation."

Annabeth nodded. She and Frank had been together for the past year and she knew he could only share certain information about cases. Annabeth picked up a piece of toast and started to butter it. "Lottie stopped by last night," she said lightly. That wasn't unusual since she and Lottie were close friends.

Frank watched Annabeth continue to butter her toast. He knew where the conversation was going.

She continued. "Patrick, she said you've taken an interest in the movies as of late."

Patrick almost spit out the coffee in his mouth. Annabeth smiled and took a bite of her toast.

Frank played along. "What's this about movies? See anything good?"

Patrick sighed. "She was asking about a lady I've started to see. She works at the theater, as the piano player."

"Well, tell us about her," demanded Annabeth.

"She's very talented," he said and thought of her gymnastics after the movie. Before they could ask more questions, he added, "She has long dark curly hair and big eyes, and I can't wait to see her again."

"When will you see her next?" asked Annabeth.

"Sunday."

"You have that case tonight," reminded Frank.

"Oh, Frank, leave him be. I'm sure he's worked it out."

"Don't worry, I will be there."

Frank looked at the dark circles under Patrick's eyes. "You going home and back to bed? You'll need to be alert for your shift."

Patrick looked at his watch and grimaced. "Yeah, that's a good idea. I need to head there now." He started to pick up his plate, and Annabeth stopped him.

"I'll do that. You get going."

"Thank you," Patrick said and felt the tiredness he'd held off coming back.

"I'll walk you to the door," Frank said. Once at the threshold, he handed Patrick the stack of papers. "When you have a chance, start going through these. Don't do it now."

"I'll get some rest first," Patrick promised, taking the papers from his friend.

"Come see me on Monday and we can compare notes on the statements."

"I will." He slipped on his jacket and put on his hat.

Frank held the door open, and Patrick exited. After he shut the door, he walked back into the kitchen. Jojo had gone to his room.

"Was it bad?" Annabeth asked as she added labels to her cooled-down jars.

"It was messy."

"Go to bed, baby. You've been up all night."

"I will in a bit," he said, studying the pile of statements he had to get through.

"That can wait until later. Rest now," she ordered.

"Yeah, you're right." He went over to her and kissed her.

"Off with you now," she said.

Chapter Six

Patrick felt his feet dragging as he climbed the stairs to his apartment. His next-door neighbor was exiting as he slid the key into his door lock.

"Just getting back?" his neighbor asked.

"Yeah," said Patrick.

"Long night?"

"Yeah," Patrick said, putting a hand up to cover a wide yawn.

"Well, have a good morning," called the man as he headed downstairs.

"I'll try," Patrick said. He pushed the unlocked door open and stumbled to his bed. The papers landed with him.

Chapter Seven

The car jerked and Jean reached out to steady herself. They were swerving on the road.

"Merle! Stop the car!" Jean said sharply.

"What?" Merle mumbled. Her head was down in her coat and her eyes closed.

"Merle, wake up!" Jean reached over to grab the wheel and put her other hand on her sister's shoulder to shake it.

"I'm awake! I'm awake!" Merle said crossly, barely opening her eyes, and grabbed the wheel, causing it to jerk to the left.

"Pull over!" Jean ordered.

That finally woke Merle up, and she managed to get the car to the side of the road. When they stopped, Jean said, "We can't keep going at this pace. You need rest."

Merle bit her lip and looked behind them. "Do you think we're far enough away?"

Jean didn't think so, but she wanted Merle to rest. "How about showing me how to drive this thing and then we can take turns."

Merle sat up straight, trying to wake up. "Let me get out for a moment. I need to walk around."

"We both do." They got out and walked around the car

together. The sun had just started to rise, and the roads were empty.

"Merle, do you think we're doing the right thing? Running away?" Merle didn't look at her; Jean thought she didn't hear her. "Merle?"

"Yes," her sister said simply. "You still want to learn to drive?"

Jean nodded. They took their places with Jean in the driver's seat.

Merle began with, "Okay, turn the switch on the dash so you can pressurize the gas tank. The gas tank is located at the back of the car, below the back seat. To get it moving you have to pump about three pounds of pressure into the gas tank to force gas into the carburetor. There's a hand pump by the driver's left foot, on the floorboard, to create the needed pressure."

Jean paid attention and followed the instructions; it took a few tries to get the car moving. They started off slow, so slow that Jean asked, "Can we go faster?"

"We can, but the roads aren't great. I had to go slower last night when I couldn't make out the path."

"I can see better now; can I speed up some?" asked Jean hopefully.

"Sure," Merle mumbled again as she sank deeper into her coat and closed her eyes. "Are you okay if I get some rest?"

"Oh, yeah," Jean said excitedly. "I got this." She pushed the gas pedal and glanced at her sister. *Sleeping*, she thought. The opportunity was too good to pass up and she pushed down on the pedal harder. The wind whipped her hair back and she felt alive. Their future, that's where they were headed.

Chapter Eight

Patrick woke abruptly, the afternoon sun streaming into his bedroom. "What time is it?" he whipped his head toward the clock. It was only 2 pm. "Whew!" It felt much later than that. He stumbled up and headed to the bathroom. *A bath,* he thought, and ran the water into the tub. He reclined for a few moments before straightening to grab the washcloth and soap. A little while later, he drained the tub and dressed. Sufficiently refreshed, he moved to the kitchen for something to eat.

He fixed a sandwich, grabbed a beer, and walked into the living room to eat. After he took a bite and a swig of beer, he looked around the room. *Where are they?* He kept scanning the room. He ran through his actions that morning. *Bedroom!* He sat his plate down and moved there quickly. His eyes settled on the pile of statements scattered on the bed. He glanced again at the clock. *I have time,* he thought. He gathered them up and took them to the living room to review.

He settled down in a chair with his sandwich and picked up the top statement to read. As he read through the statements, he saw each had the same format: who, what, when, and where. Some were short with just a statement of the person's name and that they hadn't seen anything. The more he read, he saw patterns start to develop. A young blonde woman stood out. Many people had said the Strathmores had been seen many times over the past six months with a young blonde woman.

"Was it the same woman each time? Was there anything else that described her?" he muttered to himself. As he read further, the descriptions all ran together: pretty and blonde. *Not much to go on. Who is she?* he thought.

Patrick kept digging through the stacks and finally found a few that referenced the woman in a silver dress. That sparked something in Patrick's memory. *Silver dress, blonde, pretty. Could it be?* He thought of Jean's sister. *No! That can't be right. There's lots of girls who are blonde with silver dresses.*

Though Jean did mention her sister liked to go to parties, often arriving home late. It wouldn't hurt just to confirm she wasn't there. That would resolve it. Yeah. He glanced at his watch and thought, *Not tonight.* The time had flown and it was already close to 5 pm. He needed to get to the precinct and join the men for the stakeout that night.

The statements were moved to the side table. It was time to concentrate on the case he'd be working on that evening. It involved a gangster who worked as an informant for the police. The information provided by the informant hinted that there was to be a slug war that evening and high-level gangsters would be there. His main task was to prevent lives from being taken—either by gangsters or civilians.

He put the statements out of his head and dressed swiftly for the long night ahead of him. He picked up his gear and drove to the precinct. The car was left at the curb, and he hurried up the stoop and into the station. "They're waiting for you," said the officer manning the front desk.

"Yeah, on my way." He could hear the voices and headed toward the full room. As he entered the sergeant standing in the front of the room called to him. "Patrick, great, we need you to give us a rundown of what we should expect tonight."

He stepped up to give his report. "Thanks, Ben. Our informant indicated that there's a war on tonight. It may involve a major gunfight on Grand and Forsyth streets. We already have men watching the area, so we'll join them and continue to monitor as the gangs arrive."

"Who can we expect?" asked Smith.

Patrick turned the board around, revealing pictures. He pointed to each. "Billy Lustig, 'Pinchy' Paul, 'Little Rhodey' Roch, Punk Madden, and Moe Jewbach. They'll be followed by their gangs. We want to stop anyone from getting killed."

"Can you tell us why this is happening now?" Ben asked.

"It's a slug war," Patrick explained. "With the emergence of labor unions, the street gangs began to be hired by companies as strikebreakers and to discourage union activity."

"Sir," Smith brought up, "don't the unions also have sluggers?"

"They do. They're used primarily as protection from these strikebreakers to go after scabs and to recruit, by force if necessary, new union members," Patrick finished.

Ben stepped up again. "This task force is only there to observe and document which groups are working together. We want to keep this as peaceful as possible and have no casualties. Do not fire without being told. Let's get going."

The men moved to start gathering up their pistols and shotguns. They didn't want trouble, but they wanted to be prepared just in case. Patrick followed suit and picked up a shotgun. The young officer next to him was loading his pistol. "Hey!" protested Patrick. "This will be a free for all with Tim involved."

Tim grinned. "I hope so." He stood, putting his gun in the holster.

Patrick raised his eyebrows at Ben.

Ben called over, "Jeff will be there; he'll keep an eye on him."

Patrick nodded. Jeff was an experienced officer and would calm the boy down. He pulled out his pistol and made sure it was loaded. The group quieted as Chief Wembley walked into the room. Patrick was surprised to see Frank with him.

"Gentlemen," Wembley began, "we'll need everyone on the same page tonight. We need to be calm. If any shooting starts, we want to be in control and start taking the men into custody. We don't want to overreact and start shooting back."

"What if they're shooting at us?" Tim asked.

The chief ignored him and continued. "The word is that the gangs are fighting for control. There's a lot of money being paid by both sides in these wars."

"Will it end tonight?" asked Jeff.

"Not as long as the companies keep paying for protection. We're just trying to keep the peace. Be safe out there."

The officers formed into groups to go to the designated location. They were loaded into several wagons and transported downtown. They split up and surrounded the area. Patrick's team sidled up to the far side and moved into the alley. "Over here," called a low voice. Patrick guided his team with hand signals down the alley.

"Anything happening yet?" Patrick asked the officer.

"Everyone's here. No violence yet. You can see from here." Patrick looked over into the streets. There were several groups standing around, but they weren't talking to one another.

That changed in seconds as guns were drawn and the men they were watching scattered. When the sound of gunfire rang out, Patrick said, "We need to move!"

"Wait! I was told we were just going to watch. I don't want to go out there! I thought we were going to watch," the officer repeated to himself.

Patrick grabbed the man by the shoulders. "Things have changed, Parker! We need to provide protection."

"We were told not to shoot without instructions. We don't want this to turn into a shootout," Parker protested.

"It already has," Patrick replied shortly.

"Patrick! We need to go!" Frank called from behind him.

Patrick turned to his team. "No shooting. Keep your weapons raised but no firing, understood?" He made eye contact with each of them, then looked toward the other teams in the alleys surrounding the ongoing gunfire. The signal was given, and the officers moved in teams to surround the gangs. They all exited at the same time, guns drawn. Amazingly, each member of the two gangs dropped their weapons. The men were sullen but allowed themselves to be taken without force.

Frank called over to Patrick, "Anyone hurt?"

"None so far. I'll continue to check." There was a doctor on standby, but everyone hoped he wouldn't be necessary. Patrick walked up to the last group to be taken in. "Any injuries?"

"None that we can find."

Patrick looked at the group and smiled when he saw who they'd gathered up. It was none other than Benjamin Snyder, the usual procurer of personnel for the slugger activities. Patrick approached him and murmured, "Well, well, look who we have here, Benny Snyder in the flesh."

Snyder sneered at him. "Think you have a prize, do you? I'll be back on the streets by morning."

Patrick nodded and said, "I have no doubt." And he didn't. The unions would get Snyder out and he'd be back on the streets continuing his job. The police only involved themselves when the public might get injured. They didn't expect to get much out of him, but their goal had been accomplished. No one had been injured.

As the groups were transported downtown, they passed the movie house on the way. Patrick looked at it wistfully and thought, *Tomorrow. I'll see Jean tomorrow.*

Snyder saw his gaze. "Got an interest in the movies?"

"No more than anyone else," Patrick said noncommittally. Snyder was not a man he wanted involved in his personal life. He was a very bad man. He'd been hired out to various racketeers over the last decade. "Why do you do it?"

Snyder knew what Patrick was asking and shrugged. "It's a living."

"Is it though?" Patrick sounded doubtful.

"You'd be surprised." Snyder looked disdainfully at Patrick's clothing and dusted off his obviously expensive jacket. He had several New York police officers in his pocket, but this one didn't seem corruptible. He didn't want to waste any effort on the other man.

It took hours to process them and take them to their cells. The officers were unloading their firearms. Patrick removed his coat and set his empty shotgun and pistol on a table next to Jeff's guns. "That went well."

"It did," Jeff agreed.

"Don't know why we bothered," Tim said from across the room.

"Ah, ignore him. He's just disappointed he didn't get to shoot anyone," Jeff replied.

"Well, there is that," Tim admitted. "But I heard those guys'll be out by the morning. Doing the same thing they're doing now."

Jeff frowned. "If that's true, why the task force?" he asked.

"It was the guns," Patrick said. "We couldn't let innocent people die in a gang war. We had to provide some protection."

"But it could happen again?"

"Yeah, I think so. Though I think they'll think twice before going to war with each other. At least in the streets."

"So, it's just probably a matter of time before we do this again?"

"Probably, though I wouldn't be surprised if next time it's much worse. The confusing thing is that both sides are hiring men from the gangs; the companies to stop the unions and the unions to stop the scabs."

"Scabs?"

"They're workers brought in to do the jobs of the union workers on strike. The unions hate them and will do almost anything to stop them from getting into work."

"So, the gangs don't care as long as they get paid?"
"Exactly."
"This doesn't sound resolvable."
"Nope."
Frank walked up to the men. "Good job tonight."
"Thanks, Captain," Jeff said and grabbed Tim by the collar. "Come on, we're headed out for a beer."
"I'm for that," Tim said.
Frank helped Patrick load the guns back into the cabinets. Once they were locked, Patrick asked, "Wanna go for a drink?"
"Aren't you tired?"
"I will be," he admitted. "But for now I'm up."
"Then I'm with you. Do you have the witness statements with you?"
"Not with me," Patrick said. "We can get them on the way."
"The sun's coming up," commented Frank as they passed a window.
"Yeah. You know. we're spending a lot of these early mornings together. No offense, but if I wanted to spend a romantic time with anyone it wouldn't be you," Patrick told his friend.
Frank grinned. "Same to you, brother, same to you. You know what? Instead of that drink, how about we get some breakfast?"
"Isn't that too much on Annabeth? Company two days in a row?"
"She'd rather we were there than not."
"Then I'm in."
They walked to Patrick's car. Patrick took the wheel and Frank cranked the engine. Once it was running, Frank jumped over the door. As they drove to Patrick's apartment, they passed Landry's bookstore. Frank looked over at it.
"I was surprised that Henrietta wasn't in the middle of things tonight."
Patrick glanced at his friend. "Since having the baby, she's been involved more at the school."

"A teacher," Frank said musingly. "Who would've thought? That must have been a relief to the family."

"Yeah, Mama and Aunt Emma have a lot less worry with both Lottie and Henrietta settled." Henrietta was almost a sister; she'd moved in with their family when he was twelve.

Frank asked, "And what about you?"

"Settling?" Patrick thought of Jean again. "Haven't had much interest."

"Lottie mentioned you were seeing someone."

Patrick gave his friend a sideways look. "You've stayed close to her."

Frank shrugged. "No reason not to after we stopped seeing each other. There's no hard feelings."

"There wasn't?" Patrick remembered some long conversations and a lot of drinking discussing his sister.

"I think I liked the idea of Lottie. Once I got passed it, I realized it was always Annabeth. I could see a future in her eyes."

"Have you had any trouble since you got together?"

"No, not here. We feel protected in Greenwich Village, but if we're anywhere outside of the Village we get stares and comments."

"Does that bother you?"

"I think it bothers Annabeth. She wants people to see her, not us. She's making headway as a businesswoman, and I'd hate to get in her way."

"What about traveling?"

"She wants to for her business. Maybe go to some fairs to generate more interest in her products." Frank grimaced. "The anti-miscegenation laws could get us arrested in certain states."

"Times are changing," Patrick replied.

"Are they, though? Did you know that the House of Representatives just voted against interracial marriage."

"I didn't know that. I'm sorry."

"Me, too. I want to be able to marry Annabeth and start growing our family."

"You know, some people are moving to France. They don't have the same prejudices of interracial marriages that we do," Patrick said. He didn't want to lose his friend but understood the man's need to marry the woman he loved.

"Trying to run me off?" Frank asked lightly, though there was no malice in his words. They'd been friends for a long while.

"Just listing the options."

"Yeah, but that would be running away."

"Are you thinking of marriage?" asked Patrick.

Frank sighed. "It seems to be a bad word these days, even without the race issues. Women want more freedom."

"This area does foster that notion." He looked over at Frank. "Have you asked her? How does she feel?"

"I haven't," his friend admitted.

Patrick let the conversation drop as he pulled the car to a stop in front of his apartment.

"I thought we were going to my place?" Frank exclaimed in surprise.

"I need my half of the statements," Patrick reminded him.

"Oh, must've slipped my mind. I'll just wait here." Frank settled back in his seat and pulled his hat down over his eyes.

Patrick ran up the stairs and into his apartment. The statements were where he'd left them. He scooped them up and walked quickly back to the door. The lock clicked behind him, and he moved back downstairs to the car. He jumped in and Frank pushed up his hat.

"That was fast."

"Take these." Patrick handed the pile to Frank and pulled the car back onto the street. It jerked and moaned a bit the short distance to their destination. He stopped the car, and they got out and walked inside the apartment house and up the stairs.

Jojo must have heard them and opened the door before they reached it. "Company again, Ma!" he called and ran off.

Patrick raised his eyebrows.

Frank waved in Jojo's direction. "Don't mind him."

"Frank, is Patrick with you?" Annabeth called from the kitchen.

Patrick answered for him. "I am, if that's okay."

"Always," she called back. "Jojo, come set the table!"

"All right, Ma. On my way."

Frank grinned at the response, and they followed the sound of running feet to the kitchen. Once again, the kitchen smelled of candles and breakfast.

"It always smells nice here."

"Yes, it does," Frank replied as he bent to kiss Annabeth. "Good morning."

She leaned in for a long moment and then tapped him on the chest and said, "Enough of that now. We need to get the food on the table." Everyone pitched in to help. Patrick and Frank gathered the toast and jam butter. Jojo carried the platter of biscuits. The eggs and bacon were put on trays and Frank hurried to take them from Annabeth. She smiled slightly and said, "Jojo, the milk, please."

The boy walked to the refrigerator and took out the pitcher. "Glasses, please," reminded his mom. He retrieved four glasses and carried them to the table.

Patrick poured the milk into the glasses and held his up to Frank. "Is milk the drink you were offering earlier?"

Frank laughed as Annabeth and Jojo looked on confused.

Chapter Nine

"The sun's coming up," Jean observed. "Why don't we pull over and get some rest?" They'd been driving for hours. "I think we're far enough away now."

Merle didn't slow down the car; she just gripped the wheel tighter. "I'm not sure."

"I am," Jean said firmly. "We need to stop."

"I'd like a few more miles behind us."

"Fine," Jean replied but kept an eye on her. "How long do you think?"

"To California?"

"Yes."

"At this rate, probably a few months."

"A few months! But it seems like we're going so fast."

Merle shrugged and thought about what Jean had said. "I think it's time to ditch the car."

"Ditch!" Jean rubbed a hand on the leather seats. "Surely we're not going to just abandon it?"

"Well, maybe not ditch," her sister admitted. "We need to try to sell it and get our stake for California."

"And then what?"

"We'll take a train. That would cut the time back to two weeks."

"Weeks rather than months?"

"That's what I'm thinking."

They continued to drive. "We'll need a spot where a car like this might be serviced," Merle said.

"Do you think they'll question where the car came from?" *Could we be traced this far out?*

"Not with the price I'll give them."

Jean mulled that over and watched as the scenery went by.

Chapter Ten

Patrick stood with his empty plate and Annabeth told him, "Just put it in the sink." She was working on her candles, adding wicks to the glass jars.

Frank joined him at the sink. "Meet me in the living room?"

Patrick nodded. "Thank you for breakfast again, Annabeth."

Annabeth smiled at him. "Any time."

Patrick put his dish in the sink and then went to the living room. Frank took the opportunity and kissed Annabeth. "Thank you for breakfast."

She leaned in and kissed him. "You're welcome."

He pulled himself away regretfully and moved to follow Patrick. He heard Annabeth call out, "Jojo! Go brush your teeth!"

"All right, Ma."

Patrick sat on the couch, pulled his statements out, and placed them next to the ones already on the table in front of them. He began sorting his into separate piles.

Frank joined him on the couch. "Okay. What's in each stack?"

Patrick pointed to the first. "This one is discards, mostly drunk responses."

Frank picked up the one on top and read out loud. "Here's one from Parker: 'Ma'am, did you hear anything?' Her response was, 'My heartbeat.' Parker - 'Heartbeat?' Her response was, 'It just is so loud tonight. Can you hear it?'" Frank shook his head. "Yeah, not much here."

"They're fun to read, but absolutely no value," Patrick said.

"And this pile?" Frank asked and tapped the next one.

"The mysterious blonde woman pile." He turned to Frank and asked, "How about you?"

"Mostly like your drunk pile, though I did have a few about a mysterious blonde, too."

Patrick nodded, took the papers from Frank, and started reading them. "Hmmm, the stories sound similar. A blonde who was seen at several parties and in the company of the Strathmores for the past six months." *Is it Merle?* he wondered. *There's no real evidence that it was her.*

"No one knew the blonde's name?" Frank continued.

"Doesn't seem like. She'd mingle with the party guests and then go off with the Strathmores. Looks to be no interactions with any other guests at the parties."

"Where did she go with the Strathmores?"

"No one was sure about that."

"Where were the other guests?"

"Mostly downstairs."

"So, she was probably upstairs."

"It makes sense," Patrick agreed. "We didn't talk about this final stack."

"What's that one?"

"The household staff."

"Anything interesting?"

"The chauffeur indicated that a car was taken."

Frank sat up quickly. "Taken? By whom?"

"It doesn't say," Patrick said and handed him the paper.

Frank read it silently. "We need to talk to him. Do you have the maids' statements?"

"Here they are." Patrick gathered up the final statements and handed them over.

"Hmm," Frank said as he flipped through them. "They said they didn't know anything about the activities of their employers." He tapped the first one in the stack he held. "This one is the upstairs maid, Mabel."

"Yeah?"

"She would've helped Mrs. Strathmore undress and probably spent the most time with her."

"You think she's covering something up," commented Patrick.

"I think so."

"Another person to interview." Patrick looked Frank in the eye. "This mystery blonde, there was something familiar about the description."

"Someone you know?" Frank's eyes narrowed.

"I'm not sure," Patrick admitted. "The blonde hair and silver dress sound familiar. I would rather not accuse anyone based on that broad description."

"We don't want to accuse anyone without evidence. Will you tell me if anything else points to that person's identity?"

"Of course."

"Okay, the next steps will be to talk to the staff."

"If they're still around."

"The officers I assigned to monitor the staff are still in place. I don't think it's going to be an issue."

"When do you want to re-interview them?"

Frank yawned. "First, we need to get some rest. Meet at three?"

Patrick grimaced; there went his afternoon with Jean.

Frank noticed and asked, "Problem?"

"No, just some plans I need to move around." *Jean will understand,* he hoped.

Jojo walked into the room and flopped into a large chair across from them.

"Jojo, can you deliver a note for me?" asked Patrick.

"Sure, but it'll cost you."

Frank frowned at the boy. "Jojo, we should help friends without compensation."

He crossed his arms and looked mutinous.

"No," Patrick protested, "he's right. He's doing me a favor. How about 50 cents?"

Jojo brightened. "I think we have a deal."

Frank reluctantly smiled at him. Jojo was a natural salesman, a lot like his mom.

Jojo directed, "Write out what you want me to deliver and give me the address."

Patrick pulled out his notebook and pencil. "It's a note for an employee at the movie theater."

"That's not far. I'll go over on my bike."

Patrick jotted down the reason that he wouldn't be able to meet Jean and promised to come by the theater as soon as the case lightened up. He folded the note and handed it over. Jojo stood up and approached him. He reached out with one hand to take the note and his other was palm up.

Patrick got the message. "Oh yeah, here you go." He dug out the two quarters and flipped them to Jojo.

He grabbed them and said, "I'll run it by later."

"Be sure it's before three."

"I will," he promised. Jojo left the room to finish his chores.

"Who was the note for?" Frank asked, sitting back.

"Just someone I met."

"The piano player?" Frank raised his eyebrow at him.

Patrick just yawned broadly.

"Home with you, get some rest," Frank said, yawning himself.

Patrick stood and stretched. "Where do you want to meet?"

"I will meet you at your place at three and we'll head over for the interviews."

"Sounds like a plan."

"Can you drive?" he asked.

"Yeah, it's not far."

Patrick walked to the door and called out to Annabeth, "Thank you again for breakfast."

She exited the kitchen, wiping her hands on her apron. "Any time." She looked at Frank. "And you, off to bed."

"Yes, ma'am, on my way," Frank replied as he went over to kiss her.

She turned to Patrick. "You, too."

"On my way home now," he confirmed and opened the door to the hallway. He was tired and his movements sluggish. Once in his car, he turned the key and walked to the front of the car to crank the engine. It rattled and jerked as he moved to drive it out to the streets toward home.

Chapter Eleven

A knock on the door sounded, and Patrick called from the kitchen, "Come in!" He stuck his head in the kitchen doorway and saw Frank. "In here. Want coffee?"

"I do," Frank said, following Patrick to the kitchen. He rubbed his neck and sat at the kitchen table. "I'll be glad to be back on a normal schedule."

"Yeah, me, too." Patrick walked to the stove to get the coffee pot. He moved it to the table, retrieved a cup for Frank, and filled it. "Sugar?"

"No, just black. I need to wake up."

They both drank quickly. "Ready," asked Patrick.

With one last gulp, Frank sat his cup down and said, "Yes." Patrick grabbed his jacked as they walked out the door. With the door locked behind them, they walked downstairs to his car. The trip to the Strathmore's house took longer than it had a few nights ago; there was more traffic in the streets at this time of day. When they were finally clear, they headed to where the murders had taken place.

"You think the maid will be here?" Patrick asked.

"She better be," Frank replied. "I'll check in with Kelly. I think he was on duty watching the house." Patrick drove the car onto the long drive that cut through the large green lawn. The area was as empty as the early morning.

Kelly saw them coming and walked down the marble steps toward them. "Captain, we were expecting you." He nodded at Patrick. "Hey, Patrick."

Both men nodded at him. Patrick switched off the car and they got out to follow Kelly back up to the house. He opened the door for them to enter. Frank turned to him and asked, "Have you seen Mabel Clarke?"

"No, sir, not this morning."

Frank nodded. "That's fine. We're here to interview her. Keep your position and continue to monitor the area."

"I will," Kelly said, taking his position by the front door. Frank and Patrick continued inside.

The house manager came toward them at a steady pace. "Sirs, do you have more questions?"

Patrick eyed the man and remembered what his statement had detailed. He'd had his hands full with the multiple party guests and hadn't met the mystery woman.

"We need to talk to Miss Clarke," Frank told him.

The man's composure broke, and he pulled out a handkerchief to wipe his head.

Patrick and Frank shared a glance. "Something wrong?" asked Patrick.

The question didn't seem to alleviate the man's stress, and his hands were shaky. "She didn't show up for breakfast this morning. I went to check her room, and it was empty," he admitted.

"She knew she wasn't supposed to leave?" Frank phrased it as a question, but he meant it as a demand.

"Yes, that point was quite clear. She and I discussed it after you left."

"Did anyone else leave?" Patrick asked.

The manager drew himself up and regained his composure. "No, sir, they did not. My staff is aware of their responsibilities."

"All but Miss Clarke," muttered Patrick.

The butler shot a glance his way but chose not to respond.

Frank took over and said, "I was told that Mr. Strathmore's parents would be seeing to the house."

"Yes, we received word this morning that we're to maintain our positions. The house will be kept in the family and fully staffed."

"Will everyone stay on?" Patrick asked.

The house manager nodded. "Yes. Most of us have been here since the house was retained by the family, more than 20 years ago." He frowned briefly. "That is, all but Mabel."

"When did she start her employment here?"

"She's relatively new to the house. She's only been here about two years."

Patrick looked at Frank over at the butler. "Can we look at her room?"

"Yes, but you won't find anything. When we checked on her, the room was cleared out."

"Cleared out? Everything?"

"She didn't even leave any trash," the butler replied.

"We need to check it anyway," Frank told the man.

"This way please." Frank and Patrick followed the butler to the back staircase that went down to the servants' quarters while the house manager dismissed the rest of the staff. They walked down a long hallway that had doors closed on both sides. They passed two closed doors and stopped at a third. The butler took out his key.

"You locked it?" asked Frank.

"We secured it, in case you needed to view the room."

Patrick and Frank entered and confirmed the butler's words. The room was empty except for a single bed, a dresser, and a small desk. "There's a window," said Patrick, walking over to it. "And it's unlocked."

"Could she have gotten through that to exit the premises?" Frank asked the butler.

The butler, who stayed at the door, laughed suddenly and covered it quickly with a cough. "That window is a little small for Mabel."

"Yeah, I think you're right," Patrick agreed. "How do you think she might have left the premises?"

"Your officers covered both exits, but there are many *larger* windows she could've used."

"Okay, we've seen enough here," said Frank. They left the room and made their way back to the foyer. "Did any of the other staff know that she'd left?"

The butler stopped. "The house manager and I have questioned the staff, and to a person, they denied knowing anything about Mabel leaving."

"Did you believe them?" Patrick asked.

"I've known this staff for many years so, yes, I do believe them," the man said and walked away from them.

"What now?" asked Patrick as they followed him out.

Frank shrugged.

The butler said over his shoulder, "You might try her male friend's home."

"He isn't staff?" Frank asked.

"No, we preferred he didn't come here. He's not the most honest sort, as he's often in and out of prison."

"Do you know his address?"

"Yes, Mabel would complain about how long it took her to get to him since we wouldn't allow him here." The butler walked to a small table in the foyer and wrote quickly. He handed the paper to Frank. "This is his address."

Frank handed it to Patrick. "We need to head there immediately."

"Thank you," Patrick told the butler as he read the paper.

"Yes, thank you," said Frank.

"Sir, we would just like to know what happened here and why," the butler said.

"We'll share as much as we can," promised Frank. He waved to Patrick, and they started out the door. He stopped suddenly and turned back to the butler. "Have the Strathmores always had parties like the one the other night?"

The butler sighed and sat in a chair near the small table. "Yes, for years. They've become more decadent over the years and often people would show up who didn't have any connections with them."

"We'll let you know when we determine what happened," Frank told the butler. The man hadn't moved from his position. "Patrick, are you ready?"

Patrick nodded and led the way out the door. After the car was cranked, Frank joined him in the car. "Got the address?" Frank asked.

"Here." Patrick handed the paper to Frank.

Frank studied the address. "Hmmm. Not close by."

"No, it's back in the city."

"I hope she's there."

"Me, too. You know the way?"

"I do, it's on the dodgy end of Greenwich Village." They drove quietly and stopped about a block from the building. "What're you thinking" Frank asked, as he looked toward the apartment building.

"If she hears us, she's going to rabbit. Probably right out the window."

"I know," Frank muttered. "Chasing her down four flights of fire escape is not something I'm looking forward to."

Patrick smiled slightly. "Stairs or fire escape. Which one do you want?" he asked.

Frank looked at his friend. "Well, partner, I think you're younger and in better shape."

Patrick's smile grew. "Figured you were going to say that." He reached into the back of the car and pulled out his umbrella.

"Expecting rain?" Frank asked.

"You never know."

They walked toward the building. Frank went to the front door and Patrick around to the fire escape. He used the umbrella hook handle to reach the ladder and pulled it down to him. He climbed slowly and meticulously toward the floor where Mabel was supposed to be located. He stopped one floor beneath her apartment. *Might as well meet her here*, thought Patrick. He hung his umbrella on the rail in front of him and folded his arms.

There was a loud noise above him—glass breaking and a scuffle of steps rushing down the metal steps. Patrick was ready and casually grasped the top of the umbrella, leaving the bottom hooked to the rail. A woman came down the fire escape, not looking where she was going. She hit the umbrella hard and fell back with an "Oof." He grabbed her easily by her coat and held her tight.

She shook her head and focused on him. "Hey, what're you doin', you big lummox? Let me go," she said, shaking her fist. Her Irish brogue was strong.

"No, I don't think so," he said. He pulled out his badge and his gun and showed them to her. "I think we'll go back upstairs. My captain has some questions for you."

She glared at him. "I won't be saying anythin'."

"Yeah, well, we'll see about that. Now, up with you." He pointed up to indicate the direction.

"You got her?" Frank called from above.

"I do," Patrick replied. "Now, up," he repeated to the woman. She looked mutinous but pushed herself up and trudged back upstairs.

By the time they returned to the open window, Frank had cleared out the glass that had been broken during her escape and the duo climbed back into the apartment.

"Is anyone else here?" Patrick asked, looking around the small place. The kitchen and living area were in the same room and the bed was against a far wall.

"Not that I could find," said Frank.

"Where's your friend?" Patrick asked the woman.

"He's got nothin' to do with this," she said defensively, folding her arms over her chest.

"That didn't answer the question," Frank said.

"He's back in prison," she muttered. "He left me money to keep the place. He wants to come back here when he gets out."

Frank let that go. "Sit." He directed her to the kitchen table.

Her mouth was pulled tight, and she started to rub her arms but didn't follow his direction.

"I don't know nothin."

Patrick grabbed her arm and pulled her into a chair. He leaned toward her and said in a soft voice, "I don't think you are being honest about that, Mabel."

"You were the upstairs maid to Mrs. Strathmore?" Frank leaned in next to Patrick.

She pushed her chair away from them and cocked her head. "Yes," she said slowly.

"You were there the night of the party?" asked Patrick.

"Your officers told you that. Why do you need me to confirm?"

"Let us ask the questions," said Frank.

Patrick continued. "Did you go to Mrs. Strathmore's bedroom that night?"

She slammed her hand down on the table beside her. "I don't want to talk about it."

"Why not?" asked Frank. He moved to sit across from her.

"They were good to me. The only thing they ever asked of me was to keep my mouth shut!" she shouted at them.

"They are gone now," said Frank, his voice low. "We want to get some answers for the family."

"They won't want them," she muttered miserably. "It'll be only hurtin' 'em."

"Why not let us make that decision?"

She sighed and unclenched her hands and spread them wide

on the table. "Okay, ask your questions. I'll do the best I can to answer."

Patrick sat next to Frank and said, "A woman was described in some witness statements: a blonde seen in the company of Mr. and Mrs. Strathmore during the past three months."

"It was more like six months," she muttered.

"Who was she?"

"At first, I didn't know. I thought she was like the others and would just be around for a week or two."

"Others?" asked Patrick.

"Yeah. There was always a girl with the two of them, the whole time I've been with the family."

"What was her relationship with the Strathmores?"

"She stayed with them."

"With them." *Them?*

"Yeah, they'd all enter that large suite, and I'd bring in the drinks and food. They were in their bedclothes when I was in the room."

"All of them?" Frank tried to temper his tone; he didn't want to seem too surprised.

"Yeah. Once I found the three of them in bed together."

"Did they see you?"

"No, they weren't wearing any clothes and were occupied."

The men didn't ask by what.

Patrick asked, "Had their relationship changed any in the last few weeks or months?"

Mabel frowned, thinking back. "The missus was gettin' more tense. Usually, the parties were fun for her, but she didn't even greet her guests that night. She and the mister often would go around the room greeting everyone before heading upstairs."

"Was the girl with them? As they circulated?"

"No, she came into the party and talked to others and then they'd meet upstairs at a set time."

Frank turned the conversation back to Mrs. Strathmore. "How could you tell Mrs. Strathmore was more tense?"

"She yelled and was more frantic that morning."

"On the day she died?"

"Yeah," Mabel replied, wiping her tears. "And her jewelry changed."

"How so?"

"Well, each morning, we choose her clothes and jewelry for the day and the night. Over the last few weeks, I'd noticed there was less jewelry to pick from."

"Did you ask her why items weren't there any longer?"

"I did. I forgot that she didn't like to be questioned."

"What was her response?"

"She wasn't happy. She threw a vase at me and told me it was none of my business," she said, frowning.

"Was there something else?" Frank prodded.

"That night, when I came up to the room to get the Strathmores ready for bed, that woman, the blonde, was wearing the missus' necklace. The one I had noticed was missing that morning."

"Can you describe it?" asked Patrick.

"It was lovely, square stone emeralds with diamonds gathered around each one. They glowed in the light."

"When was the last time you saw the necklace?"

"The day before. The missus was wearing it when she got ready for the evening's events."

"Hmm," Frank muttered.

"Do you think she killed them both?" Mabel whispered; her eyes wide.

"We don't know enough right now to comment," Frank replied.

"The blonde woman, did she have any distinguishing marks?" Patrick asked.

"About a month ago, she needed help," Mabel said, moving her hand to her arm.

"What kind of help?"

"It was her arm; someone had bitten her hard enough to break the skin."

Patrick's eyes widened at this. "Which arm?"

"The left one, about here." She rubbed her arm again. "I sewed it up the best I could; she wouldn't go to the doctor." She stared into space, lost in her thoughts. She turned her gaze to Patrick. "You know, she didn't cry at all, and I know she was in a lot of pain."

Patrick closed his eyes; he knew who it was. *It was Merle! Jean's sister!*

Frank didn't see Patrick's reaction and continued with the questioning. "You have no idea what her name is?"

"I'm sorry, I don't."

"Okay," Patrick said abruptly. "We don't need anything else now. We'll leave you here." Frank looked at his friend with raised eyebrows. "We have what we need," he said, meeting Frank's eyes.

Frank looked at Mabel. "Since we have what we need, we'll leave now." They stood. Frank looked over at the woman. "We'll need you to go back to the house. You've nothing to fear. I understand your jobs are still there."

"Really? I was so scared; I didn't want to be sent back to the old country. There's nothing left for me there."

"Yes." At the door, Frank whispered to Patrick, "What do you know?"

"I'll tell you when we get there," Patrick replied in the same tone.

"Get where?" Frank asked, frustrated.

Mabel interrupted their conversation. "Patrick, how long since you've been back to the auld sod?"

He knew she meant Ireland. He turned to her. "I was born there, but I only remember my life here."

Her eyes turned dreamy. "I miss it. It was wonderful, and then it wasn't."

"I've heard that. Your accent, why is it different from the other night?" he asked.

She shrugged. "The Strathmores wanted refined help. They wouldn't be wanting a common Irish potato farmer mixin' with their high and mighty friends, now, would they?"

Frank tapped his friend's shoulder, and he followed him out of the building. When they got to the car, Frank spoke up. "I didn't know you were born in Ireland."

"I was. My parents brought me over and we settled in Chicago."

Frank frowned. "But I thought your parents were already in Chicago." He tried to remember what Lottie had told him about her family. "Wasn't your family bakery established long before you were born?"

"My *adoptive* parents, Tim and Dora Flannigan, are in Chicago. I went to live with them after my parents were murdered."

"Patrick, I didn't know. I'm sorry."

"Thanks, it was a long time ago. I don't remember much about them."

"Do you have any plans to go to Ireland?"

"One day," he said. He'd been thinking about it, but he was unsure of how Tim and Dora would react. Even though he had been adopted, he didn't feel anything less for them; he was part of a family. Patrick changed the subject and asked, "Did Jojo drop the note off for me?"

"I don't know," admitted Frank. "He has a sleep-away with Lottie and Elise. He was promised some motorcycle rides."

Hmm, thought Patrick, *will Jean and Merle be there? Could it be that easy?*

"Just when are you going to tell me why you ended the interview so abruptly?"

Patrick pulled in slowly to the front of the theater. He turned to Frank. "How about now? This is what I know. The woman I'm seeing has a blonde sister that I've seen in flashy clothes."

"That could be anyone these days."

"I thought that," Patrick admitted, "until Mabel mentioned the scar on the woman's arm. I saw it when I was at the theater."

Frank sat back and considered the new information. His reflections were interrupted by a short, round man yelling at a teenager. They exited the car and leaned back on it to observe the fight.

"Move that sign over here!" the man ordered, pointing to his right.

"But you just said to move it to this location," the boy complained.

"Just move it!"

The duo watched the boy drag the heavy sign to the spot the man referenced. He froze then, waiting for the next direction.

Patrick jumped into the conversation before the man told the boy to move the sign again. "Excuse me."

The man didn't turn away from the sign; he pushed a hand toward Patrick. "I'm busy. I don't have time for you." He looked at the boy again. " You…"

The boy knew what was coming and said with a long-suffering sigh, "Where now?"

"Back to where we had it, over by the booth."

"*Every* time. You do this *every time*," the boy complained.

"Shut your yap and just move it."

Frank and Patrick watched the boy move the sign yet again and waited. The old man finally turned to them and said shortly, "There isn't a movie tonight." He looked back to the sign. "No, that ain't right either."

The boy hefted the sign up again and moved it back to the position it had just come from.

The man glanced back at the two men. "You still here?"

"Are Jean or her sister here?" Patrick asked.

The man frowned heavily at the question. "They're gone."

"Gone?"

"Yeah, I got a note. Hey, Jerry, bring Jean's note to me." The young man ran over to them, reached into his back pocket, and handed the older man a folded piece of paper.

"Can I see it?" asked Patrick.

"Sure."

Patrick took it. It was short and to the point. 'We've decided to go back home. We won't be returning.'

The old man grimaced. "And just like that, I'm out an entire staff." He looked at them consideringly. "You wouldn't be able to play the piano, would you?"

"Not me," Patrick replied, gripping the note fiercely and thinking of Jean. *Where is she? Have they run away?*

The man looked at Frank hopefully. "Nope, not me," Frank told him.

The man sighed and pushed back his hat. "Yeah, well, I need someone by tomorrow or we ain't opening."

Frank tapped Patrick on the shoulder. "We should go."

Patrick nodded. He held out the mangled paper. "Would you mind if I kept this?" he asked.

"Yeah, sure. It's no use to me." He turned to the boy again and yelled, "What're you doing? Why's the sign over there?"

"Old man, I'm not moving it again!"

Frank and Patrick left them to their argument and got the car started. "Funny thing, I actually can play the piano." Frank chuckled.

"Want me to tell him?" Patrick asked, nodding at the arguing duo.

"No, that's okay. I'm quite busy with my current job. Where to now?"

"The girls' apartment."

"Want to give me some more information on these two women?"

Patrick gripped the wheel and stared ahead. "Jean Cooper and her sister Merle worked at the theater. I've seen Merle a couple of times, usually when she was on her way to a party."

"What kind of people are they?"

"I think good," Patrick said hesitantly. "Merle has a flashy personality, maybe a bit of an opportunist. Very protective of Jean."

"And Jean?"

"Quieter, she has big dreams. I don't think she's involved with Merle's party life."

"You know the address?"

"I do." Patrick thought of his and Jean's walks. *Is she gone? Is that all I'd have of her?*

It was a little while later when they arrived. Frank got out quickly and started toward the building. He turned to ask Patrick a question and found him still sitting in the car; he hadn't moved from his position. Frank walked back over and leaned in. "Something you need to talk about?"

"What?" Patrick asked. "No, I'm okay." He got out and followed Frank inside. The apartment building was old but looked taken care of.

"Not the best neighborhood," observed Frank.

"No, but they couldn't have made much at the movie theater."

"Another reason for Merle to look for other ways to make money," Frank commented.

They walked through the door. "I don't know which one is theirs," Patrick admitted, looking around the building. A young boy sat on the stairs with a knife and a piece of wood. Patrick walked over to him. "Hey, we're looking for Jean Cooper's apartment."

"Fourth floor. Second door on the left," the boy said, not looking up from his task.

"Thanks!" They headed upstairs.

"They're not there," he called up to them.

They stopped. "How do you know?" Patrick asked.

"Saw 'em leave early yesterday morning; took everything with them."

"What were you doing at that time of morning?" Frank asked suspiciously.

"Delivering papers. Got to make some change. I came down behind them."

Frank looked at Patrick. "Is there anyone who can let us in?"

"Sure, my pops is the building manager," the boy said. "He can do it." After the pronouncement, the boy didn't move.

"Will you go and get him for us?" Patrick asked in exasperation.

The boy folded up his knife slowly and stood. "I might...for a price."

Frank leaned toward the boy and shook his hand at him. "You're talking to police officers."

He shoved his cap back. "Yeah? So what? I have the information you need and that makes it valuable."

"Are all the kids like this?" muttered Frank.

Patrick smiled slightly. "How about a quarter?"

"That'll do."

Patrick flipped it at him. The boy caught it deftly and moved to the door nearest the stairs. He opened it and called out, "Pops! Some coppers here about Merle and Jean."

An older version of the boy walked out, pulling up his suspenders over his short-sleeved white shirt. "Who are you?"

Frank pulled out his badge and showed it to him. "We're looking for Jean and Merle Cooper."

"Why?"

"They might have information we need."

He sighed. "They were good tenants. We liked them. Let's head up." The man trudged up the stairs, his eyes concentrating on each step. The walk took longer than the drive had. Frank and Patrick followed and didn't comment. He had a key and opened the door for them. "Lock up when you leave, please."

"We will, thank you." Frank and Patrick walked into the small room.

From the hallway, the man called, "The furniture was provided, belongs to the building."

That was all that was left in the small room. Patrick went to the kitchen and opened the doors. "Empty," he called. There was nothing, not even a scrap of paper on the floor.

"Clean," Frank confirmed.

Patrick pushed the small closet door shut and saw something on the wall. He took it down. "Well, there is one thing."

"What is it?" asked Frank, walking over to him.

"It looks like one of the pictures we saw at the theater today, a movie picture."

"Yeah, it looks like a lobby card. They worked there and probably got it for free."

Patrick didn't comment as he studied it. *The note said they were going home. I don't think so. Jean had said there was no going back. They didn't have anyone left there.* He tapped the picture. *Hollywood was her dream. Would she and Merle head out there?*

"Theories?" Frank asked his friend.

"I think Merle was the third person in that room, and I think their disappearance answers that question."

"You think she was involved with both of the Strathmores and possibly blackmailing one or both of them?"

"And she provided the final push to a woman who was unhinged."

"The jewelry. We'll need to get an inventory and find out from Mabel if anything else is missing."

"The jewels and the car would be a way to finance their way out of New York."

"We'll need to talk to the chauffeur. How did Merle get access to the car?"

Patrick took off his hat and slapped it on his leg. "Dammit, why didn't they stay?"

"Yeah, this whole thing's a mess. It would've been much easier if they'd stayed. Now, we'll have to put information about them in the papers."

"I thought that all the evidence points to a murder-suicide."

"It does, but we still need answers," Frank agreed. "I'd like to talk to Merle."

"I'll write up the article and get it submitted," Patrick said.

"It should include a description that two women are part of the tragic events and wanted for questioning."

"I agree. I'll head to the newspaper office and get started."

Sorry, Jean, Patrick thought. *I wish you'd come to me before disappearing.*

Chapter Twelve

Jean drove her shift and saw lights ahead of them. *A city, finally.* There'd been a lot of small towns along their way that had allowed them to rest, pick up groceries, and keep on the move. She nudged her sister. "Merle, I think we're in a big enough city to try to get rid of the car."

"Good," Merle muttered, struggling to sit up. "I want to get out of this thing. I don't know what the big deal is about cars. They're bumpy, uncomfortable, and we've had to stop for water and gas all the time."

"I'm also worried about the tires," Jean added.

"Why?"

"Last time we stopped, I thought they were looking a bit thin."

"Well, that's just great. One more thing that's probably going to take money to fix," Merle complained, yawning broadly and sitting back in her seat. "This car was meant for city driving. Just drive until you see some kind of shop." The sun had gone down, and it was getting dark. That would work in their favor. They drove through the city at a slow pace. "There." Merle pointed to a garage on their right.

"That one?" Jean asked doubtfully. "It looks rundown." She stopped the car just short of the entrance.

"Just a gut feeling." The garage did have a run-down appearance, but when you looked closer there were cars that looked expensive parked inside. *This is the one*, thought Merle.

Merle could read people and Jean trusted her instincts. "Okay, then we stop here." Jean pulled into the area in front of the garage. A man in overalls strolled out with his hands in his pocket. He let out a slow whistle. "In here." He waved her into the garage.

Jean followed his direction and pulled into the building. The man immediately went to close the doors behind them and turned on the lights.

Jean tapped her hands on the wheel, a thread of doubt making its way through her. "Merle, is this a good idea?"

"It is," her sister said firmly. "Just, let me handle this."

Jean tried to relax her hands on the steering wheel and waited.

The man was much younger than Merle had originally thought. She watched his slow stride as he came toward them. *Sandy hair and a lanky body, just my type,* thought Merle. She quickly ran her fingers through her hair and smoothed down her top.

"Nice car," the man said, running his hand over the hood and kneeling to examine the tires.

"It is," she agreed.

He stood up and leaned against the car. "Lozier Model 77. You want to make a deal?"

"What makes you think we might want to sell?" asked Merle coyly. These types of deals were her specialty.

Oh, he liked this game. He leaned toward her and said in a low voice, "I know who you are." Both women just stared at him.

Jean shot a glance at Merle, her eyes wide.

Merle raised an eyebrow. "You think you have something on us?"

He turned and moved to a small room off the large garage. When he returned, he had a paper with him. "I know I do," he said, holding up the paper for them to view. Across the front of the paper, the words shouted:

TWO WOMEN!! A YOUNG BLONDE AND HER SISTER WANTED FOR QUESTIONING IN DOUBLE FATALITY!!

Jean grabbed it from him, reading closely. Both of their names were listed! She couldn't get past that; they seemed to know everything, including the fact they'd taken the car. *How did they know? Who saw us?*

Merle didn't reach for the paper. Instead, she turned to the man. "So, you have an offer for us or what?"

He took the rag out of his pocket and rubbed an imaginary spot on the side light, next to Merle. "Maybe I do."

"What is it?"

He studied the car and moved to the engine. He propped the hood open and lowered his head inside. "Start it up," he called.

Jean looked at her sister and she nodded.

Jean started it up. He stayed under the hood for a long while. When he finished, he pulled his head out, wiping his hands on a rag. "You can turn it off." Again, Jean followed the instructions. He walked around the car, eyeing the black chassis with red pin striping, the white wicker door inserts, and the black tufted leather interior. "The tires have some wear."

"We HAVE been moving around a lot the last few days," Merle said laconically.

"Yeah, that would do it," he agreed.

Merle watched and waited and, when he seemed to have completed his evaluation, she asked him, "Ready to make a deal?"

He smiled slowly at her and said, "Follow me."

Merle returned that smile and reached for the handle to get out of the vehicle. Jean started to follow her. Merle turned and said, "Stay here. I'll take care of this."

"You're sure?" Jean asked, the frown deepening on her forehead as her eyes moved from the man and back to Merle.

"I am," Merle said confidently, opening the door to get out.

She hesitated briefly before closing it and turned to Jean. "Don't come in, no matter what you hear."

"But..." Jean protested. "What if you need help?"

"Oh, hun, I won't need any help," Merle said and winked before turning and following the man. The door slammed shut, jarring Jean, but she stayed where she was.

Jean could hear a heated discussion behind the closed door, and then something fell or was thrown. What followed was silence. *Should I go in? No, she said wait.* She stared at the door intently until it finally opened.

"You can come in now," Merle called.

Jean jumped out of the car and headed to the room. When she entered, she saw the man on one side of the desk with his head in his hands and her sister in a chair on the other side with a large smile.

"Are you okay, Merle?" Jean asked as she looked at them. *What happened here? Had she... No, no. Or had she?*

"Oh, I'm just fine, aren't I, Jesse?" her sister said with a smile.

He lifted his head. "I'm not."

"That's not any of my concern." Merle held out her hand and said, "The money we agreed to?"

He sighed heavily. "I'll bring it out to you."

Merle lowered her hand. She knew a dismissal when she heard it. "Jean, let's go back to the car." Merle had to drag Jean out.

"What happened in there?" Jean whispered.

"I got us the money to get us to California," Merle said confidently.

"But what did you *do*?"

"I did what I had to do," said Merle. *Well, had is a little strong,* she thought with a small smile. *It was rather pleasant.* She drifted a moment and saw Jean was still staring at her. She straightened up and said briskly, "I have to get us to a safe location and that takes money."

Jean sighed and let that go. "How much did you get?"

"Enough to get train tickets and set us up in California," she said triumphantly.

"Did you take all of his money?" Jean asked with wide eyes.

She laughed huskily. "No, honey, he's playing a game. He knew the minute we came in how much that car was worth."

"How much is it worth?" Jean asked. Her knowledge of how much things cost didn't extend to cars.

"Five thousand," Merle replied. "Minimally, it costs a lot more to purchase a custom car like this new." Jean's face lost all color and she wavered on her feet. Merle grabbed her by the shoulders and said in a firm voice, "Pull yourself together. We have to finish this so we can get out of here." Jesse came out of the office, his head hung low as he walked over to them. Merle released her abruptly to take a plain wrapped package from him and handed it to Jean. "Open it, Jean. "

"You don't trust me?" Jesse asked, grabbing his heart and pretending to be hurt.

Merle didn't spare him a glance as Jean opened the package. "Would you?"

His expression changed with a wide smile. It changed his whole countenance. "No. No, I don't think I would," he murmured.

Jean didn't understand what was happening. *Why is he smiling now?* She looked at her sister as she held out her hand to Jesse and said, "It was nice doing business with you."

He took her hand and brought it to his lips. "It's been my pleasure."

Merle let her hand linger and then pulled it away gently. "Time to go." She turned to Jean. "Help me get our things." They pulled the bags out of the car as Jesse moved to pull the boxes out of the back.

He stared at them for a long moment and finally shook his head. "Wait a minute. There's no way you won't get caught. You won't be able to go out and about like that."

"Like what?" Merle asked.

He walked over and looked at both of them. "Your descriptions and names are everywhere. You need to change your names and appearances if you want to move around undetected."

"Name change, yeah, I thought of that," said Jean. The newspaper had scared her.

"Appearances?" asked Merle.

Jesse studied Merle. "That blonde hair has to go. You should dye it."

"My hair?" Merle asked disconcertingly. She reached up and touched it and, for the first time since all of this started, she looked uncertain. Jean reached out her hand to her, but Merle didn't take it; she just stared at Jesse.

"And you," he said and turned to Jean.

"Me? My hair is already brown." She touched her hair, behaving similarly to her sister.

"No, not your hair. Do you have any pants?"

"I do. Why?"

"You might put them and a basic shirt on." He walked back to his office and threw a man's hat her way. She grabbed it mid-air. She examined it and said, "Thanks... I think." She put it on.

"No, not like that." Jesse moved to her and adjusted it on her head. "Now, keep your hair tucked in and your collar turned up." He turned back to Merle. "And you, I have someone who can get you the dye and a place to stay for the night."

"Why would you do that?" she asked suspiciously. She gripped the money tighter. *Is this a scam?*

He saw the move and tried to reason with them. "Look, the longer you're hidden, the longer I have to get rid of the car. And I do plan to get rid of it at a significant gain on my part."

Merle nodded grudgingly.

Jean said, "Thank you."

He nodded. "Let's go."

"Is it close?" Jean asked. Their bags and boxes were heavy, and she didn't think they could carry them far.

"It is."

The three gathered the bags and boxes. Jesse led the way out of the shop through a side door. "Wait," Merle said. She turned her back to Jesse and put the money inside her blouse before they continued out the side door. The night had gotten darker, and Jean stayed close to her sister.

Merle kept quiet and hoped they hadn't made a poor decision by stopping there. *Is this our new beginning or our end?* She felt a sense of trepidation as they walked to the small house next to the garage. Jesse opened the gate for them and waited. Jean started to follow when Merle grabbed her arm.

"Well, come on," Jean told her. When Merle wouldn't move, she whispered, "Come on. You trusted the man before in the office. Why not now?"

Merle heard the taunt, straightened her shoulders, and walked forward. "Jean, aren't you coming?"

Jean rolled her eyes. "Right behind you, sis."

They walked through the gate and up to the house. Just as they stepped onto the small porch, the door opened. A small woman with short dark hair spoke. "Jesse, what're you doing here, and who are these people?"

"They need a room for the night," he explained. He leaned toward the woman. "It's important to me."

She looked them over. "Only if they pay in advance."

Merle took over from there, feeling more confident. "We have it."

The woman looked at Jesse and he nodded. She moved back. "Okay then, come in." They entered with their belongings. She eyed the bags and boxes and said, "You can set those in the small closet over there." She motioned to the staircase.

As Jean and Merle carried their belongings to the small closet, the woman grabbed Jesse by the ear and dragged him back onto the porch. "Who are these people?" she demanded.

"Oww, jeeze! Stop, sis. Please."

She gave his ear a final twist and released him. "Well, explain."

He rubbed his sore ear and said, "They're business contacts, Billie, and they're on their way out of town."

Billie raised an eyebrow at the terms he used. She'd dealt with his 'business contacts' before. "Fine, but you're responsible for them."

"I can do that."

Billie squinched her eyes. "And stay away from the blonde."

"Too late for that," he muttered under his breath.

"What?"

"Nothin'. Nothin' at all."

Billie shot her brother a dirty look. "Time to get them settled."

"I need to talk to you after. I have an update on our plans."

She nodded and waved him back into the house. The sisters stood with one bag each. Billie went to the stairs and called to them. "Come with me." They followed her up the small stairway and she pushed open the first door they found on the second floor. "This is your room, and the bathroom is down the hall." They walked into the room and looked around. "There's two beds. Will this work for you?"

Jean and Merle each sat on a bed. Their tiredness was apparent. Billie felt a softening for the two ladies. *What's their story?*

"Billie," Jesse called from downstairs.

"On my way," she called back. She turned to them. "I'll be back to check on you." She closed the door, and they could hear her descending the stairs.

"At least it's clean," said Merle, wiping her fingers on the side table between the beds. Jean wanted to sleep more than anything, but she felt she had to keep an eye on Merle.

There was a knock on the door and Billie came in. "This is for you," she said, handing a bottle to Merle.

"What is it?"

"I hear you need to change your hair. This will change it."

Merle reached up to touch her hair and chewed her lip. She

understood the reasoning, but her hair was integral to who she was.

Jean stood and moved to sit next to her. "I'll help."

Merle took a deep, shuddering breath and nodded.

"How long has it been since you both ate anything?" Billie asked, giving the sisters a thorough review.

"A few days," Jean admitted.

"I'll make some sandwiches for you."

"Would you like me to help?" asked Jean. She started to stand. She didn't want them to be any more trouble than necessary.

"No, wait here. I'll get it back to you."

"Thank you for your kindness," Jean told her, sitting back on the bed.

Billie nodded and left to prepare the food.

Merle sat studying the bottle.

Jean put an arm around her. "It'll be safer for us to change our appearances."

Merle laid her head on Jean's shoulder. "I know."

They sat like that until they heard a knock on the door. Jean got up to answer it. Billie was there with a tray of sandwiches and two glasses of milk. Jean took it from her. "Thank you."

"Breakfast is at eight o'clock."

"Do you need your money now?" asked Merle.

"Let's discuss it tomorrow morning."

"We'll be there."

Billie nodded. "Good night." She closed the door as soon as she left.

Jean took the bottle from her sister. "Eat first and then we get some rest. We can work on that in the morning."

Merle looked relieved at the reprieve. Jean sat the tray on Merle's bed and they both picked up their sandwiches to eat. Neither talked; they were starving, and the food they'd found on the road hadn't been filling. They drank down their milk and Jean picked up the tray to take it downstairs. "Merle, you go to the bathroom first and I'll go after you."

"I guess I should." Merle moved to the bag by the door and laid it on the floor to open it. "A bit of a mess in here," she said.

"Couldn't be helped." Jean walked down the stairs. The light from under the door led her to the kitchen. She could hear voices as she pushed open the door. Billie and Jesse sat at the table. They stopped talking as soon as she entered. Billie stood and took the tray from her.

"I wanted to thank you for the food and a place to stay," Jean told her.

"That's okay. Sometimes we need help," replied Billie.

"Can you tell me how far we are from the train station?"

"A few blocks," Jesse spoke up from the table. She nodded and turned to leave. "I'll bring my car to help you move everything over."

She turned back and smiled in thanks. "See you in the morning." She hurried upstairs and into their room. Merle entered a few minutes later, sat on her bed, and began brushing her hair

"Your turn."

Jean reached into the open bag to retrieve her bedclothes. "Thank you," she said and started out.

"Any problems downstairs?"

"No. Jesse said he'd help us get to the train station in the morning."

"Oh, that's nice." Merle yawned. "Hurry up. You need to get some rest, too."

"All right." Jean grabbed her night things and ran to the bathroom. The bathtub was inviting but she knew she'd fall asleep. Instead, she gathered a clean rag and washed her body. She brushed her teeth, pulled on her gown, and walked back to their room. The lights were on, and Merle was asleep. Jean closed the door and, for extra security, turned the lock on the door. Satisfied, she moved to the bed and lay down. She was asleep before her head hit the pillow.

Chapter Thirteen

"Jean!" Merle called. "Jean, you need to wake up."

"Hmm, no. I don't wanna drive to California. It's too far," mumbled Jean.

"Up now. Come on." Merle shook her sister's shoulder.

"Didn't you just tell me to get some sleep?" she complained, not opening her eyes.

"I did, but that was about nine hours ago."

Nine! Jean's eyes snapped open at that remark. "Are we late?"

"Late? No, though it's seven o'clock and we have to dye my hair before we leave."

Jean's eyes searched her sister's face. "You changed your mind. It won't bother you?"

"I hadn't slept much, and I overreacted. I got us into this mess and, if I have to sacrifice my hair color, then so be it."

Jean nodded and got up.

"Follow me to the bathroom?" In the bathroom, Jean looked at the small box. It read **Brodie's Imperial Hair Dye Permanent Color**. "The dye goes into the hair, we wait some time, and then wash it out." She frowned, "I think we should test it first."

"We don't have time," Merle said philosophically. "Besides, it'll eventually wash out."

"And if it doesn't?" Jean knew how much her hair meant to her.

"Then it'll grow out," Merle said determinedly. Once they finished and cleaned up, Merle was left with a wet head of dark hair. "I'll have to give the lady of the house some money for towels," Merle murmured, taking a look at the stains.

"We can do that. For now, keep the towel wrapped around your head. Hopefully, it'll dry before we leave." Merle nodded and wrapped the towel around her hair.

They walked back to the bedroom, got dressed, and repacked their bags. Jean sat on the bed. Now that they'd had some sleep, she started to think about their destination again. "Hollywood," Jean murmured excitedly.

"And now it'll take a lot less time to get there. And we'll have enough money to live on for a while," she said looking down.

"It'll work out," Jean said determinedly.

She raised her toweled head and said determinedly, "It will. We'll be on the train today, this morning."

"That's a relief."

Merle touched her still-wrapped towel head. "Now or never," commented Jean. She took the towel off, Jean threw her a brush. Merle caught it and ran it through her damp hair. They gathered their things and headed downstairs.

"Breakfast," called Billie from the kitchen.

They left their luggage in the hallway and moved to the kitchen. Jean stepped ahead, pushed the door open, and they saw a table full of food. Jesse and Billie were eating.

"Well," Jesse said when he saw Merle. "That's a change."

"Yeah, you were right. I need to be less recognizable."

"And you?" Jesse asked Jean.

"Pants and a hat. Check," she said and gestured to her legs.

"You girls eat," Billie said. "You have a train to catch."

"Yeah, we do," confirmed Merle.

The sisters sat and began eating quietly, each consumed with their future plans. Jean looked around the small kitchen; there were boxes on the counters and opened cabinets. "Are you going somewhere?" she asked. The room hadn't looked like this last night.

Billie leaned back in her chair with her coffee. "Same as you. It's time for us to move on."

No one wanted to share their story, so they finished their food without further conversation. Jesse spoke up. "I have the car outside to take you to the station."

"Not…" started Merle.

"No, no. This one is my work vehicle. I'll move the other car at night."

"Good." Merle pulled out some money; it was from her savings. The other money was hidden, and she didn't want to show where it was to the group.

"You keep that," Billie said.

"But you said last night that we couldn't stay unless we could pay."

"Yeah, well, I said a lot of things last night. Now, I'm saying be safe and on your way."

"Thank you."

Jean stood and walked over to Billie and hugged her from behind. "Thank you."

"Yes, well, that's fine," Billie replied and patted the arms wrapped around her.

Merle stood. "Jean, we have to go now."

Jean stepped back. "You're right."

"Be safe," Billie told the two sisters.

"We will," called Jean. They walked into the hall and saw the bags and boxes were gone

"Where are they?" Asked Merle, looking around wildly.

Jesse's voice could be heard from outside. "Come on! We need to get goin'!" They went quickly to the door and found the packed car waiting.

"Well, come on," Jess called to them.

They hurried over and climbed into the front seat. Jesse drove quickly, dodging early morning delivery drivers on their way to the train station. He pulled to a stop and turned to them. "Well, this has been a good time. Don't mention me to anyone."

"Same for us," Merle said.

Jean reached for the door handle and said, "Come on, we don't want to miss the train!" They got out and went to retrieve their boxes and bags.

"Wait," Jesse called. He got out and walked around the back of the truck. Merle waited for him.

"We have to go," Jean implored, looking at the people rushing into the station.

"Give me a moment, please," Merle requested. Jean frowned and moved away from them. Jesse and Merle had a low, intense conversation. When it finished, Merle carried her bags and walked over to Jean.

"What was that about?" Jean asked her sister.

"Nothing. It was nothing," Merle muttered.

Jean frowned. That nothing seemed to bother her, but they didn't have time to discuss it now. They started walking toward the crowds entering the station.

"Merle!" Jesse called. They stopped and turned. Jesse ran over and took her hand. "Maybe we'll meet up again one day," he murmured. "You know, I always had a thing for blondes. "

Merle gave him a studied glance. "Yeah, maybe we'll meet up again."

Jean was anxious to leave. "Let's go."

Merle pulled her hat down over her face. Hers and Jesse's hands separated, and she joined Jean. They carried their luggage and boxes toward the ticket counter. Merle turned and watched Jesse drive off.

"Merle," Jean said in a low voice.

Merle turned to the frowning Jean. "What?"

"You know what. That's what got us into this mess in the first place."

"Hmph. I was just watching."

Jean just grabbed her arm and pulled her to the counter.

The clerk looked at the sisters. "Where to?" he asked.

"California, Hollywood," Merle said firmly.

He processed the tickets and gathered their paperwork. He returned with a quoted price. Once they paid, the tickets were theirs. A train horn sounded. "You might want to hurry. That's your train there. You'll have several connections. The trip will be eighty-three hours to San Francisco and then a transfer the rest of the way." The horn sounded again. "Go now!"

They listened to him and dragged their luggage and boxes on board. A porter ran up. "Can I help you?"

"Yes, we should have a cabin," Merl said, handing him their tickets.

He glanced at the tickets. "Let me take some bags."

"That would be great." Merle handed her bags to him.

"Follow me." He took the bags and walked them to their cabin. He opened their door. "Get settled, ladies. We're starting to pull out."

The sisters walked in and placed their luggage above the seats. The train jerked and started to move. "We're off," said Merle as she slumped into her seat. "What do you think it'll be like?" she asked, staring out the window.

"Hollywood?"

Merle nodded.

"From what I've read, it has been developed. There are still a lot of rolling hills and orange groves. The first studio was Nester Films but now many others are setting up shop. What'll we do first?"

"I've been thinking about that. We'll need a place of our own. A house, I think."

"A house of our own?" said Jean. They'd never had one. Their homes had always belonged to someone else. Even their parents had leased their land to raise horses. When they passed, Jean and Merle had to sell the horses to pay for the lease to close out. They'd had almost nothing when they moved to New York.

Merle had plans. "Oh yes, a house of our very own. We have enough money and time to set down roots. Ones that can't be taken away."

Jean sat back. "A house. Do we really have enough money?"

"If we don't have enough, then we start selling the jewels."

Jean said, "We'll need jobs first thing. I expect I'll be able to find work in a movie theater there playing the piano."

"No," Merle said sharply. "You won't do that."

"Merle, I'll be able to pitch in when we get there."

"No, you won't. We moved to New York because of me. You had to settle there. You're not settling in California."

"But..."

"No, it's my turn to take care of us."

Jean nodded. "So, we settle and then we go get jobs."

"We do."

Jean asked tentatively, "What happened in that office with Jesse?" Merle looked away and stayed silent. Jean stared at her for a long moment and then said, "Can you please find another way to negotiate in the future?"

"Yeah, I just might do that."

"Eighty-three hours, almost four days, and then we move to another train in California." They sat back and watched the scenery rush by.

Chapter Fourteen

Strathmore house

Patrick walked around the various cars in the garage. "You take care of all these?" Jim, the chauffeur, leaned over a car, shining its hood while talking to him. "You said one is missing," Patrick inquired.

"Yes, the Lozier 77."

Patrick wrote that down. "And who do you think took it?"

"I'm not sure..." The man trailed off.

Patrick tried a different tactic, "Did you see Merle Cooper around the cars?" Jim mumbled something unintelligible. "What was that?" asked Patrick.

"I taught her to drive it. She'd come down and visit me before she left in the mornings."

"Was it just that car?"

"Yeah, she said it'd been promised to her."

"Had it?"

"I don't know, but she seemed pretty sure about it. She thought she'd be taking it soon."

"How did she get the keys?"

"She knew where I kept them."

"How did she know that?"

"I told her. We were friends, you know? We talked about stuff, and she hung around sometimes."

"Just friends."

"Yeah, that lady had too many other relationships going on, if you know what I mean. I think she was relieved I just liked talking to her."

Patrick closed his notebook. "That should be all for now."

"She was a nice lady, you know," Jim said. "I hope she comes out of this okay."

"So do I."

Patrick thanked the man and walked slowly to his car. He cranked it and then got behind the wheel to drive back to the station.

The papers had carried the story and requested information about Jean and Merle. So far, there hadn't been any reports of either the car or the sisters. He walked into the precinct and put his notes down on his desk.

"Patrick!" called Frank.

He looked over at his captain. He stood in the doorway to his office.

"Don't get comfortable. We have to head back to the Strathmore house."

"I just got back from there," Patrick complained.

"We need an inventory of the jewelry that was taken."

Patrick picked up his jacket. "This case is taking up all of our time," he grumbled.

"You know that society deaths take priority."

"Want me to drive?"

"Why do you think I called you?" Frank smiled

They signed out and headed back to the house. There was no

one outside the house, as the officers that had been at the house had been reassigned. Frank knocked on the door.

The door opened, revealing the butler. "Sir," he said. "The house manager would like to speak with you."

"Of course," said Frank.

They waited and Patrick nudged his friend. "Over there."

Frank followed his glance. The house manager stood talking to a couple in a room on the far side of the foyer. He nodded to something they said and approached Frank and Patrick.

"We need to inventory the jewelry that may be missing," Frank began.

"Yes, sir, it's just..." The manager waved his hand toward the opposite end of the foyer.

Frank looked in that direction at an older man standing at the doorway. "Who is that?"

The house manager dropped his voice, "It's the parents, sir."

"Whose parents?" asked Patrick.

"Mr. Strathmore's."

"When did they get here?" asked Frank.

"A little while ago."

"We'll need to speak to them."

The house manager started to step back but hesitated and muttered, "Watch them, sir."

Frank frowned, and Patrick mirrored his expression. "Wonder what he meant by that?" Patrick asked.

"They have money and lots of it," muttered Frank. "They'll expect that we'll do as we're told."

"Not likely."

"I agree. It looks like they're moving into another room." Frank called out to the couple still standing in the foyer. "Just a minute, Mr. and Mrs. Strathmore, we need to speak with you." They seemed to not hear him and walked into the room without turning. Frank got impatient. "Patrick," he said and waved him forward. They entered the room the couple had entered. The couple sat and the maid had begun to serve the tea. They still hadn't acknowledged their presence. Frank wasn't going to be polite. "We need a word with you."

Neither looked up from their tea. "Can you hear me?" asked Frank.

"Oh, they can hear you," a voice came from behind them. They turned toward a young man who was splayed out on a couch, his attention on a ball he threw up and caught. "They just don't want to acknowledge you."

Frank had enough. "We'll see about that." He walked to the table where their tea sat and slammed his fist down. They finally turned their eyes to him. "Now that I have your attention."

"Do we have to talk to him?" Mrs. Strathmore asked.

"Hey, Ma."

Mr. Strathmore did respond to that. "Please don't address your mother that way."

"Mother, *dear*," the boy sneered. "I believe these are policemen."

That drew the man's attention. "What've you found out about our son's murder?"

"Finally," muttered Patrick.

No one offered, but Frank and Patrick took two chairs by the piano and moved them close to the couple. The boy continued to toss his ball and didn't move from his current location. "I'm Captain Frank Griffin and this is Detective Patrick Flannigan. We're working on getting the facts organized at this time," Frank said.

"That doesn't answer my question."

"No." They glanced at the boy on the sofa. "Did you want us to go over that now?"

"Of course," Mrs. Strathmore said, disregarding the young man.

"Don't worry about me. I'll find out anyway," said the young man.

Frank nodded to Patrick. Patrick pulled out his notebook and covered the time of the party and the couple's deaths.

"What about the girl?" the boy asked.

"Girl? What girl?" Patrick asked. *Do they know about Merle?* The newspaper had only said they were wanted for questioning.

"My brother was rather twisted," he said.

That got Mrs. Strathmore up and moving. She pulled out a cigarette and lit it. She moved in a jerky manner, her agitation showing. "Just stop it, Stuart! You don't know what you're talking about."

"Don't I? I've been to their 'parties'; I think I have a better idea than you of what was going on."

Patrick turned his focus to Stuart. "Were you here the night of the party?" Stuart stopped talking and started to throw his ball again. All his focus was on catching the ball. "Were you here?" repeated Patrick.

She took a pull on the cigarette and released a cloud of smoke. As it settled, she said, "He was here that night."

"*Ma*," Stuart screeched. "I thought you said..." His voice trailed off and the ball fell and hit him on the head.

She ignored her son and turned to Patrick and Frank. "We turned a blind eye to the life my older son was living. Stuart was at the party, but he arrived at our home by eleven that night."

"Curfew," muttered Stuart, rubbing his head.

Mr. Strathmore leaned back with a sigh. "We messed up with Robert and we're trying to prevent the same thing with Stuart."

"Making much progress with that?" Frank asked as he watched the young man start tossing the ball again.

"We shouldn't have allowed the interaction with his brother."

That brought the boy to his feet. "You don't own me! You let Bob have his own life!"

His mother turned to him and said, "And look where that's gotten us." That shut him up. He sat and put his head in his hands. "When will the body be released?" she asked.

Patrick corrected her. "There were two bodies."

"I suppose we'll also have to take care of her as well."

"Does she have family?" Patrick asked.

"No one that matters."

"Could you tell me what you mean by that?" Frank asked.

"She was an orphan," the woman said shortly. "She wasn't good enough for our son. She led him into this life."

"No, she didn't," corrected Mr. Strathmore. "If anything, she went along to keep him happy. He was always like this. Testing the limits. He needed someone stronger in his life."

"We couldn't control him," Mrs. Strathmore admitted. "He'd been such a good boy and so smart. If we'd just been stronger parents and stopped him from getting involved with the wrong people."

"How much do you know about his personal life?" Frank asked tentatively.

"We know almost nothing." She turned to the son and said, "Stuart." The sullen boy didn't respond to the command. "Stuart!"

Stuart dropped his hands to his knees. "I don't want to share his secrets."

Patrick tried. "He won't care now. We're trying to piece together what happened. Anything you know could help."

"You're right," Stuart agreed. "There was a girl involved with Bob and Catherine."

Mrs. Strathmore was startled by the news. "What're you talking about? What girl!"

"Margaret, sit down. And, Stuart, you keep your mouth shut," Mr. Strathmore ordered.

"Sebastian, you knew about this?" she accused, not moving from her position.

"Put that nasty cigarette down and sit," Strathmore commanded. He turned to his son. "And you just stop talking."

They did as he asked. Frank and Patrick realized the quiet man had more control over the two than they'd thought. "I knew about Merle. I had an agreement with her." His wife was shocked into silence and Stuart had his mouth open in shock.

"What type of agreement?" asked Patrick. *What was Merle involved in?*

Strathmore sighed and looked at his wife. "You wanted Bob and Catherine to break up and I wanted him straightened out." She nodded and took his hand. Stuart just stared at his father with clenched fists.

Frank murmured to Patrick, "We'll have to watch that one."

Patrick turned his eyes to the boy. He could see the boy's anger was increasing. Patrick asked, "What did you do to make this happen?"

"I met Merle at a local bar. Don't ask why I was there. I watched how she dealt with the men. She was strong and I could see she could handle herself."

"What happened next?"

"I asked her to attend one of the parties here and get close to him."

"What was in this for her?"

"The car. I signed it over to her."

Not stolen, Patrick thought. *It was Merle's all along. That's one less thing to worry about.*

Stuart stood up and yelled, "You gave away Bob's car to some floozy!"

"Not Bob's car, mine. It was mine and I could do anything with it that I wanted."

"Was Merle successful in her endeavors?" Patrick asked.

"Bob and Catherine were fighting a lot," Strathmore admitted. "So, I had hope."

"How did you know that? Did Merle tell you?"

"No, she and I didn't talk. I didn't want to be seen with her."

"Was Mabel your contact?" Frank prodded.

"Yes, it was her. She was the one closest to Catherine." Strathmore stood and walked to the window. "I didn't know things were getting so volatile, or I would've ended it and gotten Merle out of there."

"We think that Merle was also blackmailing Catherine by threatening to expose her and Bob's relationship."

"Why would this woman be blackmailing Catherine?" asked Mrs. Strathmore, perplexed. "Her relationship was with our son."

"No, we have reason to believe that she was in a relationship with both of them," stated Patrick.

"Both of them?" Mrs. Strathmore stuttered and sat down. "Did you plan that?" she asked her husband.

"No, I just thought she might get close to Robert and make Catherine jealous. He was always looking around, even after his marriage. I knew I just had to get the right person in there. I didn't foresee both of them being involved with her."

"Oh, the scandal. We won't survive this," his wife wailed, holding her head.

Mr. Strathmore sat back down and dropped his head back on the sofa. "What happens now?" he asked.

"We already have the newspapers looking for the car and Merle and her sister Jean."

"Why her sister?" Strathmore asked.

"Whatever happened that night," Frank said, "scared Merle so much that she decided to run away and take her sister with her."

Strathmore pulled his head up. "Keep us informed."

"We'd also like to speak with Mabel," Patrick added.

"Why?" asked Mrs. Strathmore. She just wanted these people out of her house.

"We have some questions," Frank said noncommittally.

The man waved at his wife. "Let them be. Go ask your questions."

Patrick nodded. He and Frank walked back to the foyer.

"Sir," the house manager said.

"We need to speak with Mabel."

The manager's composure broke for a moment, and he clenched his jaw.

"Is there something wrong?" asked Frank. "Has she gone again?"

"No, she hasn't gone, but I don't think you'll get much out of her."

Frank frowned. "Has someone influenced her?"

"That's not for me to say, sir," the manager replied but his eyes darted to the room they had just come from.

Frank nudged Patrick. He nodded. "We'd like to speak to her anyway."

The manager sighed. "She's upstairs in the bedroom. They asked her to start cleaning out Mrs. Catherine's things."

"That's fast," Patrick commented.

"Yes," the man agreed and was silent after that.

Frank and Patrick got his meaning. All things related to the late Catherine Strathmore would be removed and her personage would be scrubbed out. "As if she'd never been there," commented Patrick.

"Rough family," Frank said.

"Exacting," Patrick said. He thought of his own family and how they accepted even the most outlandish things from their children. Support from them was something he never questioned.

"Let's head upstairs," directed Frank. Patrick followed him up. They didn't notice Stuart lurking in the doorway, watching them. "What do you think we'll learn?" Frank asked his friend.

"Nothing, if she was paid off," Patrick said shortly.

"We'll see."

They entered the bedroom without knocking. Mabel was in there, holding up dresses in front of a mirror.

"What're you doing, Mabel?" Frank asked.

She screeched and scrunched up the dress as she whirled around to face them. "Jaysus, you scared me," she said and sounded out of breath. "I'm cleaning out Mrs. Strathmore's things like I was asked."

"Did they also ask you to try on the clothes?" taunted Patrick.

"I like nice things. I'm a normal person," she said defensively, rolling the dress up in a ball.

"Hmm," Patrick said non-committedly. Frank looked around while he started his questions.

"Have you compiled an inventory of the jewelry that was taken?"

"All of the jewelry is accounted for," Mabel said, turning away from him.

"No, not all of it. What about what was given to the girl?" She didn't seem to know Merle's name and he didn't want to bring it up.

"I don't know what you're talkin' about," she said and walked to the drawers.

"You told us that the girl had been given a necklace on the morning of the last party held here."

"I never said that."

Frank decided to change tactics. "Who told you to lie to us about the jewelry?"

She stopped but didn't turn. Her hand shook, and she clenched them tightly. "No one," she said.

"You're sure?"

She turned abruptly. "You see how they are, how much money they have. Whatever they say goes."

"Sit down and let's talk," said Frank. She sat on the edge of the bed and waited. "Tell us what you know."

"They don't seem affected by their son and his wife's death, just the bad press." Frank and Patrick looked at each other and back at her.

"How much jewelry is missing?" Patrick asked.

"At least five necklaces and some rings." The duo were taking notes and she continued. "They don't care that the girl has them." She wrung her hands and asked fearfully, "You won't mention this to them? I need this job."

"Did they threaten your job?"

"Not in so many words. The older Mr. Strathmore just said it would be good if I kept my mouth shut."

"The missing jewelry, none of it was considered stolen?"

"Not in the way you think. I heard the girl talking to Mrs. Catherine. She'd admire something and casually mention Mr. Strathmore's parents or the newspapers."

"Nothing specific?"

"No, but the threat was enough for Mrs. Catherine. She knew Mr. Robert's parents would use anything to break them up. They didn't like her and wanted her out."

"Do you think the girl was in the room when they died?"

"I do. It would've been odd if she wasn't still here. That night, she arrived early. Mr. Robert asked me to sneak her into his bedroom."

"And Catherine?"

"I wasn't to tell her. He wanted me to distract her."

"Do you know why?" asked Patrick.

"He wanted time alone with her."

"Had he done this before?"

"He had," she admitted. "It was getting to be more and more often."

"What did Catherine think of the girl?"

"I think she also had strong feelings for her, but she knew where the money came from. Between her love of money and the girl, the money was stronger. She was starting to feel like the one left out, that she was being left behind."

"What do you think happened that night?"

"I was in Mrs. Catherine's room, doing my best to distract her."

"What made her go to the bedroom?"

"We could hear the two of 'em. It was too much for her. I did my best to hold her back, but she broke away from me. She grabbed her gun and ran out of the room."

"What did you do?"

"I ran downstairs. I didn't want to be involved."

"That's enough," said Frank. "Mabel, thank you."

"You won't tell them I talked?" she stuttered.

"No, we won't." They left her sitting on the bed.

Patrick muttered, "The car was a gift."

"The jewels were a gift," Frank supplied.

"What now?"

"We wait and see if Merle and Jean are found, we still need to give us some answers."

Chapter Fifteen

The train pulled into the final stop. They'd been able to rest and eat and now they were at their destination. Jean stepped off the train with her sister close behind her. She couldn't believe it; they were in California! She hadn't expected the bustling station. "There's so many people," she murmured.

"Yeah, all the more reason to get settled quickly," Merle said, looking around.

"We need to find a builder or a house for sale."

"We need to be careful, though. It looks like this place is growing. People will try to take our money."

Jean nodded. They couldn't trust anyone. They gathered their luggage and boxes.

"Why Hollywood?" asked Merle.

"It's where movies are made."

"No, I mean, why are they here? And not in the East."

"Better weather would be my guess, but it's because of Thomas Edison."

"The lightbulb guy?"

"Yeah, Edison owned all the patents for the cameras to make motion pictures, so no one could make movies without going through him. Filmmakers flocked to Los Angeles to get away from him. Some even fled to Mexico when Edison threatened lawsuits."

"Is it still illegal?" Merle asked. *Did we jump from one problem to another? This was supposed to be our sanctuary.*

Jean laughed. "No, we made it just in time. William Selig stayed in the country long enough to settle with Edison. They were partners at first and then split off this year. There's lots of groups that make movies now. Selig is just one of them, though he was the first, and without him, we probably wouldn't be here."

"You know a lot about the movie business," Merle stated. "How do we get in?"

Jean stopped to think. "We go to where they make movies. There's Nester Studio, The Selig Polyscope Company, Balboa Amusement Producing Company, and others. But we can't show up like this," she said, referencing the load they were carrying. "We need to keep moving." They walked what seemed like miles with cars passing them on dirty roads. Coughing, they continued.

"You're sure we need all of these?" Merle asked tiredly after a while. She was seriously thinking about just leaving their things on the roadside.

"Our things? Of course we need them. We can make it, Merle, just keep going."

A car passed them and stopped abruptly a little way down. It reversed and Jean said, "Back up, Merle. We're about to have company."

"Man or woman?" Merle asked.

She squinted toward the dusty car. "Man I think."

"Well, this can handle this," Merle said, setting her bags down.

"Just don't close any doors," Jean muttered under her breath.

"What?" her sister asked. She'd pulled out her compact to check her makeup.

"Nothing, I said nothing."

Merle glared at her and turned to watch the driver roll the

window down. It wasn't a man; it was an older woman, her gray hair escaping her brown hat.

Jean started to laugh lightly and then it turned into a belly laugh. "You were saying?" she gasped. Merle found her sense of humor and laughed along with her.

"If you two are so happy, I'll just leave you here to eat the dust," the woman said. She started to roll her window back up.

"No, wait! Please," Jean said, trying to stop her laughter. "We need help. Can we get a ride with you?"

"Throw your bags in the back." They did as she asked and moved to sit with her in the front seat. "Where are you headed?" the woman asked.

Merle looked at Jean. Jean shrugged. "We aren't sure. We need a place to stay."

"Hmph. Well, maybe I can help with that."

"How so?" Merle asked.

"I'm Hannah and I just happen to have a boarding house. You two interested?"

"Depends on the rates," Merle replied, ever the negotiator.

"I think we can work something out. Besides rooms, breakfast and dinner are provided."

"We'd like to stay with you," Jean said, nudging her sister. They needed somewhere to figure things out.

"Are you here to work in the movies?" asked Hannah.

"How did you know?" asked Jean.

"Once you are here a while, you will see how many people are coming here to do just that."

"I would like to try and get a job at one of the studios," said Jean.

The woman grunted and continued to drive. About fifteen minutes later, they pulled onto another dusty road and up to an old house. It looked to be four stories tall.

"Is it always so dusty here?" complained Merle, watching the dust pile up on the truck as they sat there.

"Yeah, it's mostly sunny and then it rains and floods. And

then that dries in the sun and the wind blows and more dust comes." The woman opened her door, and they continued to sit and stare ahead. "Were you goin' to join me?" she asked, tilting her hat back.

That finally moved them. "Yes, yes, of course," said Jean. They got out and reached in the back of the truck for their things.

"You can leave those; my son can get them out later."

"That's okay," said Merle. She motioned to Jean. "We'll take our things with us." They gathered their bags and boxes and made their way into the house. Once inside, they marveled at the difference—everything was polished and clean.

The woman saw their stares. "I like my home to stay clean. What are your names?"

Jean thought frantically. Their real names were still plastered all over the papers. She suddenly hit on the perfect names. *Our middle names.* "I'm Annie Spencer and this is my sister Marie."

Merle smiled, recognizing what her sister had done. "Yes, that's it."

Hannah didn't question the names. Many people had moved to California to start new lives, and many had changed their names in order to make a clean break from their old one. "Well, come up and see the room, girls." She walked toward the stairs and called out, "Mattie!"

A small woman came out of what must have been the kitchen. She was holding a bowl and stirring the contents with a wooden spoon. "You called?"

Hannah waved to the sisters. "We have new guests, Marie and Annie. Girls, this is Mattie, she's in charge of the kitchen."

Mattie's firmly-lined face didn't change with the introduction. "Welcome, dinner's at five sharp."

"Thanks," Jean said. She hoped they were still there at that time. Merle might not approve of the rooms. *Though, so far,* she thought, looking around, *this seems like a nice place.*

Merle had noticed that also, and there hadn't been a price

given as yet. She knew the woman didn't owe them any favors; this was a business.

"One or two rooms?" Hannah asked over her shoulder.

"One," said Jean at the same time that Merle said, "Two."

Hannah stopped and turned to them. "I have enough rooms for two if that's what you want. "

"It is," said Merle.

Jen frowned at her sister. They'd always shared a room. *What changed*?

Merle ignored her and, once they were on the third floor, Hannah opened the door to one of the rooms. It was simple with a double bed, dresser, and a small table. To Merle and Jean, it looked like much more: a sanctuary and a place to rest.

"Would you like to see the other room?" Hannah asked.

"Yes, please." They followed her across the hall, and she opened the door for them to review. The only difference was the quilts on the beds.

"How much?" asked Merle. The last thing she wanted to do was leave, but they had to protect themselves.

Hannah squinted her eyes and studied the girls. After a moment, she named a price. It was reasonable and Jean waited for Merle's approval.

Merl nodded. "We can pay weekly."

"Whatever works for you. But you have to pay upfront."

"Oh, we will." Merle turned the knob on the bedroom door she'd selected. "Got a key for these rooms?"

"I do," Hannah said and pulled out the keys. She removed two and handed them over to the sisters.

"Are these for individual rooms?" Merle took the key offered and inserted it in the lock to test it.

"They are. You're a suspicious one, aren't you?"

"It's nothing personal. You don't know us, and we don't know you. It's better if we protect ourselves," Merle said pragmatically.

"Yeah, that makes sense." Hannah dropped the rest of the

keys into her pocket with a clang. "Need any help moving those things in?" she asked, looking at the pile of luggage and boxes.

"No," said Jean, "we have it."

"Well, I'll leave you to it. Don't forget dinner." Merle didn't comment as they watched her go back downstairs.

"Why two rooms?" Jean asked as she bounced her key in her hand.

"I thought we might like some privacy for the first time in our lives," Merle said, diverting her eyes.

Jean watched her for a long moment and finally said, "If that's what you want."

"It is."

"Okay then." Jean moved her luggage to her room and came back for her boxes. She dropped to her bed. *Things are already changing. I hope we did the right thing in leaving New York.* Thoughts of Patrick floated in. For the first time in weeks, she let herself think about him. *Would we have ended up together?* She nodded off. The packing could wait until later.

"Jean, wake up."

"What!" She sat up quickly. "Do we need to leave again?"

"Leave? No, silly, they're calling us for dinner."

"I slept that long?" Jean asked and looked out the window. The sun had started its descent.

Merle took her hand. "Jean, we're here. We aren't going anywhere until I find a house for us."

"And jobs. I might look at the local theaters and see if they need a piano player," she suggested for a second time.

"No. You're not doing that again." Merle was firm on this topic. "We're going to make your dream come true."

"But what if we start to run low on money?"

"We have enough," her sister assured her. A bell rang downstairs, reminding them to come down for dinner. "Come on, let's go down."

Jean pushed her hair back and stood. She grimaced. "Ugh, I could use a shower."

"After dinner, now come on."

Jean stood and got a good look at Merle. "You look refreshed," she accused.

"Yeah, well, I didn't sleep the entire time," Merle teased.

They walked down the stairs together, arm and arm. The dining room was on their right. When they entered, they found a table full of food surrounded by all types of people.

Hannah saw them and called, "Marie and Annie, Sit! Make some room there." The table was mostly men with sleeves rolled up showing tanned, muscled arms. Each one's features were different; some with dark curly hair, straight brown, and a wavy auburn. They sat.

"Welcome," said the man on Jean's right. He smiled and his teeth gleamed against his tanned skin.

"Thank you." She held out her hand to him. "I'm Annie." She touched her sister's arm. "This is Marie."

"I'm Harry. When did you get here?"

"Just today," she replied, taking a tray that was being passed around the table. There were vegetables, meat, and biscuits. She took a helping of each and saw that Merle did the same. The food on their trip was never warm enough. Merle smiled at the men but didn't flirt. *Again*, thought Jean, *changes. What else should I expect?*

Hannah called over to them. "Marie, Annie, this is my son Robbie." Her son was older than Jean expected; he looked to be in his late twenties. Hannah continued. "He works at Selig Studio. He can answer your questions."

"Hey, we work at the studios also," said the man on Merle's left.

Harry asked, "Why don't we introduce ourselves?"

The girls nodded.

"Harry Brown."

"Paul Johnson." The man across from Merle.

"Charlie Bandy." The man sitting across from Jean.

"Jerry Smith." The man on Merle's left.

"Nice to meet you all; we're Annie and Marie Spencer." Merle smiled but didn't add to Jean's statement.

"Are you interested in working in the movies?" Jerry asked, digging into his dinner.

Merle spoke up. "Annie's always wanted to work in the movies."

"Not you?"

"I just want to work," she said. "It won't matter where."

"What do you do there? Are you all actors?" Jean asked the men.

They laughed and Harry said, "No, we work in various jobs. I work making and tearing down sets."

"I work in transportation," Jerry added, "mostly repair and replacement of parts."

"And you?" Merle asked the two men across from them.

"We two," Charlie said, referencing Paul next to him, "work with livestock and provide them to sets and stuntmen. We provide our animals to all of the studios."

Merle nudged Jean under the table. Jean acknowledged her with a nod.

Harry looked over at Jean and asked, "What do you want to do?"

She looked down at her plate; she didn't want to say. Finally, she looked up and said, "Right now, I just want to get started in the business and work my way up."

"Hmm," he said. He looked over at Charlie and Paul. "Didn't you say you were looking for someone to help with the animals?"

"Can you ride a horse?" asked Charlie.

Merle started laughing. Jean grinned and said, "As a matter of fact, I'm pretty good with horses."

"Where does that come from?" he asked.

"Marie and I were raised on a ranch."

"Then I have something for you. Can you come with us tomorrow to the barns? I'd like to see how you handle the horses."

"I'd love that," Jean said excitedly. She'd missed working outdoors.

"Marie," Harry said, "you mentioned you need work also."

"Yes, definitely."

"Why not come with me tomorrow and see how things work on the set?"

"I'm not sure I'm going to be able to help build sets," she said doubtfully.

"Not to worry. I think there might be something else for you," he said cryptically.

"Thank you," she said quietly. Her normal nature was to flirt and be more outgoing, but she realized that persona hadn't done them any favors.

Jean glanced over at Hannah. Her mouth was tight, and she glared at the men who took over the conversation. She stepped into the void. "Robbie, Hannah mentioned you also work at the studios. What do you do?"

He preened a bit and Hannah smiled encouragingly at him. "I'm a driver."

"In the movies?" Jean asked.

Harry snickered. Hannah glared at him, but Robbie ignored the man and answered, "No, I drive for the top directors, actors, and actresses."

"Really?" Jean asked. "Do you drive Patty Dove?" Jean had seen the famous actress' movies back in New York and hoped to meet her.

"I have," he said triumphantly.

Harry tapped her under the table. She didn't show that she got the signal. She'd have to follow up after dinner. "That's quite a job," she said.

He smiled happily and Hanna looked on approvingly. The group finished their dinner and took their plates into the kitchen.

Merle asked Jean, "Would you like to go for a walk?"

"I would."

LIGHTS, CAMERA, MURDER!!!

"Mind if we tag along?" Charlie asked. Harry and Jerry stood with him. Jean noticed Paul headed back upstairs.

"Sure," said Merle tentatively and looked at Jean. She didn't appear to mind. Jean continued to look up the stairs.

Charlie's gaze followed her. "He likes to be alone after dinner." Jean nodded. Harry opened the door, and they all walked outside.

Jean heard Robbie complaining. "But, Ma!" She didn't hear Hannah's follow-up.

The group started out in the front yard and walked down the dark road. "It's so dark," Merle commented.

"No worries," said Jerry, "I have a flashlight." He pulled it out and turned it on. They followed the brightly lit path in front of them. Jerry and Charlie walked with Merle. And for once, she wasn't smiling and flirting. She seemed more sedate. Harry walked next to Jean.

"What's up with Robbie?" she asked.

Harry pulled out a cigarette. "Do you mind?" he asked. When Jean shook her head no, he lit it. "Hannah is protective of Robbie. She can get defensive if you say anything against him."

"I'll remember that," promised Jean.

He blew out smoke and asked, "Where were you two before California?"

"Out east," she commented evasively. She didn't want to share more than that with a man she'd just met.

Harry let it go. He had his own story that he wouldn't share easily. He asked, "Going to surprise Charlie and Paul with your horse skills tomorrow?"

She laughed, her voice low. "Yes, I think I will. "

"I can't wait to hear how it goes."

She smiled. They continued to walk. Jean rubbed her arms; it had started to cool down. "It's nice here," she commented.

"Yeah, it's mostly sunny. Gives us lots of days to film."

Harry dropped his cigarette and stepped on it. He noticed

Jean's interest and laughed. "Yeah, you'll always be able to find me by the chewed-up cigarettes."

"How long does it take to make a movie?" she asked curiously.

"A couple of weeks, depending on setup. Also, it depends if it's a serial or a movie."

"Do you build new sets for every movie?"

"No, they reuse as much as possible. We also keep warehouses for furniture and for shooting indoor scenes."

"Are you working on a movie currently?"

"Yeah, there are several set changes for this movie."

Charlie heard them talking and hung back to say, "At first, we'll want you working with the horses. If you prove yourself, then eventually you might be able to deliver horses to the set."

"I can't wait."

He smiled slightly. The group turned and headed back to the house. They said goodbye at the second level, where the men's rooms were located. The sisters kept on walking to the third floor. Merle walked ahead of Jean. When she started to enter her room, Jean stopped her. "Merle, can we talk?"

She sighed and stared at the key she'd put into the lock. "I'd rather not."

"I think it's important."

Merle turned the lock and pushed the door open without saying a word. Jean shrugged and turned to her own door. She started to enter when she heard behind her, "Well, what're you waiting for, an invitation? Come in already."

Jean turned and went to her sister and hugged her tightly. "Enough of that, come sit with me." Merle held Jean's hand and sat on the edge of the bed with her. When Jean didn't start, Merle said, "Well, you got me here, so talk."

Jean began tentatively, staring at their clasped hands. "Merle... are you okay? You seem so different since we got here."

"I'm trying to be different here. I think the way to do that is to not get involved with men."

That comment made Jean raise her head and ask incredulously, "Forever?"

Merle smiled slightly. "No, not forever, silly, but long enough to get us settled." She laid her head on Jean's shoulder. "You know I don't have a good track record with men or women. We just don't need that complication."

Jean wrapped her arms around her shoulders and said, "You know, you have a point. The last thing either of us needs is that kind of complication. We need to build our new life here."

Merle lifted her head and asked, "Jean, I haven't asked, but what about Patrick?"

Jean stood and walked over to the tall dresser opposite them. "What about him? He's back in our old life. Something we left behind."

Merle picked at the bed cover and didn't look at Jean when she asked, "Was he someone special?"

Jean sighed this time and turned to her. "I thought he might have been, but it was early. We barely knew each other."

"And I stopped anything that might have happened."

Jean walked over to her sister and took her chin in her hand, forcing her eyes up. "Just stop with the martyrdom. We're in this together. You didn't force me to come with you. I chose to. And you chose California for me."

Merle lay back on the bed. "I'm just so tired. I feel drained of everything."

Jean dropped down beside her and said bracingly, "You just need rest."

"Do you think they're still looking for me?"

"Us, you mean."

"Maybe."

"The newspapers only said we were wanted for questioning. Of course, the police might get us for taking the car or the jewels."

"They can't use the car against us," Merle said, staring at the ceiling.

"Why not?" Jean asked, raising herself on her elbow.

"It was a gift. I gave the paperwork to Jesse."

"A gift from who?"

"I wasn't just blackmailing Bob and Catherine. I was hired by Bob's father to try to break them up. The car was my payment."

Jean was nonplussed. "Why would he do that?"

"He and his wife didn't like their daughter-in-law, Catherine. They felt she made him more volatile. She was unstable and he was hoping it would lead to them divorcing," Merle explained. "I knew that going in."

"Were you supposed to get that close to them?" Jean asked delicately.

Merle laughed and said huskily, "No, I was supposed to just be with him. To break them up."

"Then why were you with both of them?"

"I don't know. After that first night, I could've found an excuse to get out, but I enjoyed it. I enjoyed them both, together," she admitted. "From now on, I need things much simpler."

Jean saw that Merle's face looked drawn and pale. "You need to go to bed. I'll see you in the morning."

"Your exciting day," her sister teased. "Everything you've waited for."

"It is," Jean said and continued to stare at her. Finally, she stood and walked to the door.

"Goodnight, sis," said Merle softly.

"Night." Jean glanced back and saw Merle hadn't gotten up. Jean frowned and hesitated at the door. Merle was normally a driving force; she'd have to keep an eye on her. As she pulled the door shut behind her, her sister's voice called out.

"Jean."

Jean stopped and went back into the room. "Yes."

"Set the lock on my door and yours. We don't know these people and we don't know who we can trust."

"Yes, you're right." She engaged Merle's lock and walked across to her room. She entered the dark room and turned on the lights. "Lock the door," she muttered and moved to engage the locks. "Tomorrow, it's our start here. Wow, the movies!" She hurriedly got ready for bed. Her last thought as she drifted off was *Horses*.

A knock on the door brought her straight up in her bed. Jean looked at the window. She could see that it was still early. She grabbed her wrap and called out, "Who is it?"

"It's me."

She opened the door and found Merle there. "Did you need something?" Merle was dressed similarly to Jean in her night clothes.

"I don't have anything to wear."

Jean drug her hand through her hair. "Come in. What do you mean you don't have anything to wear? We brought all of your clothes with us."

Merle grimaced. "We didn't bring anything that would fit in here. Can I borrow a skirt and top or a dress?"

Jean smiled slightly. "Okay, that shouldn't be an issue. I'll be in pants mostly." She moved to her closet and pulled out the high-collared shirt and blue skirt. It was light enough for the California weather and would be okay in a business setting. She brought them over and handed them to her sister.

"Thank you."

"Let me know if you need anything else."

"Once we get settled, we'll get some new clothes," Merle promised. She carried the items out the door.

Jean got her things and went to the bathroom to get ready for the day. Back in her room, she pulled on her shirt and pants, as along with some well-worn boots—her uniform from her ranch days. She brushed her hair into a low ponytail and grabbed her hat. She pulled the door shut quickly and locked it before heading to Merle's. She knocked and heard, "Come in." She went in and found Merl tugging at the waistband of her skirt.

"What's wrong with this thing? It doesn't fit," Merle asked.

"Really? We normally wear the same size." Jean went over to

her. She looked at the band and said, "I can split it and you can wear a belt. It should cover it up."

"You think so?" Merle asked hopefully. She wanted to blend in and find a job.

"Of course, it won't take a minute." Jean went back to her room to retrieve her scissors. The cut was made quickly, and she released the waistline. Merle breathed a sigh of relief. She tucked in her shirtwaist and added a wide belt.

Jean walked around her. "Perfect, it can't be seen at all. I can fix it more permanently tonight."

"Thanks. I guess I just ate too much junk on the road."

"And too little exercise," agreed Jean. "It'll come off quickly once we start work. Ready?" Merle held out her hand, and Jean took it and accompanied her downstairs. Charlie and Harry joined them on the second floor. "Where's Paul?" Jean asked.

"Already downstairs, I think he's sweet on Carrie, the kitchen helper," commented Charlie.

"No, I just think he likes the extra food." Harry laughed.

"Hey," called Paul, "are you talking about me?" He stood in the doorway of the dining room, holding a biscuit.

"See, already at the food," complained Harry with a smile.

"Better hurry, there's not much left," Paul said.

"Oh, shush, there's plenty," Hannah said, stepping from behind him. She waved. "Come sit and eat."

They followed her directions and sat down at the full table. The food was passed around quickly.

"You girls going with the guys today?" Hannah asked.

"We are," Jean replied. "And I can't wait."

"There'll be plenty to do. We'll get the horses organized and over to the set," Charlie said.

"Will I go to the set with you?"

"Maybe."

"What do you do while they're shooting? Go back to the stables?"

"No. One of our main jobs is to manage the horses and make sure they're safe during shooting," Paul added.

Jean frowned. "Safe? Do they hurt the horses?"

"The actors, and I use the term loosely, don't always treat them like they should be treated."

"What do you do if that happens?" she asked, her hands clenched.

"I've threatened to remove the horse from the movie."

She nodded and thought about that; she'd seen a lot of movies and hadn't thought about the possible injuries the horse suffered during shooting. Some had gone over cliffs or into water. She'd watch the stunts more closely in the future. No animal should be hurt in the process of shooting the movie.

Charlie pushed back his chair. "Annie, we need to get moving. You ready?"

Jean took a bite of eggs without acknowledging his question.

"Ahem, Annie," Merle said loudly. "Harry asked you a question."

Jean realized what happened. "Sorry about that. Ready when you are." She followed him with her plate to the kitchen. She returned to the dining room, kissed Merle on the cheek, and said in a low voice, "Good luck."

Merle grabbed her hand and said, "You, too, *Annie*." Jean got the hint and nodded.

"Let's go," Charlie called from the foyer.

Jean grabbed her hat and ran to meet him and Paul at the front door. "How are we getting there?"

"My auto is over there." Charlie pointed to a black vehicle on the side of the house.

"What kind of vehicle is this?" she asked as she walked around it.

"Galion-Godwin truck."

"A truck?"

"It makes hauling things easier."

She looked in the cab. "There's only two seats."

"No worries, I'll ride in the back," Paul said, jumping into bed of the truck.

"How do you move the horses to the set?" she asked.

"We have a place close by and we sometimes ride them over," said Paul.

"Hey," called Charlie, "Paul, are you going to crank the engine?"

"I got it." Jean took the crank from Harry and went to the front of the truck to crank the engine. Once it was running, she joined him in the cab. "What can I expect today?" she asked.

"When we get there, I'll walk you through the location, introduce you to the others working there, and then we'll get the horse ready for the day."

She nodded and asked, "Who are the other people working there?"

"Jack Steen and Sean O'Malley are probably already there. They're good with the horses and have a background similar to yours," Paul called from the back.

She held her questions until they got to the work location. The trip was about an hour when they pulled into a long road with barns at the other end. "The studio's that way," said Charlie, waving his hand to their right.

They pulled up and parked by an open paddock. "This way," Charlie told her. They got out and headed into the barn. Two men stood talking in the middle of a room with stalls lining the walls.

Some of the horses neighed a greeting. "Can I go over and see them?" Jean asked excitedly.

"Sure," Paul said. He wanted to observe her with the animals.

She approached slowly, making sure the horses could see her. When she reached a mare, she put her hands close to the animal's nose. When the horse smelled them and snorted, Jean took the opportunity to move closer. She lightly petted her on her lower neck. "Will you let me pet your muzzle?" she murmured. She reached up and stroked the horse's face. She talked in a low tone and rubbed her forehead; the mare nudged her again. "You like that, do you?"

Paul nodded and said, "She looks like the real deal."

"Question is, can she ride?" Charlie asked.

"Who's that?" Jack asked as he walked over. "New girlfriend?"

"No," said Paul. "We need the help, and she has experience with horses."

"What kind of experience?"

Jean heard the question and moved toward them. "I worked on a ranch from the time I was fifteen. We ran cows, horses, and some smaller animals."

"Annie, this is Jack and Sean. They do the same work, take care of the animals and deliver them to the sets."

"Can you ride?" Sean asked.

"I can."

"Fine, saddle that horse you were talking to and show us what you can do in that field," requested Paul.

"Good idea," Charlie said. "Do you mind, Annie?"

"No, of course not." They didn't know her, and she was in line for a job that could go to someone else. "Saddle?" she asked.

"Over there." Paul pointed to the tack room.

She went to the room he indicated to retrieve the items she'd need. The men didn't move to help her. She knew if she wanted the job, she'd need to be able to manage the gear herself. The saddle, blankets, and harness were just inside. She inspected each and carried the heavy gear out with no trouble. Her muscle memory was in place. She walked back to the mare, handling her gently and calmly. Her stall had room to add the blanket, saddle, and harness.

She knew the horse would test her by pushing out her stomach when she tightened the saddle around her middle. If she didn't have a tight enough fit, the saddle would fall off, taking Jean with it. Jean slapped her lightly on the rear and the horse let out the air she was holding. She immediately tightened up the straps. She continued to talk to the mare in a soothing tone and walked her out to the main area where the men stood watching.

Paul looked over at Jack and Charlie with raised eyebrows. "So, she knows something. Can she ride?" asked Jack.

Jean ignored the comments, walked the horse to the field, and opened the gate. She moved the mare inside and pulled herself up into the saddle. She cantered a bit then coaxed her into a run.

"Is that all you can do?" goaded Charlie.

She leaned down and asked the mare, "Do you know any tricks?" She backed the horse up a few steps and had her do a bow.

"All right, time for fun and games is over," Paul said. "Annie, move her back to her stall and brush her down. We'll be taking her with us today." He turned to the other three. "She's with us from today." When Jack looked like he might protest, Paul eyed the man. "Problem?"

"No, I can't say I do."

"Fine, you and Sean take those two to the Selig set. They have a stunt set up this morning," Paul directed.

Jean heard that and took a chance. "Can I go with them?" Even if Jack didn't approve of her, she wanted to see a movie being made.

Jack glared over and Charlie rushed to answer him. "You can come with me today and observe. First, though, we need to muck the stalls and put out food for the other animals."

Paul nodded his agreement. "You two, keep going," he said to Jack and Sean. They went about their business and Paul went to his office.

Charlie walked up to Jean. "No worries, Annie. Paul approved of you, so you have a job."

Jean went back to working in the stall. She mucked it clean and transferred the debris to a wheelbarrow. Charlie had brought a load of clean hay over. Once it was transferred into the now clean stall, she moved to the next. When she and Charlie had finished cleaning, she pulled out a handkerchief to wipe the sweat from her forehead and asked, "What next?"

Charlie leaned on his shovel. "Feed the animals."

Paul came out of his office with a clipboard. "I'll take care of that. I need you and Annie to take the horses over to the set."

"Why so early?" asked Charlie. "I thought our call was after lunch today."

"I rode over and checked. The shooting's going well, and the schedule got moved up."

Jean gasped; this was her chance! She was going to a movie set!

Charlie grinned at her. "Follow my lead and don't talk too much."

"I'll do that."

"Go get Betsy, the mare you rode earlier, and I'll get Belle. They're both easygoing. We'll ride them over, so get her ready. We'll leave in about fifteen minutes."

She walked to the tack room and got the items she'd used earlier. Betsy snorted at her as she put on the blanket and then the saddle. She moved around to secure the bridle and led her out.

Charlie was waiting on his horse. He nodded when he saw her. "Follow me." They walked out of the barn and climbed into their saddles. "The sets are just over that hill," he said and nodded ahead of them. "We have one trailer that can be towed by the truck, but that's used for short distances. We prefer to be close and ride over; it gives the horses good exercise and loosens them up before the scene."

"Do you know what movie we're in today?" *Will it be an action movie?* she wondered. *Will I meet any stunt people?*

"Yeah, it's an easy one. The horses will be in the background of the scene. Just props today." He saw her face drop. "Hey, don't worry. There'll be more excitement on other films."

Chapter Sixteen

Merle and Harry at Selig set

"Just stay with me," Harry told Merle.

She looked around at the people running by her. "Is everyone late for something?"

"Nah, things just change quickly." He pointed to each building. "Those are sets, where I'm working. I'm assigned to that one over there." They crossed the road and went through a side curtain. Merle didn't know what she expected, but this was a surprise. The set was different parts of a house: a bedroom, a living room, and a kitchen. She followed Harry through the rooms, and he started to gather wood. "We finished last night if you want to look around."

"It looks so real," she said, observing her surroundings.

"Looks can be deceiving," he commented.

"Yeah, that's true." She thought of the façade that Bob and Catherine had created back in New York. The two didn't know each other at all. *And I manipulated them for my own means.* She sighed as she walked around touching the furniture.

"I need to get to the shop, just behind this area. Are you okay here?" Harry asked.

"I think so," she commented softly, still studying the detail on the set.

"I'll be back here if you need anything."

People started coming in, dressed in formal wear: the men in top hats and the women in satin dresses. "You there," called a small man with a clipboard. "What's your part in this movie?"

Merle put a hand to her chest. "Me?"

Harry heard the question and ran back into the room. "Sorry, Tom, she's with me."

Tom took his pencil and tapped his board. "We can use her."

"Me?" Merle repeated.

Harry lowered his head and said in a low voice, "Just follow his directions. This'll be your first job in the movies."

She nodded and waited for the man to provide direction.

Tom walked around her, looking her up and down. "Is that what you have to wear?" he asked.

Merle looked down and smoothed her shirt into her skirt. "Yes."

Tom tapped his pencil again. "Okay, it should work. All right, when the scene starts, pick up that tray behind you." Merle turned and saw a large silver tray loaded with food. "A party's going on and you'll go through the crowd offering food."

"Okay, what then?"

"Just follow the director's instructions."

"You aren't the director?"

Tom pushed up his dark-rimmed glasses and said, "One day maybe, but for right now, that excitable man by the camera is the director." He waved his hand behind them.

Merle looked in the direction Tom indicated and saw a small man jumping up and down while screaming at the man working the camera. "How will I know he's talking to me?"

"Oh, you'll know. Believe me, you'll know," Tom said, walking away from her.

"Harry?" she started, looking around for her friend. "On my own." People kept entering the space from all sides of the set. In total, there were about thirty people at this party.

The director called out. "Okay, group, this is a party. Start talking, start drinking. Start having fun. Serving girl, move around with that tray."

There's my instruction. She grabbed the tray and balanced it on her right hand. Immediately, she was bumped from one side to another.

"Keep doing that, keep doing that. Everyone, jostle the girl with the tray around more." The bumping got worse, and Merle struggled with the tray. "Start dancing; couples, get together," the director called. At that moment, someone pushed her hard from the back and she spun around with the tray. She managed to stay upright just as a man swung his arm toward another man. She dodged them and managed to get to the side of the room.

"Okay, Helen... One of the ladies wants your man. Alan, the women are fighting over you." The actress he had addressed followed his direction and tore the hat off another woman in front of her. The other girl's response was to rip the other's pearls from her neck. Several people slipped on them and fell to the ground. Alan walked over to Merle and spoke low in her ear, giving her instructions.

"But the director..." she stuttered.

"Leave that to me. Will you do it?" he asked.

What do I have to lose? She nodded and waited for the instructions. It came almost immediately. "Start the fight!" the director yelled. Merle went to the dessert table where she'd picked up her tray. There were several pies there. She grabbed two, Alan had moved to the front of the crowd. She got in the line of fire and yelled over the crowd, "Drop!" The man in front of Alan dropped down and she had a clear shot. She threw one pie directly at him, hitting him squarely in the face. The crowd stopped moving and watched the man move two hands to his face to remove the pie.

The director yelled out, "Keep going!" Merle had the second pie and threw it at him again, hitting him in the chest. "After her!" called the director. Alan started to chase her around the crowd until they formed a tight circle around her.

"Jump up and down and try to find her." He leaped with the help of the people and continued to run around. "Now, group, let her out." They made an opening and Merle ran out. "Alan, catch her!" He caught her with one hand and pulled his other from behind his back. It was a pie! Her eyes widened, and she threw her hands up to try and protect her face. It didn't help. The pie hit her square in the face. She started to laugh, and everyone followed her lead.

"Cut!" The director ran over. "Alan, that was perfect."

"Did you get it?" Alan called over to the cameraman while he wiped off his face with a towel and tossed one to Merle.

"Everything!" the man called back triumphantly.

"Next time, tell me," requested the director.

"You know, George, it works better if it's spontaneous," said Alan. "I think we need to work on the pies. Those seemed a bit heavy," he added, shaking pie out of his suit.

The director called for his assistant. "Tom!"

"Yes, boss," Tom said.

"Look into a pie that can be thrown with better accuracy but not so heavy. We don't want anyone to be hurt."

Tom tapped his clipboard. "Greenbergs might work for this. They're in Glendale."

"Check with them and we'll do some tests."

"Alan!" a female voice screeched.

The men around Merle grimaced and the director rolled his eyes at Alan. "This is on you. Fix this mess."

"No worry," Alan said and pulled out a cigar. "I know how to handle her." He nonchalantly lit his cigar and approached Helen.

Her tense posture changed with something he said and she started to smile.

"What did he say to her?" Merle asked.

"Best not to know," Tom replied.

The director studied Merle. "Tom, with that new scene, we'll need to change the setup for the next one." He pointed to Merle. "Bring her over here."

"He means you," Tom said. They walked over to the director's chair next to the camera. "His name is William Stone," Tom muttered.

The director sat sprawled with his cloth hat pulled low on his forehead. "You did good. Can you do that again?"

"Do what?" Merle asked, confused. "The trays, the pies?"

"Yeah, that. You've got good instincts. You ever worked in the movies before?"

"No, this was my first one." She didn't mention she used to work in a theater that played movies. She figured that was irrelevant.

"Come back after lunch." Stone waved to Tom and left with the cameraman to discuss the next setup.

"We have another scene outside, then we'll come back here," Tom said, scribbling on his clipboard.

"What'll I carry in that scene?" Merle asked him wryly.

He looked at the clipboard. "Flowers, I think. You'll also need a change of clothes. Go see the costumer; she should be able to help you." He looked up from his clipboard at her. "You know, you'd be more attractive as a blonde."

She reached up to her hair. "Yeah, I've heard that before."

"Also, go see the accountant and tell him you're on the payroll for the film. He'll make sure you get paid."

Merle smiled. *What a strange place. Just like that, I'm now working in the movies?* "Yeah, sure, I'll do that." She walked off and found Harry. "Harry, I think I just got a job."

"Told you she'd do well," Harry said to the man beside him. "Marie, this is Rich."

"Yeah, she sure has the looks," observed Rich.

"Thanks. I think," she replied.

"Just stating a fact," said Rich.

"What did they tell you?" Harry asked.

"I need to see the accountant to get on the payroll for the movie and then I need to see the costumer to switch outfits for the next scene."

"Can you handle this while I run her over to the accountant?" Harry asked Rich.

"Sure, but hurry back, we need to switch this up for when they come back inside." Harry started walking quickly away. Rich looked at Merle and said, "Follow him."

"Oh." Merle ran over to follow him. When she caught up, she said, "Thanks for this."

"It's no problem. We all had some help when we got here, and I wanted to return the favor. You did good today, really thought on your feet."

"Um... not to sound dumb, but what did I do exactly?" she asked. She was still confused about how she'd gotten a job on a movie.

"Just follow direction and that will do most of the work. They have the story and will let you know if you don't do what they want."

"So much of this seems spontaneous."

"It just looks that way. The main actors have rehearsed for days, and they bring the extras in on the day of the shoot."

"Oh, I have so much to learn."

Several small buildings lined the streets. "The accountant is over there," Harry said, nodding toward the building on the right.

"And the costumer?"

"Down that way." He pointed to his left. "Just look for the signs."

"Thanks!" She started off.

Harry called to her, "Meet us back here. We'll go to lunch."

She was suddenly ravenous and said, "I'll be here." She

hurried to the first building. The streets seemed to be full of people and cars. She maneuvered her way through them to the door. *So many people work here,* she thought. She pushed the door open and entered the office.

A man sat at the desk surrounded by books. "What do you want?" he barked at her.

"Tom, the assistant director of the movie that I'm apparently in now, told me to see you."

"I know who Tom is." He sighed heavily. "Another extra. Figures. Did he say which movie you'll be working on?"

"No, but it stars Alan and Helen."

"That one? The one with the party scene?"

"That's the one."

"Fine, sit. I have some paperwork and will cut the checks at the end of shooting. If they change your status from extra to something else, see me immediately. We'll need to review the contracts again." He threw the contract at her. She caught it deftly and began to read it. "Just sign the bottom," he ordered.

She didn't look up from the paperwork. "I'd like to read it first."

"That's a first," he muttered and threw up his hands. "Fine, read. I have nothing better to do."

She ignored him and read it carefully. It was clear; the time on the movies would be calculated and her pay would be based on that. It seemed fair and, if things progressed into a more complicated contract, she'd have someone else review it with her. "Pen?" He held it and she took the offered pen and signed the paper.

"For each movie, a new contract will be required."

"I understand."

"See me after the shoot is complete."

"Thank you."

"No use thanking me; it doesn't help with this mess I'm working on."

Merle left the man to his unending work and went to find

Rich, and Harry back at the workroom. They were sawing wood and building walls.

"What's the set this afternoon?" she asked.

"The jealous wife's house," Rich told her.

"Where were we this morning?" she asked.

"The mistress' house," said Harry.

She looked at the set they were changing. "You use the same set over and over?"

"Yeah, less cost that way. We just redress them as needed."

"Let's finish here and we'll go to lunch," Harry suggested.

"Okay," she said and stood undecided about what to do while they finished.

"You can go watch the shoot while we finish."

"Where are they?" she asked.

"For this film, I think it's a street scene," Rich said. "Watch out and stay behind Stone, the director. That will be the safest place."

Merle nodded and walked toward the stairs and down to the grass. She was dizzy and grabbed the handrail. She took deep breaths. *Just a little hungry, that's all.* She followed the noise; the cars were being moved down the street. She did as Rich said and stood behind Stone. He called action and there was a loud bang as the two cars hit one another. The men jumped out of their cars.

"Now argue," the director called. She watched the men throw their arms out and yell. The film wouldn't catch the sound, but the audience would know that they were fighting. "You hate each other! You're in love with the same woman! Now, you," Stone pointed to the second man, "you run toward your lover's home. Alan, you follow!" They did as they were told and ran down the now deserted street and disappeared.

"Cut! The next scene will be back in the house."

Tom showed the director his clipboard. "Yeah, I guess we have to." Stone called out, "That's lunch! Come back at one for the next scenes. We want this wrapped up today."

One day's worth of work, Merle thought. *Well, it's a start.* She started to walk back down the road to where her friends were working.

"Hey, you," called Tom. "Did you get the paperwork signed?"

"I did."

"Good, we'll want you in the afternoon scene. Have you been to the costumer?"

"Oh shoot, I forgot. I'll head over there now." She hurried off to the costumer. She didn't want to keep the guys waiting for lunch. She went to the small buildings Harry had pointed out earlier and knocked on the door. "Come on in." She entered and found the building was one large room; every inch was covered with fabric, sewing machines, and various outfits on rails lined the room.

"What ya need," asked a rather garish looking woman. She wore no makeup and her hair looked to be held up by twisted wire clips. Her clothes were a bright red shirt and a skirt with red and pink flowers. She caught Merle's look and said, "Don't let the clothes fool ya. I know what I'm doing."

"Of course, I'm sure you do," Merle said as she continued to examine the clothes on the table on the racks. "These are beautiful; the workmanship is amazing."

The woman saw that she was being truthful and not just buttering her up. "What're you here for, girlie?"

"Tom told me to get with you about the next scene."

"That would be Alan's movie?"

"Yes, I think so. Today was my first day."

"Do you know which scene you'll be in?"

"The next one back at the house. I believe it's now the wife's house."

"You an extra?"

"I am. I believe he said I'll be holding flowers. And in the last scene, I was a serving girl."

"Hold it," said a young girl of about eighteen running a sewing machine. She stopped her work and stood. "Ma, it was her."

The older woman frowned at her daughter and back at Merle. "You were the pie thrower?" she asked incredulously.

"Yeah, that was me."

"Wow," said the girl, "you're already famous. Did Alan mind that you hit him in the face?"

"It was his idea," Merle admitted.

"Hmm, get back to work, Sammy."

"Yes, Ma," Sammy said with a roll of her eyes.

"And, you," she pointed to Merle, "come with me." She led her through the room. "I'm Dorothy Lipton, and you are?"

Merle stuttered a little and said, "Marie Spencer."

"*Marie*," Dorothy stressed. "I think you might be another character. So, let's give that to them." She reached for a full rack of clothes and pulled out a lighter-colored skirt and top. She looked at her closely. "What's up with your hair? You should lay off the dye, it's going to ruin it."

"Will it?" Merle asked worriedly, putting her hand to her hair. "I just did it as a lark," she said lamely.

"You did, huh? Next time come and see me and we'll do it properly. You're a blonde I'm guessing?"

"Yeah, and I do miss it."

"I get that. Well, for today, how about brown? It'll come off softer on camera. And a hat, I think. Let me get your measurements." Dorothy pulled out her measuring tape and took them quickly. "That's it. Come back after lunch and we'll do a final fitting."

"Will there be enough time?" Merle asked with worry.

"There will be if you go now." Merle watched her and nodded. "Now to work," Dorothy said as she moved an outfit she'd picked out for Merle to a stand. Pins in her mouth, she started to reorganize the outfit.

Merle returned quickly to the set where the guys were working. Harry saw her. "We need to get goin'. Time's tight for lunch."

"I'm ready." The group headed to the Harry's car and then

drove into a small town nearby. "It doesn't look crowded," she observed, observing the small parking lot with a few cars.

"Most actors are fed on the set," Rich explained, "but extras and crew have to get their own."

"That doesn't seem fair," she commented.

"Yeah, well, actors get the movies made. We can be easily replaced," Harry said laconically.

They went into the small café and sat; food was ordered quickly. While they waited, Merle spoke up. "I appreciate all the help getting a job. Even though it's a short one."

"Oh, I think you'll get more," Rich said.

"Have you heard something?" she asked. The waitress came over with their food and prevented Rich from answering. Once the food was set on the table, she left and the three began to eat. Merle tried again. "What've you heard?"

Rich swallowed a bite of his sandwich. "Tom came by and asked if you had a stable living condition. I told him you did, and he said he'd want to talk to you about more films after this one's wrapped."

She let out the breath she was holding. "That... that sounds amazing." She thought about Jean. *How did her first day go? Will she be upset that I'm already in the movies? Did I accidentally steal her dream?*

Chapter Seventeen

Jean on the set

"Look over there," Charlie said. Jean looked in the distance and saw a camera and crew. "It's an outside scene today, so we'll put the horses nearby so that they're in the scene. Once we get them settled, we'll back out and you can watch how the process works."

She studied the area. "Do we head down there?"

"Race you to the tree?" he asked.

She didn't respond. Instead, she applied pressure to her horse's flanks and took off. She heard galloping behind her and bent her head to the horse's neck. That gave her the speed she needed to pull ahead and beat him to the tree. Laughing, she pulled the mare to a stop.

"You're fast!" Charlie laughed.

"I've missed this," she admitted, patting Betsy's neck.

"Well, you'll get plenty of time with them on this job."

A man with a clipboard ran over. "You're late and we're about to start."

"We had to get the horses ready," Harry explained.

"Yeah, whatever. Get them tied to that tree. The actors are on their way." With that, he left them to return to the director.

"Who was that?"

"He's the assistant director, Kevin." Harry climbed down. "Come on, we have a job to do." He waved to Jean to follow him. She dismounted and walked after him.

After the horses were tied up in the shade, she asked, "Where can I watch?"

"Let's go behind the director. Best seat in the house." He strode off and she hurried after him the short distance across the field.

The director, Kevin, and the cameraman ignored them. Kevin called the actors to set. A man and a woman came out of a tent. They went to stand by the tree.

The director called to the actors, "Your fathers don't want you together and she's about to be torn from you!" The actors used their eyes and hands to communicate their feelings. Jean turned to the cameraman and leaned in to watch through the lens. "Good, good. Now, untie the horses and walk them to the water." They did as they were told and, once they stopped, the director called, "Cut! That's a wrap." Turning to the cameraman, he said, "Cal, let me know when I can view the film."

"Right, John, I'll have it for you in about an hour."

The director nodded and walked off toward his car and driver, Kevin following.

Jean watched him go and saw a man waving to them. She squinted toward him. "Is that..."

"Yeah," Harry answered, "that's Robbie."

Kevin returned to them. "You can take the horses away now. They won't be needed anymore today." He started to walk off.

Harry called to Kevin. "The other movie starts tomorrow?"

Kevin checked his clipboard. "Yes. We'll need two more horses, ones that aren't scared of trains."

"What did he mean by that?" Jean asked.

"The horses for the stunt tomorrow. Some horses don't like the noise or movement of trains. We have some trained specifically to interact with trains. We don't want the actors or horses to be hurt."

"Stunt! Tell me what's happening tomorrow?" Jean demanded excitedly.

Chapter Eighteen

Merle back on set after lunch

Merle climbed out of the car and the three walked toward the set. Tom ran into her. "Oh, I'm sorry," she apologized.

"I don't know why you're sorry," Harry grumbled, "He ran into you."

Tom ignored him. "Shouldn't you be in costume?" he asked Merle.

Merle looked around and saw others returning to the set. "Of course, I'm on the way now." She took off at a run to get her costume.

"You didn't have to pressure her," Harry said to the assistant director with a dark frown.

"Hey, I'm just doing my job," Tom said, stepping back from the other man.

Harry stepped toward him, and Tom took the opportunity to turn and run.

"You scared him," commented Rich.

"Meant to," he replied. "Let's get to the set."

Rich raised his eyebrows and followed him.

Merle ran through a crowd that was going in the opposite direction. "Hey! Watch it!" called a tall man in a top hat.

"Sorry!" she said and continued to push through.

She got to the costume shop and knocked. The door swung open, and Dorothy stood there with her hands on her hips, "A little late, aren't you?"

"Yeah, sorry. Do we have enough time?" Merle asked, wringing her hands.

"We'll make time. Get in here and go behind the screen. Strip down to your slip."

Merle followed her directions and quickly stripped. A dress was thrown over the edge of the screen. "Come out and I'll get you buttoned," Dorothy said. The costumer stood at the small stage, waiting for Merle. The door swung open behind her, banging into the wall.

Tom yelled, "Is she ready yet?"

"Just about. Now, out!" She didn't raise her voice, but her tone carried an undertone of steel.

Tom blanched and pulled his hat down. He turned and went out the door.

"He listened to you," Merle said wonderingly as she stepped onto the small stage.

"He knows better than that. I can hold up entire movies. I've done it, too." She smirked.

"Do you and Sammy sew all of these yourselves?"

"We're on a budget. I bring in additional help as needed," Dorothy commented as she put a final stitch in the hem.

"You know, I'm pretty good with a needle and thread," Merle said tentatively.

"Are you now? I'll have to keep that in mind. You're done now; turn for me." She put a short brown wig on Merle and, as a final touch, pinned a flower on her dress. She stood back and looked at her. "Do you need shoes?"

"I have those." She pointed over to her brown shoes.

"Those are fine. Bring all this back after the scene is complete."

"I will," Merle promised. She stepped over to the costumer and kissed her quickly on the cheek. "Thanks for the lovely clothes."

Dorothy turned red. "Go on, get outta here. They're waiting."

Merle exited and slammed into Tom. "Let's go," he said, grabbing her hand, and they ran to the set.

"Where the hell is she?" Stone groused.

"Here, boss," Tom spoke up, "just behind you."

Stone turned toward the duo. "You, girl, over there." He pointed to the set.

Tom muttered to her, "He wants you by the stairs on the set."

Merle nodded and went to where they told her. One of the men working on the set handed her a bunch of flowers. *I guess my job is to hold things.*

"Remember, ladies and gentlemen," Stone began, "this is the wife's house, and her husband and boyfriend are going to slam into the door. Helen, you're on the staircase reacting to them." He paused. "All right, everyone, ready? We're set to go. And... Action!" he called.

Merle stood with the flowers, not knowing what to do. She saw an empty vase on the side table and walked to it and started adding the flowers to it. The door slammed open, and the two men fell in together.

"Helen... you see them fighting but you don't know what to do. React in horror," Stone said. Helen performed the direction with her hands on her mouth and eyes wide. "Now... run down the stairs!" Helen ran down to try to stop the fighting men. They didn't see her and accidentally knocked her back onto the stairs. "You with the vase, help her out." Merle thought quickly and instead of running over, she took the vase and conked both men on the head. They fell and Merle ran over to help Helen up from her prone position.

"Scene changed," the camera man muttered

"Keep it going," Stone said.

"We're off script," Tom put in.

"I don't care, this is better!" Stone yelled at the set. "Flower girl! Lead Helen out of the room. Tom and Alan, grab their ankles. Ladies, fight them off." Another man ran into the room.

"Helen," the man said, "I'm here for you."

The two men stopped fighting and they both yelled, "Who are you?"

Helen turned and said, "He's the one I chose." She shook the two men's hands off her leg and ran to the man who had just entered. They hugged and kissed while the two men on the floor looked on with open mouths.

"Cut. That's a print," Stone commanded. "Someone get that flower girl over here."

Merle walked timidly to the director. "Yes, sir?" she asked.

Stone sat back in his chair and looked at her for a long moment. "You changed my scene," he finally said.

"Uh, well," she stammered, "I wasn't here for the rehearsals and I just... I just went on instinct."

Stone laughed. "That was some good instincts."

Helen sauntered over. "Who's this, Billy? I haven't seen her before."

"She was an extra earlier. She was the maid who hit Alan in the face with a pie."

Helen looked at Merle closely. "Is that a wig?"

"Yeah," Merle said, pulling it off.

Helen snorted in derision. "I can see why. Keep the wig on." She leaned toward her. "Girl, that's a bad dye job." She looked at Stone. "What about the next one, Billy?" she asked, pulling out a cigarette and lighting it. "Will she be in it?"

"She has good instincts. What do you think?" Stone asked, folding his hand on his stomach.

"Bring her on as my kid sister, see how she does with a bigger role."

"What do you think? What's your name?"

"Marie. Marie Spencer."

"Well, Marie Spencer, what do you think?" Stone asked. "Want to work on the next film?"

"Yes, sir, I would."

"Good. We're starting rehearsals on Monday."

"What'll the movie be about?" *Will there be scripts?*

"We'll go over that in rehearsal."

Helen dropped her cigarette and ground it down. She whistled and an older woman ran over holding a towel and an apple. "Where have you been?" Helen demanded.

"I was waiting for you to finish," the woman stammered.

"Whatever, let's go," Helen said and sauntered away. The woman dashed after her.

"Wow," Merle commented.

"She is something," Stone said. "I liked your instincts there. But watch it. During rehearsals, I'll let you know when you can improvise just as long as it doesn't affect the overall story."

"Yes, sir."

He turned to talk to the cameraman and she found herself dismissed. She shrugged and turned back to the set. Tom ran over to her.

"Turn in the dress and report here on Monday morning."

"Do I need anything to prepare?"

"No, just be on time."

"I will," she promised. Merle quickly ran backstage to tell Harry that she'd need to get her clothes changed out.

"I'll be here," he said. He and Rich were taking down parts of the set. They were going over the set directions for next week.

"Thank you!" she said and hurried over to the costume building. She knocked on the door and was called in.

Dorothy sat drinking tea with Sammy. "I was waitin' for you," the woman said.

"Thanks for helping me with my costume."

"Eh, it's the job." She shrugged. "Go get dressed." Merle followed her direction and walked behind the screen. She came out tucking in the dress with one hand and carrying the costume in the other. "Hang that there," Dorothy said. She was bent over her table, looking at future movie designs.

"I will," Merle said as she struggled with her waistband.

Dorothy finished her work and looked over at her. "Come over here, let me check that for you." Merle walked toward her. Dorothy looked at the waistband and commented, "You blew out the seams."

"No, had to cut it to get me in it this morning."

"You gained any weight?"

"Maybe," Merle admitted. "This is my sister's skirt."

"You didn't have one?"

"Not in the style I wanted to show up on set in."

The costumer cackled suddenly. "Sounds like we have something in common." She referenced the gaudy clothes she wore. Merle laughed with her.

"I'm trying to blend in more."

Dorothy worked quickly. "There you go. I added some fabric so that the extension won't be so obvious."

Merle tugged on the skirt. "Thanks for that; it does feel more secure."

"Will you be back?" Dorothy asked as Merle slipped off the wig.

"I've been asked to be in the next movie, starting on Monday."

"Monday, hmm. That's rehearsals. What part?"

"Helen's sister."

Dorothy nodded thoughtfully. "I have the drawings for the costumes. Wanna see them?"

"Oh, yes, please." Merle followed the woman to the table. Dorothy pointed to one. "Helen's will have a deep V neck and yours will be higher."

"When will you make them?" Merle asked curiously, studying the intricate designs.

"Gonna be fast," Dorothy muttered.

"Need any sewing help?" Merle and Jean could use the extra money.

"I do. I'll need at least two girls for this. Can you come in tomorrow through the weekend?"

"I can."

"Great! Be here at eight tomorrow. We'll start gathering fabric and get a basted set done. The details will take all weekend."

Merle gathered her things. "See you then."

"See the accountant and let him know you'll have a part in the next movie."

Merle smiled. "Is he always involved?" she asked.

"In every step," Dorothy confirmed. "And you can't start until he sets it all up."

"Back to the accountant, I guess," muttered Merle. She walked to his office and opened the door.

"You again," he called from his desk. "What now?"

"I'm going to be Helen's sister in William Stone's next movie."

He sighed and started writing on the papers in front of them. He tossed it quickly at her.

She tapped the paper. "And... Um... Also, Dorothy told me I was hired as a sewer on the movie."

"You're just too much trouble. Gimme back the contract." She did as he asked, and he added several lines and tossed it back at her. "Read this one closely; there are two rates of pay to focus on."

She read through the contract and saw her pay had gone up. "Why so much more?" she asked, her pen poised to sign.

"Before you were just an extra, but now you're a named member of the movie," he explained. "The pay is pretty standard." She didn't see anything that bothered her and signed the form. She started to stand. "Here's your pay for the last two days," he said, holding out a check.

She took it without looking at the amount. "Thank you."

"No need. You did the work, you get paid. Now, get out," he said gruffly.

She folded the check, walked out the door, and headed back to the set. They'd dismantled most of the interiors.

"You're back," Harry called to her.

"I am and I'll need to come back tomorrow and the rest of the weekend."

"We'll be here also." He turned to her suddenly. "Does that mean you got some work on the next movie?"

"It does."

"That's great! What'll you be carrying next?" he teased.

"I'm not sure; I have to be here for rehearsals on Monday."

He started. "Rehearsals? Only the main cast rehearses. Maybe you got that wrong."

"No," she said, "the director told me himself."

"Hmm."

"Is that unusual?"

Rich called over. "This business moves quickly. Be careful, you can go down as fast as you go up here. Follow the directions given." He nodded toward a couch. "Why don't you go sit over there. We'll be done soon and then we'll head home."

About an hour later, Harry came over and said softly, "Merle, wake up."

"Oh, I didn't realize I'd fallen asleep. Are we ready to go?" she asked with a yawn.

"We are," Rich said. They helped her up and the three made their way to the car. Rich jumped in the back and Harry held the door for Merle. The car bumped along the rough road, and she yawned widely. "Sorry."

"Don't be, it was a long day."

"I hope Jean's went as well as mine did." Merle was worried that her sister would be angry that she'd gotten an acting job and not Jean. Coming to Hollywood and being in the movies had been Jean's dream and now Merle had stolen it.

When they got home, she went up to her room to lie down before dinner. She'd dozed off when a knock sounded on her door. Merle struggled with her robe. "Just a second. Who is it?"

"It's me."

Jean, she thought. She unlocked and opened the door. Jean stood there, covered in dirt. "Did you have a good day?" she asked hesitantly.

Jean grinned through the dirt on her face. "It was an amazing day!"

"Why don't you get showered and then come tell me all about it," Merle invited.

"I will." Jean started down the hallway, "How was your day?" she called over her shoulder.

"Umm. It was pretty good. I'll share with you once you're clean."

Merle could hear Jean's laughter as she shut her door and leaned on it. *Will she be angry with me?* she thought and walked to the bed, to wait for Jean.

It was a little while later when Jean stuck her wet head in. "Ready for me?"

"Come in."

Jean entered in a robe and was toweling off her hair. She took a chair and moved it closer to the bed. "Tell me about your day."

"No, you first."

"Oh, Merle, the horses were wonderful, and it was so nice to be working with them again. I helped to muck out the stalls. Charlie and I rode two horses and we had a grand race, which I won, by the way."

"You always did like working with the animals. Were you able to go to the set?"

"I did! The horses we rode over were used as background for a romantic movie. It was a small group with a cameraman, director, assistant director, and the two actors."

"I'm glad. What was the rest of your day like?"

"Right now, I'm working on training. We'll get scripts and

then work with the horses for the different scenes." She leaned forward excitedly. "Next week, we're going to a train set where the horses will be used by stuntmen! It's going to be so great to see it in person! What about you? Did you get to see some shooting?"

Merle looked down uncomfortably and picked at the cover. Every excited word that Jean had said dug a little deeper into her heart. "Umm... A little more than that."

"What did you get to do? Run errands?"

"No, I kinda sorta got into a movie."

Jean looked confused. "How do you kinda sorta get into a movie?"

"I was standing around with Harry and everyone and this man came up and told me to pick up a tray for a scene that was being filmed."

"So, you were an extra?"

"I was."

Jean was stunned. "You were put into movie today?"

"Yes," Merle mumbled, still not looking at her. She could feel herself getting more and more upset the more she told Jean. "It was this morning and again this afternoon." Jean looked at her with a stunned expression. Merle felt she had no choice but to continue her story and dash her sister's dreams.

"I was given a costume and went to the accounting department to sign a contract. In the afternoon, after the scene I was in, the director and the star, Helen Bixby, asked me to come on Monday to play her sister in a new movie."

"OH. MY. GOD!!" Jean breathed out in shock.

Here it comes, Merle thought. *She's going to hate me and she's right, too. She's never going to trust me, and she'll make me leave, and I will for her. I'll leave and get a job as an accountant somewhere, not that I know how to account... But anyway...* Merle realized she was rambling in her head.

"OH. MY. GOD," Jean whispered. "You're a movie star!"

"Oh, baby," Merle began, "I'm so sor— Wait, what?" she asked, confused.

Jean screeched, "YOU'RE A MOVIE STAR!" She screeched again and started jumping up and down in glee. "My sister's a movie star!"

"Wait... You're not mad?"

"Mad? Why would I be mad? Merle?" When her sister still didn't look up, Jean said again, "Merle, look at me." Merle lifted her eyes slowly. She had been expecting a frown or tears, anger. Instead, she saw a huge grin. "You're in the movies! And on your first day. That's amazing! We'll have to go to the movies when it comes out."

"Jean, you aren't mad?"

"Why would I be?"

"This is your dream, not mine."

"My dream is to be a stuntwoman." Jean studied her sister. "You as an actor make sense; you've always been overly dramatic." Merle swatted her arm. "And I'll get my dream. I'm close now."

"You will! I know you will. I have some sewing work on set this weekend. Do you want to come with me and poke around?"

"Do you think it would be okay?" *A weekend on a real movie set.*

"I do."

"Yes," Jean said happily. "Just think, both of us will be in the movies."

A knock sounded at the door. "Dinner," called Robbie.

"We'll be right down," Jean answered. She helped Merle stand. As Merle tucked her shirt into her skirt, Jean noticed the waist had been fixed. "Nice job with the repair."

"The costumer, Dorothy, helped me out. There will be extra sewing work this weekend if you are interested."

"Oh, yes, can I also see the set?"

"Of course." Merle stood and asked, "Ready?" Jean nodded and they walked down together. Everyone was at the table when they entered; glasses were clinking together.

"Congratulations to you both!" called people from the group. Hannah ran over to take their hands.

"We heard you girls both had a good start today."

Merle turned red and Jean grinned. "Thanks to the guys we have."

Paul muttered, "She's good with horses."

"You should've seen Marie carry things today," Charlie said, laughing.

Merle chuckled. "What can I say? They kept handing me things to hold: a tray in the first scene and flowers in the second."

"Well," said Harry, "there was also pie."

"Pie?" asked Jean.

"Yeah, in that first scene, I was running around with a tray and an actor told me to throw some pies at him."

"And you did it?" Hannah asked.

"She did," commented Harry. "The director liked it. I won't be surprised if we don't see more pie-throwing in the future."

"Will you be going back?" Robbie asked.

Harry commented as he passed a tray of meat around. "Marie got a second lead in the film next week."

The table quieted. "So soon?" Hannah asked faintly. It was rare for people to move up so quickly.

"Maybe one day I'll be driving you," Robbie commented.

She smiled at him. "Maybe."

Chapter Nineteen

The next morning, Saturday

"Jean, stay with me, please," Merle said as Jean barely missed getting hit by men moving boards.

"What?" her sister asked, distracted. "There's so much to see. Sets are being built and some have movies being filmed. Can I go watch?"

Merle smiled. "Yes, drop me off first and, if anyone asks, tell them you're with me." She could see that Jean wasn't paying attention. She clapped her hands. "Jean listen to me." When Jean finally met her eyes, she said, "Please don't interfere with their work. These people can get easily agitated."

She nodded and continued to look around. They arrived at the costumer's building, and she said, "First, come in. I want you to meet Dorothy and Sammy."

Jean looked over her shoulder wistfully. "I guess they'll still be there..."

"They will be. Now, come on." Merle knocked on the door and Sammy answered with, "What do you want?"

Jean looked at Merle and asked, "Are we in the right place?"

Dorothy walked up and tapped her daughter on the shoulder. "You are. Be nice, Sammy, and let them in. Hi, Marie. You can ignore her; she's grouchy today."

"Gee, thanks, Ma," Sammy said drolly.

"Just get back to work. We have lots to get done."

"Don't we always." Dorothy glared at her. Sammy held up her hands. "I'm on my way. No need to yell."

"I'll show you yelling when we get home," Dorothy threatened. She turned back to Merle and Jean. "Marie, I have a station for you and an instruction sheet." Merle walked over to the station she was assigned.

"And you are?" Sammy asked Jean.

Before Jean could answer, Dorothy called, "Back to work!"

"Dorothy, Sammy, this is my sister, Annie," Merle said as she took off her jacket and rolled up her sleeves. "She's here to look around today. She won't be in the way."

Dorothy looked Jean up and down. "Can you sew?"

"I can."

"She's good," Merle said. "But she wants to see how this place works first."

"When you finish looking around, come back and I'll get you to do some work for me."

"Do I need to take her to see the accountant?" asked Merle.

"Not today. I'll keep a log and we can turn it in next week."

Jean said, "I'd love help." She kept looking over her shoulder toward the door.

"Go on now. I see you want to explore," said Dorothy. Jean grinned and headed out. Once the door closed behind her, Dorothy asked, "Does she want to be in the movies?"

"That's why we're here."

"Hmm," Dorothy said and put pins in her mouth on the

dress form in front of her. "We have a lot to do before Monday. The dresses need additional details."

* * *

Jean ran out and looked around. *Where is the action going on?* There were sets lined up and down the road, one right after another. She heard a woman scream and walked up quietly behind the director. The movie looked like a kidnapping; the inept bad guys were attempting to get the girl down the stairs. The director yelled directions to the set, and the people followed his lead.

"Okay, the leading man enters. Where's your girl? You look up the stairs and see they're trying to get her." The hero ran up the stairs and the bad guys pushed him back. A fight started, and the bad guys started to roll downstairs. The director called, "Now, hug and kiss the girl." They did as they were told and he yelled again. "Cut! Good, good. Set up the next scene." With that order, he strode off the set.

Jean saw a man with a clipboard standing nearby. She tapped him. "Where's the next scene?"

He didn't look up as he said, "The high wire lines. We'll have a scene where they're after her again and she uses the lines to get away."

"May I follow you?"

He looked up and asked, "Who are you?"

"I'm with my sister today; she works here, and I wanted to observe some of the movie-making."

He frowned. "That should be okay, but stay out of the way." He leaned toward her. "We normally throw people out. Secrets, you know."

"Oh, okay. I won't share anything."

"Good. Come with me." The set had broken up, with a smaller group moving with the camera to an open field. "Those are the lines." He pointed to the long lines attached to two poles.

They were at different heights. "Stay with me. The director won't like having to do any retakes."

"I'll be right behind you." There was a group of people standing to the side, out of camera range.

The assistant hurried over to the director. He was already in his chair, and the cameraman had his face buried in the lens. "Jamie, move over to the pole and start climbing. Everyone, out of the scene!" the director yelled through a bullhorn. "Action!" The area cleared and the actress from the prior scene was climbing up the pole. "Cut! Stuntwoman, please."

"Oh, boy," said the assistant.

"What wrong?" asked Jean as she watched a large "woman" walk to the pole.

"That's not a stuntwoman," the assistant muttered.

The director got a good look at the "stuntwoman" and screamed, "What the hell are you doing? Come here!" A man in a wig and dress walked over. His face showed at least a day's growth of beard. "Joe, what the hell's going on here?" the director demanded. "We arranged for a woman. We're gonna want closeups when she comes down that line."

"Yeah, about that," Joe said, scratching his head and dislocating his wig. "She... uh... she wasn't well."

"Well, this won't work," the director fumed, throwing his script onto the ground.

The assistant stepped up quickly. "But, sir, we need to have this on film today or we'll be behind schedule and the accountant will want to talk to you."

The director stared hard at the man. "Accounting doesn't run this business, I do."

"I can do it," Jean said. Suddenly, everyone turned to look at her. *Oops, did I say that out loud?*

The director's eyes lit up. "Are you a stuntwoman?"

She squirmed a bit. "In training."

"Well, the best way to learn is to do it." He pointed to Joe.

"You go with him, and we'll run it through. We see what we like, then we'll do a final shoot."

Jean wanted to grin and jump in the air, but instead, she just said, "Yes, sir."

The director told Joe, "Get her the wig and go over the stunt with her."

Joe studied her and muttered, "Welp, a job's a job. Let's go." Jean had to run to keep up with his stride. "What stunts have you done?"

"Mostly stunts with horses. I can also do some tumbling."

"How's your upper body strength?"

"I keep in shape."

"Okay, this'll be more of an endurance test. You'll need to climb that pole. At the top, there's some handles that you'll grab onto. You swing out and gravity will take you all the way down. When you hit the ground, tumble off and get to your feet quickly at the end." Joe stopped and grabbed her arm. "Can you do that?"

She looked at the pole and line. "Just try to stop me."

He raised his eyebrows and smiled. "I sounded just like you on my first job." He turned and continued walking to the pole. There, he gave some final directions. "I'm stepping away now. The director will call out directions and you just follow them."

She nodded and took the wig and pins from him. She put it on. "Is it straight?"

Joe smiled at her. "Yeah, looks better on you than me. I'm off."

Jean waited with her hands on the rods sticking out of the pole. Trying to remember which hand the actress had started with, she started climbing as "Action! Bad guys, chase her to the pole!" was called. She started up the fifty-foot pole. The height made her a little dizzy. She hesitated and looked down. Just as before, the bad guys had surrounded the pole. "Start shaking it!" called the director. They did as he directed, and Jean grabbed the handles and hung on. "Okay, guys, start to climb after her. Now, you girl, go faster! Go!"

Jean grabbed the final rod and pulled herself onto the platform. The men were close; she didn't hesitate. She tucked her hair behind her ear, grabbed the handles with all her might, and swung out! There was a bounce, then she was sailing through the air. It was exhilarating! She let out a loud yell. "Whoo-Hoo!" The line came to a halt, and she tumbled to the ground. She jumped to her feet at a run.

"Cut!" hollered the director. "Come here, girl!"

Jean walked over, still feeling somewhat dizzy from the ride. "How did I do?"

He rubbed his chin and then looked at her. "Do you know what the movie is about?"

"Umm, the girl's running from the bad men and trying to get back to the man in the first scene."

"Yeah. And what were you doing up on the line?"

She thought it through. "Getting away from the bad men?"

"And what do you think your emotion is?"

"Not thrilled?" she asked tentatively.

"You're scared! You don't normally do that every day. And when you roll in on the landing, jump up and start running. The leading lady will then take your place. Got it?"

"So... I do it again?" she asked. Jean could hardly contain her grin.

"You do it again." The director yelled, "Set it up one more time! This should be it." He called to the leading lady. "Jamie, you're going to start running when she comes down. Be ready." Jamie nodded and went to her position. "And you, stunt girl, try to tone down your excitement."

Joe walked her back over to the pole. "Do you have what you need?"

"I think so."

"Just remember, act scared. And make it big; the audience needs to experience it with you. It'll all have to be done with your face."

"Got it. Act scared and make it big."

"Okay then. Hey, what's your name?"

"Annie. Annie Spencer."

"I'm Joe Cummings."

"Clear the set!" called the director.

Joe moved away and watched as she got into position.

"Action!"

Jean climbed up the pole and the bad men ran over and started to shake it. She glanced down at them and jumped onto the platform. The bad men were close behind her and the platform waved in the air. She tucked her hair behind her ear, grabbed the handles, and swung out. As she started to slide down, she gritted her teeth, widened her eyes, and opened her mouth as if to scream. She hoped it was enough. The end came quicker than expected and she bounced before rolling to her feet. She took off running and, in front of her, Jamie took over, so she slowed. The camera followed Jamie out of the scene.

"Cut! We go it."

Joe walked over to Jean and patted her shoulder. "You did good."

"Thanks. Do you think he thought so?" she asked, nodding at the director.

"He didn't yell at you. So, I think we're in the clear."

The crew around the director seemed to be moving again. "Where are they going now?" she asked.

"This film is more of a one-reeler, so it's about ten to twelve minutes. There'll be one more scene to wrap it up. Want to watch?"

"No more stunts?" she asked, disappointed.

"Nah, stunts aren't in every scene."

"Might as well," she grumbled and followed him. They joined the crew back at the house scene. Jean watched Jamie run back into the house and find her lover there. She ran over to him; he was lying on the floor with his eyes closed. They sprang open when he felt her touch. They hugged.

"Is it over?" Jean asked in a low voice.

"Just watch."

At that moment, a large man came in and started to yell. He waved the bad guys into the room to go after them. Jamie ran to her purse, handed it to the leader of the bad guys, and waved her arms to indicate they should go after the big man. They looked in the bag and nodded at each other, then ran after the big man and out of the house. The couple hugged.

"Cut and that's a wrap! Good job, everybody," the director said.

"What'd you think?" Joe asked her.

"It was confusing without the cards. Who was the big man?"

"Her father. He was trying to break them up."

She smiled, reached up to unpin the wig, and handed it to him. "Thanks for helping me with my first movie."

Joe took it. "I appreciate you stepping in." He rubbed his chin and asked, "Where do you do work now?"

"I'm working with Harry Brown and his crew. He works with the animals that're needed at the different studios."

"I've used them occasionally. You good with horses?"

"I am," she said. There was no reason to hide this from him.

"Hmm, I have a more action-packed movie coming up. Have you been on set with the horses?"

"I'm supposed to be on set for Balboa Studios on Monday. I believe it's a train scene."

"Where are you staying?"

She quickly pulled out her notebook, wrote her information on a page, tore it out, and handed it to Joe. He took it. "I'll contact you." He handed her a card—**Joe Cummings - Stunts**—and a piece of paper. "Here's my card and your accountant paperwork."

She took them. "Thank you!"

"Don't forget to get that paper turned in to the accountant. You did good work today and you should be paid for it."

"I will," she promised and slapped it on her leg and ran to the costumer's door. She knocked on it and heard a loud voice call out, "Come in!" Jean pushed the door open and walked inside. The three women had moved to the detailed work on the dresses. "So pretty," she said as she approached the dress forms.

"Watch the hands!" warned Dorothy.

"Oh," Jean said, looking down. The handles on the zip line had been dirty and it had transferred to her hands. "Yeah, right, sorry about that."

Sammy looked up. "What's that you have in your hand?"

"This?" Jean asked and held up the pay slip.

Merle glanced over. "I've seen that before. Annie, is that a pay slip?"

"It is!"

Merle jumped up and ran over to her. "What did you do? Were you carrying things?" she teased.

"No, I got to do a real stunt."

"That's all good and well," said Dorothy, "but we have lots of work still left here. Annie, go wash your hands and then come back. I'll provide you with another pay slip."

Merle moved back to her location. "Annie, hurry."

Jean nodded and moved quickly. Her hands clean, she returned. "What can I do?"

"Marie says you have some sewing skills."

"I'm pretty good."

"I need you to start attaching these feathers to the collar."

She took the feathers and held them up. "Like this?"

"Yes, that's it." Jean followed the directions. She went to work and soon had the feathers attached. "Good job, now move to the sleeves with a similar design." Jean looked at Merle with a grin. Merle winked at her and went back to sewing.

They broke for lunch. Dorothy provided sandwiches and beer for them. They sat outside and watched people in costumes walk to and from various sets. "Busy place," Merle observed.

"Getting bigger every day," Dorothy replied. "Soon, I'll have to have full-time help. Are either of you two interested?"

"I can help out occasionally like now," Merle told the woman.

"Me, too," Jean said, "but we want to see what happens with the movies."

"I get that." Dorothy glanced at her daughter. She'd laid back on the porch and propped her drink on her chest.

"You've always got me." Sammy smiled at her mother.

"Don't remind me," Dorothy said loudly. "Let's get back to work. We need to get a lot done today. Can you both come in tomorrow?"

Merle looked at Jean and she nodded. "You can count on us."

"Aren't you going to ask me?" asked Sammy.

"You live with me; you're coming in tomorrow."

"Yeah, yeah."

"Dorothy," Merle said, "we're looking for a little house. Something that we can easily take care of."

"Buying or renting?"

"Buying," Merle said firmly. She didn't volunteer where the money came from.

"Ma," Sammy spoke up, "there's that yellow house, near ours."

Dorothy tilted her head. "Hmm, yeah, that might work. The man who owns it wants out. His wife got involved in drugs after he worked so hard to keep her straight."

"Did she work in the movies?" asked Merle.

"Yeah, she did."

"I worked with her a few times," Sammy volunteered. "She was nice enough, but she liked the white powder."

"White powder?" asked Jean.

"Cocaine," Merle supplied. Dorothy and Sammy looked at her with wide eyes. She held up her hands. "No worries, I just knew some people who used it."

Was it the Strathmores? thought Jean.

"That stuff is bad news. It can take over your life and affect your behavior," Merle told her sister.

"When is he wanting to leave?" Jean asked Dorothy.

"Pretty soon, I think. He wants to go back to his family in the east."

"Can you set up some time for us to view the house?" Merle asked.

"I can," Dorothy said and squinted her eyes. "Provided you agree to work next weekend."

"Why, Dorothy, that sounds like blackmail." Merle grinned at her friend.

"Eh, I gotta get help where I can." Dorothy shrugged.

"Well, I'll be happy to help next weekend," Merle agreed readily.

"Me, too," Jean said.

"All right, enough chit chat," Dorothy groused. "Let's go back to work."

"When can we see it?" asked Merle.

"Stop by on Monday and I'll confirm the time with you."

They walked back to their work. At the end of the day, they all stood and viewed the rack of clothes they'd completed. "That was good work," Dorothy congratulated them. "I have the fittings scheduled for tomorrow. Be here at eight sharp."

They headed out together; Jean took Merle's hand as they walked over to Harry. He and Rich were drinking coffee. Harry spotted them and stood. "Ready to go home, ladies?"

"We are," Merle said for her and Jean.

Chapter Twenty

fter dinner that evening on their evening walk

"I hope the house works out," Merle said, laying her head on Jean's shoulder.

"Me, too. This is nice, but I would like our things around us."

"That would be nice."

Jean changed the subject and tentatively asked, "Merle, did you ever try the cocaine?"

She sighed and lifted her head. "Am I a terrible role model?" At Jean's exasperated sigh, Merle took her hand. "No, I didn't try that particular thing. I saw what it was doing to people I went to parties with. I saw Catherine take it; she thought it was good for her."

"It wasn't."

"No, it wasn't."

"I'm glad you didn't try it."

Merle changed the subject. "Tell me about your first role as a stuntwoman. How did it happen?"

"It was like your opportunity; I was in the right place at the right time. And the stuntman they had looked nothing like the leading lady."

Merle laughed. "I'd like to go see that house soon."

"Me, too."

"Tomorrow, back to the lot for sewing."

"Yes, the extra money can only help."

Chapter Twenty-One

T*he next morning*

Harry took the sisters back to the set the next day. "Thanks for bringing us back to the studio. I know you're off today," Merle told him.

"That's okay. I don't mind." They came to a stop, and they started to get out. "Want me to pick you up?"

"I think we may have another way home." Jean looked over at her with raised eyebrows. Merle nodded.

"Yes, we do," filled in Jean. "Thanks, Harry."

"Yes, thanks, Harry."

"I'll see you later then?" It landed as a question.

"I think we'll be busy," said Merle.

He nodded and looked at his hands, clenched on his steering wheel, before he drove off.

"What was that about?" Jean asked.

"He's getting attached. I don't need that type of complication."

"He seems nice," Jean said tentatively.

"He is, but we have plans."

Jean hooked her arm through Merle's. "That we do."

They walked to the costumer's building. "Not a lot of people today," Merle observed. The normally full streets were empty.

Jean looked around. "No, it's kind of interesting; it's so quiet. Can you get on the sets when people aren't here?"

"Did you notice the guards?"

"No, where?" asked Jean, looking around.

"They're over there and there." Merle pointed to the side of each set.

"Hmm, so no wandering around today." Jean looked down the road. "Isn't that Robbie?"

Merle looked in the direction she indicated and didn't see anyone. "Not that I can see. Were you worried about something? He does drive for the directors occasionally."

"No, not really," Jean said, still looking down the road.

"We're here," said Merle. Jean pulled her eyes away and realized they were at the small building. She followed Merle up the small steps and looked over her shoulder as Merle knocked on the door.

"She's not here yet," Sammy said from the left.

"Morning," said Merle.

"Morning." Sammy groaned and laid back down on the porch.

"Are you okay?"

"It's my back, too much bending over the sewing machine."

"Complain, complain, complain," came a gruff voice from the street.

"Hey, Ma," Sammy said.

Dorothy went over to her daughter and helped her up, her tone and her care in counterpoint to each other. "Fittings start soon. We'll have a line out here."

Merle couldn't wait to ask her friend, "Dorothy, were you able to find out if we could take a look at the house today?"

Dorothy didn't say anything as she settled into the room.

"Ma, tell them."

Dorothy smiled suddenly. "If you want to come back with us after work, I arranged for you to see the house."

Merle squeezed Jean's hand. "Thank you."

"Don't thank me. You might not like it. Now, get to work."

They each moved to their stations to focus on the detailed work. The actors and actresses started arriving within an hour. Each person took an actor or actress to fit them. Everyone wanted the process to go quickly, so there was little talking.

"Next," Merle called out. She didn't look up from the list of outfits. "What's your number?"

"Should be close to yours," said the woman.

Merle looked up and saw it was the actress from her movie. "Helen Bixby," she said. She saw Jean perk up out of the corner of her eye. "Let me get your dress." She moved to the rack and pulled the number. "Annie," she called, "can you come over and help on this one?"

Jean looked at the actor she was helping. "Would you mind waiting a moment?"

"No, go ahead. I have a book with me." He pulled it out and sat in her chair.

Jean walked over to her sister. "Helen Bixby!" she said, her eyes wide.

"Yes. Do we know one another?"

"No, I've seen all your movies."

"That's nice." She took the dress and said, "I'll be right back."

"Helen Bixby!" Jean whispered. "Did you ever imagine that we'd meet the people we saw on the screen?"

"I know."

"I need some help with the buttons," Helen called.

"Go back to your guy. I'll work with her," directed Merle.

Jean nodded and returned to the actor. He put down his book and allowed her to finish the fitting.

Merle tapped on the screen and Helen called, "Come

around." Merle went around and saw that the buttons down her back would need to be done up. She immediately went to work on them. "Who was that girl?"

"My sister."

"Does she want to be in the business?"

"She does, but she wants to be a stuntwoman."

"Is she any good?"

"She's still learning but I heard that she was in a movie yesterday and did a good job."

"I'll keep her in mind. She has a similar build to mine." They moved back to the main room, and Merle took up the waistline. Once that was completed, Merle helped Helen out of the dress.

"I'll see you tomorrow," Helen said.

"I'm looking forward to it."

Once the actors and actresses had come and gone, Dorothy called to Merle, "Marie, that final dress on the rack is yours. Go put it on."

Merle moved behind the screen and started to button up. "I'll need help with the buttons."

"I'll come back and help," Jean said. She appeared quickly and did them up. They walked outside the screen to the full-length mirror. Merle twisted and turned, looking at herself at all angles. The dress was black satin with sequins on the top.

"It's so beautiful," she said, feeling the fabric.

"It won't have to be taken in much," Sammy observed. "Let me get some pins."

"Move to the box," said Dorothy. After Merle stood on the box, they began to pin her in. "You may need to stop with the desserts for a while," she commented.

"I've been trying, it doesn't seem to help," Merle complained.

"We'll work on it," Jean said. "It's just the move and starting the new job. It's too much stress."

"Yes, that must be it," Merle said with a frown.

"Well, get it off," Dorothy ordered. "We need to make the adjustments before we can go see the house."

The house! thought Merle. She glanced at Jean and saw the same expression. "Help me out of this," Merle requested. Jean followed her to the dressing area. The dress was removed carefully and handed over the screen to Dorothy. She got dressed quickly and joined the three out in the main room.

Dorothy said, "Everyone take a costume from the rack, work on it, and then place it on the other rack as ready for the film." Each woman jumped in and, within a few hours, the last seam was done.

"We're finished," said Sammy.

"Thanks to everyone. Good work." Dorothy looked over at Jean and Merle. "I guess now you'd like to go see the house?"

"We would."

"Well, come on. Don't know what's holding you up." The sisters moved quickly to gather their things and followed Dorothy and Sammy out. "My car is over here." Dorothy motioned to a beat-up car. She saw their faces and said, "Don't worry, it runs."

"Ma likes to bump things," Sammy said sarcastically.

"It isn't me. People just won't get out of my way." They climbed into the battered vehicle and drove for about thirty minutes. When orange groves started to line the roads, she announced, "We're close now."

Jean and Merle looked around at the lush trees. "This is nice," Merle commented.

"I've lived here long before the movie people got here," Dorothy told them. "My house was my mama's house."

"And one day it'll be mine," said Sammy.

"Eventually," agreed her mother. "It'll stay in the family." As they got closer, they saw bungalows and craftsmen-built homes.

"That blue one over there is mine," Dorothy said, waving to her left.

"And mine," her daughter reminded her. Her mother grunted a response. Jean and Merle were looking at the homes around them. Sammy said, "It's two doors down from ours on the right."

"Can we go look?" Merle asked hopefully.

"Of course, we're headed there now."

"Not me, Ma. Can you drop me off at home? I'm tired."

"You're always tired," Dorothy complained. She pulled into the small driveway. "Go on." They watched Sammy enter the house. Once she shut the door behind her, Dorothy turned to them. "She's a good girl, just a little off sometimes."

"She does beautiful work," Merle commented.

"She does," Dorothy agreed, "and I'd like her to keep doing it."

"Does she want to quit?"

"I'm not sure what she wants right now. I don't think *she* knows what she wants right now." She started off and called back over her shoulder, "Come on then. We can walk over from here." They hurried after her.

"They're so lovely," Merle said, looking around the area.

"They are," Dorothy agreed. "We're lucky." The house came into view as they passed a large tree. It was yellow, in the craftsman style, but was not in the same shape as the homes around it.

Merle and Jean stopped. "Oh, no," Merle exclaimed. The houses around them had given her hope.

"Don't let the outside fool you. All of the bones are good and there are plenty of skilled men in the area who can help with repairs," Dorothy assured her.

Jean nudged Merle. "Let's give it a chance."

Merle had had such hopes that they could find something perfect. This one didn't match her vision. She took a deep breath and said, "I'll be open-minded." Merle was very conscious of the money they had. They were working, but could they afford to buy a house that would require repairs? She didn't want to rely too much on anyone. This was going to be hers and Jean's future.

Dorothy walked to the door and knocked. Then they waited. She looked back over her shoulder. "He's home."

"Hopefully, we're expected," muttered Merle. Jean nudged her again.

"We are. No worries."

The door swung open and the man who stood there was younger than they'd expected. He appeared to be in his mid-30s. His face set in a permanent frown. "What?" he demanded briskly.

"Mr. Hobbs."

"Miss Lipton."

"I have the young ladies who would like to view your home with the purpose of buying."

Hobbs turned and stared at the sisters. "You sure they can afford a house?"

"We can," Jean said before Merle could answer.

"Well then, come in." Boxes lined the walls and blocked doorways. "I have to be moving in the next week."

"How's Martha?" Dorothy asked.

Hobbs sighed. "She's better now that she's out of here; this place was no good for her. The facility took her, and they recommended that I live in the area. Thank goodness we have family around there."

Drugs, thought Jean. *They seem to be all over here.*

"Would you mind if we looked around?" Merle asked.

"Sure," he said and walked out on the porch with Dorothy.

"The inside is much better than the outside," said Jean encouragingly.

"It is," Merle agreed. She ran her hand along the wood molding on the doorway to the dining room. "The details are amazing." They continued through to the kitchen. "Not exactly clean," said Merle, looking at the stacks of dishes in the sink.

"It's fixable," Jean replied.

"Hmm."

They moved to the living room and saw the fireplace. Jean leaned down. "I don't think this has ever been used," she said. The weather was on the warmer side, but she could see them using it on the cooler evenings. "Bedrooms?"

"Let's go look."

They wandered around and saw that there were three bedrooms and one bath. "I like it," said Jean.

"What about the outside? We need to check the roof."

"I can climb up. Let's go out and look around." Merle stayed silent and followed her out. "Can I check the roof?" Jean asked Hobbs.

"Sure, the ladder is on the side there." He pointed to the side of the house. "I haven't had any leaks."

"I just wanted to take a look," she assured him. He waved her on. She climbed up and took her time walking around. There were no soft spots, and the shingles appeared to be in decent shape. It might be something they replaced in a few years. She climbed back down, and Merle went over to her.

"Any problems?" she asked in a low voice.

Jean replied in the same tone. "No, I think it's mainly paint and some wood repairs on the outside. I think we should make an offer."

"No, we should ask him what he wants first. We haven't done this before."

"But..." Jean started.

"I'll handle this," Merle said. They walked over to Hobbs and Dorothy. "We like it, though we see we'll need to do some repairs."

He studied them and nodded. "Yeah, that's true." He rubbed his neck and said, "I've been distracted in the last year. I meant to paint it. Martha always wanted it to be a lemon yellow with white trim. You'll find the paint is in the storage area out back."

Merle got down to business. "How much would you take for it?"

"Would you be able to pay me this week?"

"That depends on the amount," she cautioned.

He looked at the house and then at them. "I'd take $4,000 cash, but it must be cash."

That was much lower than Merle had expected. And that would leave them with money to buy furniture for the house. They looked at Dorothy, and she nodded quickly her approval.

"We like that, and we can meet your terms. How would this work?"

"We'll need a notary," said Dorothy, "to witness the exchange of money and ownership papers."

Hobbs nodded. "I have all the ownership papers. I'll set it up for next Saturday. Would that be okay with you?"

"We have a deal," Merle told him.

The relief on his face was palpable. "Good, good. I'll finish packing. I have a truck coming on Sunday to help me move."

Merl stuck out her hand. "We'll be here on Saturday."

Dorothy spoke. "Mr. Hobbs, let me know if anything changes and I can contact them."

"I look forward to it," he said.

The trio started to walk off, and Hobbs called out, "Thanks, Dorothy!" She nodded and waved back at him.

"The poor man," Jean said.

"Yes, he and Martha loved that house, but all of his money is going to her treatment." The sisters thought about that as they approached Dorothy and Sammy's home. "Come in for some tea and then I'll drive you both home."

Jean and Merle followed her inside. Jean said, "We'll need to get some sort of transportation, too."

"Well, I can't do everything for you," said Dorothy drolly.

Merle laughed. "What, you have limits to what you can do?"

Sammy heard the question and met them in the living room. She burst out laughing. "Not in her mind."

The layout of Dorothy's house was very similar to the house they'd just seen; wood molding gleamed, and the fireplace appeared to have been used. They also could see the space better without the boxes piled up. "I like it even more now," Jean said.

"We can see what it can become," said Merle.

"I have lemonade if you want some," Sammy said.

"Sounds good," said Jean and they followed her to the dining room. The drink was passed out and Dorothy leaned back in her chair.

"Do you have the money?"

"We do," Merle told her.

"I won't ask where you got that kind of money."

"We have nothing to hide."

"Well, it's still none of my business."

"Well, hell, I'm interested," Sammy said, laying her chin on her propped-up hands.

Dorothy looked at her daughter sternly. "It's none of your business, either."

"All right, fine," she groused. "So, when do you get the house?" she asked the sisters.

"Looks like next weekend." Merle asked Dorothy, "Can you be there?"

"Are you worried?"

"I don't like meeting people I don't know, especially with that much cash."

"You're right. I'll give you the names of several notaries. If you want, we can meet in their office."

"I'd rather do that," said Merle. Jean nodded in agreement.

"You both came here from the east?"

"We did," Jean replied. Merle kicked her in the leg as a reminder to keep it short.

"Hmm. So many people coming to be in the movies."

"Ma, stop torturing them. You're going to lose two seamstresses."

"You're right. You were asking about transportation?"

"See? I told you she'd have a plan," said Sammy.

"Yeah, we'll need something to get us from work to here," Jean responded.

"Okay, I'll ask around and, until then, you can ride in with us."

"Thanks, but we don't want to be that much trouble."

"Oh, she's got something in it for her," muttered Sammy.

"And that is?" Merle asked. She liked the woman but was

concerned with any additional debts she'd owe. She couldn't afford to be involved in anything illegal.

Dorothy rolled her eyes at the tone. "Sewing, you idiots. If I need extra hands, I'd appreciate it if you were on call."

Merle broke into a grin. "That, we can do."

Dorothy gulped down her drink and stood. "Good, now let's get you both home."

"Goodbye, Sammy," Merle told the girl.

"Goodbye, Sammy," Jean said.

"See ya."

They walked outside and loaded back into Dorothy's car. The group was quiet as they pulled into the boarding house parking area. Merle turned to her and said, "Thanks for the work this weekend."

"Be sure to get your timesheets turned into the accountant tomorrow."

"I'll turn in ours in the morning," Merle assured her. "I'll stop by for my costume in the morning."

They waved as she drove and then they entered the house. It was dinner time, and the group had already started eating. "You two are late today," Hannah remarked.

"Yeah, sorry about that." They'd decided not to tell them about the house. This was their business, and no one else's. "It was a long day, and we had to get the costumes ready for the movie."

"Will you need a ride in tomorrow?" Harry asked Merle.

"Yes, please." She didn't want to lead him on, but she needed a ride to work.

"Annie, you've been requested to bring the horse to the set tomorrow," Charlie told her.

"Really? I'll accompany you?"

"Seems the director at Balboa heard you were on a movie at a competing studio."

"Uh, yeah, that was kind of an accident."

"What, you slipped and fell into a movie?" he asked dryly.

"She was just in the right place at the right time," Merle said. This was the kind of thing she wouldn't miss. They shouldn't have to explain themselves to this group.

"You made an impression. I told him you'd need to shadow me on the first movie."

"That makes sense. What's the schedule?"

"We'll drive over at 6 am to get the horses ready and ride them to the set."

"What kind of movie is it?"

"It's a western, hence the horses," he said laconically.

Chapter Twenty-Two

T*he next day*

Jean got up early and sat on the side of the bed, monitoring the time. When it finally got closer to 5AM, she gathered her things and walked to the bathroom. She stood outside the door and started to turn the knob when she heard someone getting sick inside. "Oops," she thought and stepped back to give the person some privacy. After a long while, the door opened, and Merle walked out. She stopped at the door and leaned her head on it.

Jean ran over to her. "Are you okay?"

Merle was white as a sheet. "Not really. I haven't felt well."

"Do you need to go in today?"

"Yeah, I have an early call, and I need to turn the time sheets into the accountant."

"But..." she protested.

"Jean, I'm okay. I promise."

"Let me help you back to your room."

"Thanks," Merle said gratefully. Jean supported her to the room and sat her on the bed.

"Lie down. I'll check on you after I get ready."

"Thanks," Merle said and closed her eyes.

Jean ran back to the bathroom and got ready so she could help Merle before she left. She went back to Merle's room and found her sitting on the edge of the bed. She went and sat next to her. "Do you want me to take you to the doctor?"

"No, no, not now. I'll be fine. It's passing."

"What time do you have call?"

"Not for another few hours. But Harry will be going in earlier."

"Hannah or Robbie might be able to take you," Jean suggested.

"Can you check for me?"

"Of course. I'll do that now." Jean kissed her on the cheek and moved back to her room to finish getting ready. Pants for the day, but she also packed a skirt since she wouldn't always know what the stunt job might turn into. With her bag ready, she went downstairs and sat down for breakfast.

Harry looked over at her. "Where's Marie?"

"She isn't feeling well."

"She can't miss her call," he warned.

"She won't, but she needs a little rest this morning." She looked at Hannah and asked, "Could you take Marie to the set this morning?"

"I can't," Hannah replied regretfully. "Robbie, can you take her in with you?"

"I have time," he said, taking a bite of his toast.

Jean finished eating and grabbed some fruit and biscuits to take to Merle. She knocked quickly and entered. "Breakfast. Try to get something in your stomach."

"Thanks."

"Also, Robbie'll take you. You have about an hour."

"I'll be up. I'm already feeling better."

"Good. I need to head out."

"Hey," Merle called.

"Yes."

"Have a great day."

"You, too." Jean left and closed the door behind her.

A knock sounded at the door and Merle tightened her robe to answer it. She opened the door, and Hannah stood there. "Come in."

She walked in and said, "I wanted to check on you."

"I'm fine. I'm just worn out lately."

"Yeah, I noticed that. Have you been feeling better in the afternoons?"

"Generally. Why, is something going around?"

"You might say that," Hannah replied cryptically. "Are your clothes tighter?"

"Yeah. So, I've gained some weight. How is that part of an illness?"

"And your nipples are a different color?"

"Whoa there, I think that's a little personal, and I think you should leave now." Merle stood to move to the door.

She stayed where she was and said, "Hun, I think you're pregnant."

"No, no. I can't be..." Merle's voice trailed off. She opened her shirt enough to look at her breasts and collapsed on the bed. "Do you think so?"

"I do."

"What do I do?"

"There are options, and it appears it's early days."

"Options," Merle said faintly. Her life was effectively over. "Kill myself? That would be an option."

"There are ways," Hannah murmured. "Why don't you take some time and then get with me on the options? "

"Okay. I don't think I can deal with this now." *A baby?* she thought. *Whose is it? Jesse's or Bob's?*

"You've a little time, but don't let it get away from you."

"Thank you."

"Get dressed, go to work. Take your mind off of this for a little while."

Merle followed Hannah's directions and got dressed. She felt numb. Her poor decisions had led her to this point. *Is there really a baby in here?* She tentatively touched her stomach. She got her things together and walked to her door. She'd locked it and heard a voice call from downstairs.

"Marie! Hurry up," called Robbie. "I can't be late."

"Yes, of course, I'm coming," she called back and headed downstairs.

* * *

Charlie and Jean were on set. They'd gotten the animals fed and the stalls cleaned before moving the horse trailer to the location. Her main job was to monitor the horses and make sure the stuntmen knew how to ride. First, they'd film with the actor, then the stunt rider. Jean watched the man standing down the road from her. It was the latest leading man, Greg Harrison; he gave off a charming façade but that covered a nasty nature. She'd already seen his treatment of the assistant director, sending the man on errands around the set.

Charlie had briefed her on Harrison's nature as soon as they saw him on the set. "Watch him. He's been known to carry a stickpin and use it to try to get the horses to move." Charlie was getting the details for the upcoming scene when the actor walked up.

Greg walked over to the horses and Jean stepped in front of him. "Can I help you?"

"I just wanted to confirm which horse I'll be riding." There were two horses of similar colors in this scene. They were both ready to go and were relaxed.

"We'd prefer that you don't hurt the animals." Harrison

ignored her and adjusted his black shirt and his hat. She stepped toward him and reiterated, "You'd better not hurt the horses."

He brushed at the invisible lint on his shoulder. He "pretended" to see her and looked surprised. "I'm sorry, were you talking to me?"

She squinted her eyes. "I'm warning you."

Mack Burnett, the director, called out, "All right, people, let's get started."

During rehearsals, everything had gone well. Harrison had started off on Betsy, riding toward the moving train. Shooting was stopped so the stuntman could take over. All in all, things had gone very smoothly, and the director was happy. Charlie had been asked to go to another set to check out the animals being used there.

Jean was on her own for this final take. Greg pulled himself into the saddle, and she walked him over to the starting point. She looked up at him. "Remember what I said." He didn't even design to look down and acknowledge.

"Clear the set!" Mack called

Jean moved back out of the shot. She was wearing similar outfits to the other actors in the film in case the camera caught her. It was a precaution that was not usually needed. Everyone became silent and waited for the next direction. "All right, we're shooting this one. Action!"

Greg started Betsy moving. Everything was going just like the rehearsal and Jean let herself relax, when suddenly the horse screamed and bucked him off. She responded immediately and ran toward the man and the bucking horse. Greg was on his hands and knees, trying to get to a standing position.

Jean ran and jumped, using the man's back as a springboard to land on the back of the out-of-control horse. Betsy bucked and she held on tightly before she took off running toward the train. She let her run and put her arms around the mare's neck to try to calm her. Gradually, Betsy slowed and Jean was able to turn her back toward the set.

Everyone was milling around and talking in confusion when Burnett yelled, "Cut! You," he pointed at Jean, "come here."

"Yes, sir," she said and dismounted, speaking in a low, calming voice to the horse.

Harrison ran over to her and began shouting. "That animal is wild and shouldn't be allowed on set and this *person* should be fired!"

Mack tore off his hat and threw it on the ground, then jumped up and down on it. "Dammit! I'm not your parents. I'm making a movie! What the hell did you think you were doing running into our scene like that?" he screamed at Jean. She stood unwavering against the onslaught; she was in the right and would hold her ground.

"And you," Mack pushed past her to the actor. "Couldn't you stay on the damn horse for a few minutes?"

"That horse was out of control and damn near killed me! You saw that," Harrison protested.

"He's lying," Jean said loudly. "This jackass stuck her with a pin."

"Wha... You're crazy! You can't prove anything," Harrison charged.

Jean held out her hand. In it was a pin. "He'd been thrown off and this was left it in place. Isn't this yours?"

Harrison crossed his arms. "I've no idea where that came from," he said defensively.

"You don't?" she scoffed.

"Stop! I will be the one in charge here!" Burnett hollered. "A storm's coming in and we're losing the light. We'll film this scene in the morning. *AND*," he said, looking at both Jean and Harrison, "we better not have any screw-ups tomorrow!" Harrison nodded reluctantly.

The assistant director started calling to everyone. "We need to wrap it up and get everything back to the studio." Everyone started moving. Jean sent a final glare to Harrison and walked back to the horse. She spoke lightly to her and moved her back to the other horse. She removed their saddles, and she walked them to the trailer to transport them back to the barn.

It was her first day working a set alone, and it couldn't have gone worse. She hoped John didn't block her from returning the next day. She drove slowly back to the barn, unloaded the horses from the trailer and walked them to their stalls. The rain started as soon as she finished. Jean brushed them down and put out fresh feed and water. Lastly, she mucked out the stalls. She carried the debris out as the other guys returned from various jobs. Charlie saw her and walked over.

"Sorry I didn't come back; you seemed to have everything under control." She didn't answer as she dumped the debris outside.

"Well?" Paul asked. "Tell me."

"She's avoiding us," Charlie said.

"Did you do something to get into trouble?" Paul asked. He'd grown to like the girl, but a mistake on set could cost them money.

"Ummm... Well," she muttered. "I..."

"Spit it out," Paul demanded. "What do we need to fix?"

She looked at Charlie. "The actor in the scene today, Greg Harrison, he did well in rehearsals then..."

"Shit!" Charlie exclaimed.

"What is it, what happened?" asked Paul.

"Did he do it?" Charlie asked, not explaining to the others.

"He did," she confirmed.

"*WHAT* did he do?" asked Paul. Charlie looked on without question; he'd worked with Harrison before, and he knew what she was saying.

"That insufferable ass stuck a large pin into Betsy." She held it up; it gleamed in the light.

Charlie ran over to the horse, running his hands over her. "Is she okay? What did she do?"

Jean joined him. "I checked her out. She seems to be fine now."

"How did she react?"

"She reared up and bucked him off her back."

"And what did you do?" Paul asked. He already knew she could be protective of the animals.

"I... uh... ran over and used him as a springboard and jumped onto Betsy's back. I was able to calm her down and moved her to a safe location." The men listened to her story, and she found only acceptance when she met their eyes.

"That's a good job," Paul commended her. "Animals first, people second." The other two men nodded.

"Do I need to take the horses over to the set tomorrow?" Charlie asked, rubbing his neck. He mentally ran the different schedules through his head.

"I'm not sure. Mr. Burnett seemed rather unhappy," Jean said. *Is my new career over before it started?*

"Were you able to finish the scenes?" Rich asked. He'd walked up on the tail end of the conversation. He knew that they'd only contracted for one day on this movie.

"No." She sighed. "The rain started to move in, and they struck the set."

"What do you want to do, Annie?" Paul asked. "Do you want to switch sets with one of us?"

She stroked Betsy's nose. "No thanks. I'd like to see this through. Since this was my first movie, I'd like to finish the job." *If they let me*, she thought.

"We're busy tomorrow..." Paul started.

"Someone's coming up the drive," Charlie interrupted; he'd moved to the barn door. Paul and Jean joined him there.

"Can you see who it is?" Paul asked.

"Looks like someone from the Balboa Studio. There's a sign on the side," said Charlie.

"Oh great, I'm going to be fired in person," Jean lamented as she moved back to Betsy. The horse must've sensed her worry, because she nudged her shoulder with her head. Jean reached out to stroke her lightly. *I guess that's the end of things here*, she thought. She'd been so proud that she'd received the guy's approval to go to the set. She didn't move as Charlie and Paul intercepted the driver. It was Robbie. The group spoke in low voices. Finally, Paul called over. "Annie, come here."

She moved reluctantly outside to the truck. When she got close, Charlie grabbed her arm and pulled her to them. "This note's for you." He handed it to her.

She opened it and read. "They want me on set tomorrow! And I'm supposed to be there an hour early to meet with Mr. Burnett."

"That's it for me," Robbie said. "I'm going back. See you all at the house."

"Not if we don't see you first," muttered Charlie. They watched as he drove off.

"What do you think he wants?" asked Paul. Charlie shrugged.

"Maybe he wants to yell some more," Jean suggested.

Paul took the note. "Well, it doesn't say anything about barring you from the set."

Chapter Twenty-Three

P*atty Dove, Mack Burnett, and Joe Cummings meeting earlier that day*

Burnett and the actress Patty Dove were watching the film from that day's shooting with Joe Cummings. They watched the girl jump and use Harrison's back to get her on the crazed horse.

Patty Dove tapped Burnett on the shoulder. "I think we can use her."

"What?" Mack yelled. "She cost me time today. And time is money."

"No." She paused, thinking. "I'm sure that was Greg. I saw him jab that horse with something."

"You did? Why, that jackass!" Mack stormed.

Joe put his two cents in. "I've had her work for me on another job. I think she could work well as a stuntwoman."

"What about my new serial we are developing at Selig Studio?" Patty suggested. "There's a lot of stunts, and she's the right build for me."

Mack got where the duo were going and turned to Joe. "That *would* be better than you in a dress."

"You're right. We've had a problem getting women to take these roles."

"And the close-ups would be more believable," Mack muttered.

"Let me handle it," Joe said. *How will my other stunt women feel about a newcomer coming in and taking a big job like this?* he thought.

Burnett motioned to his assistant. "Yes, sir?"

"Send a note over to that horse girl from earlier and tell her to be at the set early tomorrow."

"It's Annie Spencer and should we mention the job?" Joe asked.

"No," Mack said. "I think putting the fear of God into her is a good thing. She shouldn't think that she got away with something."

"And what about Greg?" Patty asked.

"We'll be shooting tomorrow, and you tell that ass, if he tries anything like that again, he'll be the one cut out of the picture and I'll take it out of his hide."

Joe hid a smile. "Sounds like a plan, boss."

* * *

That night at the boarding house

As Charlie and Jean drove into the yard, his hands tightened on the steering wheel. "Want me to go with you to the meeting tomorrow?"

"No," Jean said resolutely. "I'll take the horses over and, if I get fired, I'll get word to you." She looked over at him. "Charlie, please don't tell Marie about this. I don't want to worry her."

"I won't say anything, and I'll talk to the other guys."

"Thanks, I *am* sorry for the trouble."

"You didn't do anything the rest of us wouldn't have done. Except maybe jumping on a runaway horse," he teased.

"I couldn't think of anything else to do."

They pulled to a stop and got out of the truck. "You go into the house," he said, "and I'll talk to the guys."

Chapter Twenty-Four

M*erle, earlier that day*

Merle and Robbie arrived at the set. "Thanks, Robbie," she said, getting out of the car.

"That's okay. Ma said you weren't feeling great."

"I'm much better now." She waved him off and headed to the costume shop to get her dress for the day. She raised her hand to knock, and the door opened quickly. Helen Bixby was exiting the room in her costume. "Hurry up, we want to have some good rehearsals before shooting starts."

"I will," Merle promised. *You just put the baby out of your mind*, she told herself. *I need to be normal.* She called back to Helen, "What's this movie about?"

"Sister's fighting over a man," Helen called back with a grin.

"Nothing too violent?" Merle asked hopefully.

"Maybe some hair-pulling. See you there."

"Hope there aren't any staircases in this one." Merle touched her belly and forced her hand away.

"Come in and close the door," ordered Dorothy. Merle moved inside and Dorothy handed her the costume. She walked behind the screen to change. She came out and Dorothy buttoned up the back of the dress.

When she still hadn't said anything, Dorothy asked, "Nervous about the movie?" She handed Merle the brown wig she'd worn the previous day.

"Maybe a little. I just have a lot on my mind," Merle replied as she slipped the costume on.

"It'll be fine," Dorothy said bracingly and helped her with the pins. "Just go out there and give it your all."

"Thanks, Dorothy, I will." Merle leaned over and kissed her on the cheek.

Her friend's cheeks turned red, and she said, "Now, off with you."

When she left Dorothy, Sammy continued to hand out costumes. When it finally quieted, Sammy said, "Nice girl."

"Yeah, it's a shame."

"What's a shame?"

"The baby. That girl is pregnant."

"Ma, do you think so?" she said, her face set into a deep frown.

"I know so. I hope she goes to someone she trusts." Dorothy turned to her daughter. "And, you, don't go blabbing it around."

"You have my word, Ma; I don't wish anything bad on her." Sammy went and laid her head on her mother's shoulder. "We know how hard it is to be alone in this situation."

"That we do, my dear, that we do." Dorothy waited a full moment before opening her mouth.

Sammy interrupted her by saying, "I know, I know. BACK TO WORK, SAMMY."

Her mother laughed and returned to her sewing machine. "Smart aleck," she mumbled to herself.

Sammy snickered and started cutting patterns for a new costume.

* * *

Merle hurried to the set and entered through a curtain. A small group stood around in the costumes that had been on Dorothy's racks yesterday. She hung back; the actors and actress knew each other, and she felt out of place.

"There she is." Helen stepped out of the crowd and grabbed Merle's arm. "Come on over. I want you to meet everyone." Merle found herself pulled into the group she'd avoided. "This is Marie, and she'll be playing my little sister today," Helen announced.

Rounds of "Welcome" came from the group.

"Thank you."

"All right, kids," William Stone called out. "I'm going to go over the script." He waved Tom over to hand out the scripts. "This movie is about two sisters being in love with one man. Patty, Annie, and Mike. Mike is seeing both girls, but they don't know it."

Merle frowned and opened the script. "There's words," she whispered to Helen.

"Of course there are. Haven't you seen a movie?" Helen whispered back.

"Well, yeah, but I just thought people were saying anything they wanted."

"Now, *that* would be a movie." Helen laughed. "No, we go over each scene and memorize the lines. Now, hush, we need to listen to the director as he sets up each scene."

The day was far more organized than Merle had expected. Each scene was rehearsed over and over, going through each line and what the actor's reaction would be. *That's why they got upset when I made changes,* she thought.

At the end of the day, Helen came over to her. "Good job. Tomorrow, we'll do more without the script, so take it home and make sure you know your lines."

"I'll work hard."

"I know you will."

Merle smiled and clutched her script to her. She was learning so much every day.

"Good day?" asked Harry as he walked up, wiping his hands on his shirt tails.

"Yeah, I think so. Ready to go home?"

"Gotta grab my stuff."

"I'll wait here." He nodded and headed back to get his keys. He strolled back into the room and held them up.

"Great," she said, and they headed to his car.

"I saw some of the rehearsals," he told her.

"You did? What did you think?"

"Pretty good."

"I'll get better," she said, hugging her script. She was more comfortable now she knew there was a structure to it.

They got home quickly, and Merle jumped out and ran up the stairs and inside the house. She started up the stairs and heard a voice call, "I'm here." She turned and ran over to Jean and hugged her tightly.

"You had a good day?" Jean asked

"It started bad but got so much better."

"You're feeling better?"

"So much. Do you want to hear about the movie today?" She paused and said, "I also want to hear about your day."

"Let's go upstairs first?" asked Jean.

"Sure." The excitement drained. "I could use a quick nap."

Jean checked her watch. "I think we have time for both."

"Good."

* * *

Charlie came in behind them and watched them go up the stairs.

"Got a plan?" asked Paul, coming out of the dining room with a cup of coffee.

"I don't know what you're talking about," Charlie muttered. "Don't you?" he asked and watched the man walk away.

***

Jean followed Merle into her room. "What's that?" Merle had dropped the script on her dresser.

"A script."

"A script?" Jean murmured and picked it up. She quickly read a few pages. "Why, it's the movie and there's lines for the actress and actors."

"Yeah, turns out they're actually saying what the dialog cards indicate."

"Well, how do you like that? I thought they were just saying whatever they wanted."

"I know. Me, too. Now it looks like I have to memorize lines tonight."

"Oh no, will you be able to do that?"

"I think so. We went over each scene so much today that I think I have most of it. Plus, we're going to be rehearsing more tomorrow."

"Who woulda thought it took so much to make a movie? Oh well. you always did have a good memory," she said. Merle yawned broadly. "You need to nap."

"I do," Merle agreed. "Can you wake me for dinner?"

"Of course." Jean started to leave.

"Jean, I didn't hear about your day," Merle mumbled, already half asleep.

"Later, I promise."

"Help me run lines after dinner?"

Jean locked Merle's door and went to her room. *I'm not going to spoil Merle's day. I'll tell her if things don't work out tomorrow.*

After dinner, Jean ran lines with Merle and just had to remind her a few times. The subject of her day didn't come back up.

Chapter Twenty-Five

Merle, the next morning

Merle hurried down the stairs to catch her ride in with Harry. Hannah stopped her. "Have you thought about what I said?"

"No, honestly, I haven't. I can't think right now."

"You have a small window where a decision could be made."

"I don't want to talk about it!"

Harry stuck his head in. "You coming?"

"I'm on my way." Merle turned back to Hannah. "Look, I appreciate you caring about me, but I need some more time."

"Just let me know if you need to talk."

"I will. I need to go. Harry's waiting," she said and ran out to join Harry in the car.

"You okay?" Harry asked before he cranked the car.

"Yeah, let's get going." *The sooner we're in our new house, the better.*

* * *

Jean walked the horses to the trailer. Her friends came and stood around her. "We'll have a spot for you no matter what," Paul told her.

She took a deep breath. "I appreciate that. I'll let you know if I get thrown out."

Charlie tried again. "You sure you don't want me to go with you?"

"No, you have other jobs. It's my responsibility to face my problems." She took the keys and got into the truck to head to the studio. She waved to the four men waiting in the cloud of dust.

She pulled onto the set and walked around the back to let the horses out of the trailer. Once she had them in a shaded area, she headed toward the director's building.

Greg Harrison stepped out and blocked her path. "What're you doing back here? I thought they fired you yesterday."

"Listen, you ass, this is all on you. If you hadn't hurt Betsy..."

"Betsy! That nag nearly killed me!"

Jean could take no more! She reared back and punched him in the stomach. "Get the hell out of my way!" Her tone was harsh enough to make the man take a step back. As she walked past him, she bumped his shoulder on purpose.

"Hey!" Harrison said to her retreating back.

"You'll want to leave her alone," a low voice commented.

"Now, see here, you can't tell me what to do," he said.

Charlie grabbed Harrison by the collar and shook him. "You make any more moves toward her, and you'll get it even worse than this."

"Oh yeah, like what?" Harrison demanded belligerently. He was trying to act tough but was inwardly terrified of this man.

"Test me and you'll find out."

"Fine, I won't bother her again."

The man shook the actor one last time and dropped him on the ground. As Greg watched him walk away, he knew he had barely escaped bodily harm.

***

Jean looked down and scuffed the ground with her foot. Mack sat in his chair next to the camera, studying her. Behind her, the set was being readied for the day. She took a deep breath.

"Mr. Burnett, I'm sorry for what happened yesterday. Do I have to leave the set?"

"No, in fact, we want you on a new serial."

"Sir? What's that?"

He sighed. "Serials are short movies, usually around twenty minutes, that are divided into chapters like in a magazine or newspaper."

"Oh, I've read about these in the *Los Angeles Times*."

"Good, good. We're looking at you for some of these."

"Me?"

"Don't look too excited. I'm supposed to be scolding you," Mack said mildly. She lowered her face and looked suitably downtrodden.

"Now, where is he?"

"Who?"

"Joe," Burnett called. Joe walked in, continually looking over his shoulder.

"Joe, I didn't know you were working this movie," said Jean.

"I provide stunt works for all the studios," he said, glancing around the set.

"What're you looking at?" asked the director.

"Looking for Harrison."

"He's over there," Jean said shortly, pointing toward the tree where the man stood.

Mack looked over at him. "Why's he rubbing his stomach?" he asked.

"I couldn't punch him in the face for what he did to my horse yesterday; it might show in the film. So, I punched him in the gut."

Joe grinned at her. "Thanks, but there's something I'd like to do." He strode over to him.

Greg saw Joe approaching and began to complain. "She... she ruined the scene and then she hit me." He didn't mention the additional threat that had been made to him.

"That's good. She saved me the trouble."

"What do you mean?" he stuttered.

"Mack knows you used a pin on that horse."

"No... I didn't..." Harrison started to defend himself.

"Don't even bother. We know you did it, and if you try that again, you're off the picture."

"You can't do that; you don't have that kind of power!"

"I can't, can I? Let's go have a little chat with Mack. This came straight from him."

Greg glanced toward Mack, then at Jean, and finally Joe. "I won't do it again." *Why does this girl have so many protectors?* he thought.

"Everyone to their marks!" Tom called.

Greg walked to him and Joe called after him. "We'll all be watching."

Eric, their current stuntman, was leaning on a cane as Joe walked over to him. "And what's wrong with you?" Joe asked.

"I think I sprained my ankle in all of the excitement yesterday. I tripped over a stump trying to get out of the horse's way."

Joe threw his hat on the ground. "Dammit."

Jean came up behind him. "I can do it."

Joe turned to her and then to Greg.

"We can make it work," Eric said. "And we know she has the skill." When Joe turned his back on Eric, the stuntman winked at Jean and wiggled his foot.

He isn't injured at all! He's just giving me a chance. She winked at the man.

Joe turned quickly back to Eric and saw him still leaning on his cane. "All right, go through the scene with her, then go sit down."

"What's going on?" called Mack. "We need to get this in the can today."

"I'll clear it with him," Joe said.

"Okay, you know the setup?" Eric asked Jean.

"I do. Once Harrison takes off, I'm dressed the same as him; he stops and I go past him, then they fix it in editing."

"Exactly." Eric gave his hat and vest to Jean. She slipped on the vest and plopped the hat on her head. "Annie, your hair has to be tied back, and you can't lose your hat. You're supposed to be Greg."

She took off the hat and muttered, "I have a hair band that'll work. Though I'm not sure I want to look like that knob. Thanks for everything." With the hat secured, she started to her mark.

Eric grinned. "Anytime."

Joe walked over to Mack. "We're using Annie for this scene."

"Why?" Mack asked harshly. He didn't like unexpected changes to his shooting schedules.

"Eric needs a break. And it'll be a good time to test Annie."

Mack nodded. "Fine. This upcoming serial will be a long-term project, and I wouldn't mind seeing how she takes direction. Are we all set?" he asked. "This is the final take. Greg, you're riding to save your love on the train. Train starts moving! Lights! Camera! Action!"

The camera and Mack were on the tracks opposite the train, moving at the same pace. Greg was on Laurel and Jean on Betsy. He got the horse running and everything worked like in rehearsals. After a few beats, Jean started after him. As she caught up with him, Harrison slowed Laurel until she passed him. As they got closer to the moving train, Jean's horse was steady. She rode up and saw Patty standing on the open platform of the car near the door. Jean tucked her hair behind her ear, reached out for handle of the car, and let go of Betsy's reins. Her legs were swept behind her! She struggled against the force of the wind and was almost yanked away! Patty forced her arms out, grabbed Jean, and helped pull her in. Jean started to collapse into the doorway.

"No," Patty said. "Hug me for the camera." Jean hugged her and held her tight. It must have worked, because the train started slowing. Patty stuck her head out. "Well, did you get it?"

"We got it," called Mack. "That's it, folks. It's a wrap."

"Good job," Patty congratulated Jean.

Chapter Twenty-Six

New York City Police Department

Patrick sat at his desk, working on his latest report. It had been over a month since Jean and Merle had disappeared. They'd had leads on the car, but those dried up after a few weeks. The car seemed to have disappeared, along with any information on Jean and her sister. He and Frank had moved on to other cases, but the Strathmore case remained open. His thoughts had turned to Jean more than he wanted them to.

A woman exited Frank's office, her heels clicking down the hallway. Frank slammed his door shut, the glass broke and fell to the floor. A woman police officer stood outside the office, waiting to speak with the captain. She took in the destruction and then turned and strode determinedly off.

Frank called out where the window used to be. "Patrick, come in here." Patrick walked to the door, nudging the glass aside.

He stuck his head in the opening and asked, "You want me to get someone to clean this up?"

"No." Frank sighed. He waved his friend in and walked to his desk chair. He collapsed into it and rubbed his hand on his neck. "Sit down."

Patrick opened the door carefully and followed him to the desk. "Bad day?"

"Yeah, something like that. Did you see who just left my office?"

"Wasn't that Margaret Strathmore?"

"Yeah. Yeah, it was. She wants the articles to stop. She wants to have this ended and move on with their lives."

"But we don't have all of the answers."

"She doesn't want them. She's fine with the murder-suicide story. She says nothing will bring her family back and all of this investigating is just continuing to cause them pain."

"Can we close it because she wants us to?"

"The higher-ups agree with her."

"Why would they?"

"Money makes the world go around. I'm sure the Strathmores contributed to one fund or another."

"So, now what do we do?"

"Call the papers and stop the articles. Stop looking for Jean and Merle. Next, there'll be a formal hearing where we go over the findings of the case. That will put the final closure on the whole thing." He sighed. "Patrick, did you find anything that we could prosecute Merle for?"

"I've thought about that," he admitted. "If she blackmailed Bob and Catherine, then they were fully complicit in the ongoing activities."

"And any money or jewels that were exchanged could be construed as gifts offered for services."

"Services," murmured Patrick. "We aren't going to list those are we?"

Frank laughed suddenly. "No, I don't think so."

"The Strathmores are willing to sign off on all the outstanding items involving Merle?"

"They are."

Patrick sat forward with his hands on his knees. "So, it ends."

"Yes."

"But Jean and Merle don't know they're out of trouble."

"No, they don't," he agreed. "They may just think things died down here."

"Should we put something in the paper?"

Frank shook his head. "Better to let this one die off on its own."

Jean, where are you? thought Patrick.

Chapter Twenty-Seven

Jean at Joe's office the next morning

"So, that's it? I am not going to be in the serial?" Jean asked, dejected.

"I'm sorry," Joe said. "We had a revolt with the current stunt women. This is a big role, and all of the women wanted a chance to be in the serial."

"Will I be considered for any other movies?"

"We'll see."

* * *

Dorothy took the dress from Merle and hung it on the rack. "I've set up the notary at her office on Saturday."

"I need to check with Annie," Merle said, "but I think that's perfect."

Dorothy took a chance. "Marie, if you need advice, I'm here."

Merle frowned. "I know, and I appreciate it."

Dorothy tried again. "I mean anything."

"Are you trying to tell me something?"

"She knows you're pregnant," called Sammy.

Merle's eyes went wide, and she looked from Dorothy to Sammy and back. Dorothy nodded in confirmation. "How do you know?" she asked faintly. "I haven't even told Annie."

"If you've been pregnant, you know the signs," Dorothy murmured, helping her friend sit down.

"What kind of advice do you have?" Merle mumbled.

"Hun, there's just three. You have the baby and keep it, then there's adoption, or abortion."

Merle sucked in her breath and put a hand on her stomach. "If I keep it, what'll happen?"

Sammy walked over. "People can be nasty about illegitimate children."

"It's a hard decision and one that we've both had to make." Dorothy held out her hand to Sammy. She took it and stepped closer to her mom.

"Both of you?"

"Me with Sammy."

"And me," Sammy said.

"How did you manage it, Dorothy?"

"If you decide to keep the baby and the man isn't in the picture?" Merle nodded her head. "You do what you have to do to survive. Whatever you decide, we can help."

Merle looked at Sammy. "Do you have a child?"

Sammy wiped her eyes. "No, I made the last decision. Abortion."

"Her decision was based on how she got pregnant," Dorothy filled in.

Merle picked up on the underlying sentiment. "Were you attacked?"

"I was."

"Do you know who it was?"

"Yes, but we couldn't prove it."

"I am sorry, Sammy," said Merle.

"It was a long time ago."

"Marie, you have a very limited window for this decision," Dorothy said.

"I think I'd like to keep the baby," she said softly. "Please don't mention this to anyone, not even Annie. I want to get us settled first. And I need to keep this job."

"We won't." Dorothy had raised Sammy on her own and understood the need for secrecy.

Chapter Twenty-Eight

T*wo weeks later*

Merle had put it off long enough. They had moved into their house, and it was time to tell Jean about the baby. She'd been lucky as, at her best guess, she was only a little more than a month long and she wasn't showing yet. She hoped it would be months before that happened. Her film career was going along, she'd already been in many movies and was starting to be recognized by the public. She and Jean had gone to see their movies in the theaters. When Merle appeared on screen, Jean was transfixed.

"You look wonderful," Jean told her.

"Thanks," she said softly. It was amazing to see herself up there on the big screen.

Next, they attended Jean's movie opening. The movie where she slid down the zipline and the one she'd worked with Patty Dove had come out. She was thrilled when the audience gasped as she jumped from the horse to the train and again when she sailed down the line. Even Merle was scared enough to grip her hand. "Hey, I'm here," Jean teased.

When they got home, they settled in the kitchen to drink some tea before going to bed. While they were drinking, Jean noticed Merle tapping her fingers impatiently on the table. Jean knew her sister had something on her mind and was trying to figure out the best way to say it. Jean decided to start talking and hoped Merle would spill the beans.

"Wow, wasn't that wonderful? And just think, we're getting paid to do something like that. I wish we had longer contracts, though."

"I think we have a bigger problem," Merle brought up.

"I disagree, I think we're doing good. I didn't get the Patty Dove serial, but I'm still working with the animals and you're getting bigger movies." Jean walked to the sink to rinse out her mug.

"Jean, look at me." Jean turned to her sister. "I'm trying to tell you something."

She stopped what she was doing, walked back to the table, and sat next to her sister. She took her hands and looked her in the eyes. "Tell me."

"I think I'm going to have a baby."

Jean let the words wash over her. She broke out of her stupor and grabbed her sister. "I'm here for you no matter what."

Merle shuddered and leaned into her. "I was so scared. I didn't know how to tell you."

Jean cupped sister's face in her hands. "Never be too scared to tell me anything."

"What'll we do?" Merle wailed.

"What do we do? We keep working and we raise the baby."

"Jean, you want me to keep the baby?" she said, tears running down her face.

"Of course, it's part of you."

"Dorothy and Sammy said there were ways to get rid of it."

"Is that what you want?"

"No! I just didn't want you to be burdened. People will talk and we might lose our jobs."

Jean drummed her fingers on the table. "Not if you're already married."

"Married? Me?"

"Yeah, you. We just need a ring and a good story."

"But where's my husband?"

"Away. On business. Traveling. In the military. Who knows. We'll think of something."

"And when he never comes back?"

"It would be simple enough to let it slip there was an accident for the long-lost husband."

Merle nodded slowly. "That might work. What about the certificate?"

"Courthouses burn down all the time. We just pick one of those."

"For who?"

"The invisible husband. He has to have a name; it is up to you," Jean reasoned.

"Jesse. Jesse Harrison," Merle said without hesitation.

"The guy we sold the car to?"

"Sure, if I have to have a husband, I like the idea of him. He had the loveliest big brown eyes."

"Okay then, Mrs. Harrison." Jean went to her room and returned. She took Merle's hand and placed their mother's ring on it. "Congratulations."

"What do we say is the reason I wasn't wearing it until now?"

"Just say you'd misplaced it in the move." Jean stood to leave. "Merle, who's the father?"

"I'm not sure," she admitted. "It was either Bob or Jesse."

"I hope it's Jesse's."

"Me, too," Merle said fervently.

Chapter Twenty-Nine

New York City, a few months later

"Patrick," called Lottie through the door. "Patrick," she called again and used her key to open the door.

"Maybe he's not home," Elise said. "Why don't we just go?"

The door from the bedroom swung open and Patrick stood there in a towel. "What? I was in the bath."

"I can tell." Lottie smirked. "You're dripping all over everything."

"Ah, hell, give me a minute and close the door." He walked back into the bathroom.

Lottie closed it and Elise sat in a nearby chair in the living area. "You're sure he knew we were coming over?"

"Kinda," Lottie begrudgingly admitted.

"Kinda he knows or kinda he doesn't?"

"Kinda whatever. He's been avoiding me," Lottie said defensively and crossed her arms over her chest.

"Because you've been trying to get him to go out."

"That girl has been gone a long time."

"It's only been a couple of months."

"That's a long time," Lottie countered. "He needs to get out. Meet other people."

"I'm not sure if going with his sister and her girlfriend is considered going out and meeting people. And why did you pick the movie theater of all places? And the one she used to work at? How's that going to take his mind off of her?"

"I didn't think," Lottie admitted. "I just wanted to get him out of the house."

Patrick walked out of the bedroom, brushing his hair. "Now, what's the emergency?"

Elise looked at Lottie with raised eyebrows.

"No emergency," Lottie muttered, plopping down on the couch and looking down at her hands.

"Then what's going on?" he asked, exasperated.

She looked at him. "I just thought you should get out."

"And where were you thinking I should go?"

She grimaced. "Well…"

"Yes?" he prompted.

"A movie. I heard a new serial's started and it's supposed to be exciting," she said in a rush.

He nodded. "I've heard about that. It sounds interesting."

"Really?" Lottie said, sitting up straighter. "That's great."

Elise checked her watch. "We should go soon."

Lottie also checked the time. "Yeah, we need to hurry." She stood up.

"Let me grab my jacket and hat," Patrick said and moved to his bedroom. He reentered quickly. "Let's go."

The trio exited the apartment, and he locked the door securely behind them. "We'll take my car," he commented as they rushed down. Both ladies nodded and went out the door of the apartment building. The car was parked just outside the entrance.

"Lottie, crank it for me," he called.

"On it," she said, moving to the front of the car with the

crank. Elise and Patrick climbed in. Lottie cranked it and, once the engine started, she walked back and climbed into the back seat.

The trip to the theater was easy. They took alleys and back areas to avoid the busy streets. They arrived and parked quickly. The trio headed up to get tickets. There was a line.

"Looks like it's popular," Elise observed.

"Should be fun," Lottie agreed.

The lady in front of them turned around. "I've seen this four times already; it's so exciting. I can't wait for the next chapters."

"Must be good," Lottie said. She looked at Patrick and saw him searching the crowd. "I don't think she's here," she said in a low voice.

"No, I know. I'd hoped once they were out of the papers, she'd come back." Lottie took his hand in hers. He gripped it briefly and then let go.

"Tickets?" The clerk manning the booth was the boy who had been arguing with the owner the last time he and Frank were there.

"Three, please," Patrick said, pulling out his money and handing it to the boy.

"Hey, I know you," the boy said.

"Yeah, I was here a while back. Have you heard from Jean or Merle?"

"No, can't say we have. I'm stuck here until we get someone."

"Did you find a piano player?"

"Yeah." He leaned close to the glass and whispered conspiringly, "She ain't as good as Jean was. She gave the movies such energy."

Grumbling started behind them. Patrick took their tickets and the three walked into the theater. The lobby was crowded. "We'd best get our seats," Elise said. She led and they followed her through the curtain to the theater.

"Over there," Lottie said, pointing to three seats together toward the front. They hurried to the seats.

"Big crowd," observed Patrick.

"Hope the film is worth it," Elise replied.

"Quiet now," the owner said as he walked onto the small stage. "Ladies and Gentlemen, if you get upset or too excited during the film, please exit out the back. Try not to interfere with others' viewing pleasure."

"I wonder what that was about?" Elise asked. "They've never done that before."

"Hmm," Lottie replied noncommittally.

The lights went out and the only illumination was on the piano player. She started playing as soon as the film flickered on the screen.

The movie was about a woman trying to foil a train robbery. Initially, she'd been locked in a burning building. Every time she tried to get out, the flames leapt up! Everywhere she turned were flames. The audience were making noises, wondering how she was going to get out. The girl noticed an unbroken window. There was a blanket on the ground; she picked it up and wrapped it around her. With her hair tucked behind her ear, she clutched the blanket tight and ran for the window. She dove through just as flames shot out of it. The audience let out a collective gasp. Patrick was startled. *Is that... is that Jean?* When she hit the ground and rolled away, several women screamed and the curtain in the back was opened to allow them to exit.

In the next scene, the woman was boarding a train and the men who had trapped her in the burning building saw her. They followed at a fast pace, knocking passengers down. She heard the noise behind her and quickened her pace through the cars. She jumped up onto a bench and went out through the open window. With a glance behind her, she saw that they were still following. The train had started as she hung out of the window. She managed to climb to the top of the train.

They exited both ends of the car and climbed the ladders to the top. She stopped running abruptly, turning one way, then another. She was trapped!

The woman looked for a way out and happened to look down. Running beside the train was a horse. She got ready to jump, and called "See you later, boys!" She tucked her hair behind her ear and jumped. She landed on the horse and rode quickly away. The movie was over! It had gone by quickly in just 14 minutes. The lights came up and the audience burst into applause.

"Wow! That was exciting," Elise enthusiastically exclaimed.

"It was," Lottie agreed. "Did you see her running on top of that train?"

"Then she jumped and landed on a horse."

"What about the motorcycle scene?"

"I thought you'd like that one," Elise teased her girlfriend. Lottie had a motorcycle as her main transportation.

Lottie and Elise stood; they were among the last in the theater. Patrick stayed seated. "Let's go, big brother," Lottie told him.

"No," he said. "I want to see it again." The theater ran the serials five times in the evening, one right after another.

Lottie frowned at him; something was up. "Let me go ask the owner if we can stay."

"He's over there," Elise pointed out. The man was holding the curtain to get everyone out for the next showing.

Lottie approached him. "Would you mind if we watch one more time?"

"It'll cost you."

"That's fine." She pulled out her wallet and handed him the money. She returned to Patrick and Elise. Patrick still stared at the screen. "We can stay."

"Good."

It took some time to get the customers settled and the movie started again. Lottie watched the film, wondering what he saw. When the scene with the burning house came up again, she saw his hand gripped tightly into a fist. When the train scene came up, he hit his leg with it.

"What is it?" she whispered.

"After," he muttered.

The movie ended and the lights came up. They waited for the people to leave. Lottie and Elise turned to Patrick. "Well?" asked Lottie.

He turned to her. "That was Jean, in the movie."

"Jean?" Lottie asked doubtfully. "Maybe you just miss her too much."

"No, I'm sure."

"Her name wasn't listed," Elise said.

"Doesn't matter. It was her. I know it."

"How do you know it was her?" his sister asked.

"Initially, I thought it was me just seeing her in every character, but just before she did a stunt, she tucked her hair behind her ear. It's subtle. She probably doesn't even know she's doing it."

"I didn't notice that," Lottie said.

"That's because you're not a trained detective like me." Patrick grinned.

"Oh, har har."

"So, what about the hair thing?" Elise asked.

"I've seen her do it before. The night we met, here in this theater, you two had gone and I'd come back to get my hat."

"I remember that," Lottie said.

"Jean was on the stage copying every move from the woman in the movie we had watched and, just before Jean somersaulted off the stage, she tucked her hair behind her ear." He stood quickly. "I'm going there."

Lottie shook her head. "Where?"

"California, of course," he said and strode out.

Lottie and Elise followed closely behind him. "But your job's here," Lottie protested. "Your apartment's here. You only knew the girl for a short time."

"It was long enough."

"For what?" she asked exasperated.

"For me to know that she's special."

"She certainly is," Elise said. "Did you see that jump onto and off of the train?"

"Wow," Lottie said. She was beginning to believe Patrick. "All that was her."

"Just to play devil's advocate, since my girlfriend is a lawyer, you don't think just maybe you've been thinking about her so much that you're seeing what you want to see?" Elise reasoned.

"No, it was her," Patrick said. "I'm sure."

"All right, looks like we're getting you to California," Lottie said.

Chapter Thirty

New York City Precinct

"California?" Frank asked. "Now?"

"Yes," Patrick said firmly.

"No."

"No?"

Frank held up his hands. "No, I mean I need you right now. We're in the middle of several cases."

Patrick nodded. "You're right, I have responsibilities here. But I'll be leaving as soon as these are settled."

Frank sat down at his desk. "I will support you no matter what. When you are ready, I will send you with a reference."

The time seemed to drag to Patrick, but he left knowing he was leaving his cases in the best possible state.

It was a few weeks later. Patrick and Lottie stood waiting at the train that would take him to California. "Take care of my car until I get back," he said.

"You know I will," she said. "Are you sure you have to go? There are girls here."

"They're not Jean."

"No, I guess not," she muttered, her head hung low.

He grabbed her in a hug. "Hey, I'm not abandoning you. I'm just taking a trip."

"You'll be back?" she said into his neck.

"I'm not sure," he admitted and let her go. "Lottie, if this was Elise, what would you do?"

"I'd do everything I had to do to show her how much I cared for her."

"And..." He smirked

"Yeah, yeah, I get it." She put her hands up to his face. "I'll miss you, big brother."

"I'll miss you, little sister. Keep my apartment; you never know."

"I will."

"There's my train," he said and ran toward it.

"Bye, Patrick!" she called, waving to him.

He turned one last time and grinned before boarding.

Chapter Thirty-One

California, at the Selig Studio

Patrick had looked into the studio that had produced the serials he'd seen Jean in. He paid the taxi driver, grabbed his bags and hurried over to the gate. The guard looked him over and asked, "Name?"

"Patrick Flannigan," Patrick said, straining to look over the man's shoulder.

The guard consulted a list. "I don't have your name on this paper, and if you ain't on it, then you ain't going in."

"He's with me," a woman's voice said behind him. *Is that?...* Patrick whirled around and saw it was Merle!

"Here to arrest me?" she asked softly.

"Why don't we go over there," Patrick said, pointing to the side of the gate away from the guard. She followed and held out her hands to him. "You can put those down. There's no charges."

She lowered her hands and raised an eyebrow at him. "Then what brings you here?"

"What else? Jean."

"You make a cross-country trip when you didn't even have one date? What are you here to do, profess your undying love?" she scoffed. He didn't comment; he just stared at her. "That's the reason!" She stopped with the banter. "Fine, you're here for Jean and nothing else?"

"I wouldn't mind hearing what exactly happened with you and the Strathmores, but that can wait."

"What? The car? The jewels?"

"Those were confirmed as gifts by the Strathmore family."

She thought about that. "They were that."

Patrick looked toward the gate again. "So, can you take me to Jean?"

"Yeah, I can."

His mouth curved slightly, and he started toward the gate again. "Not that way," she called to him.

"Then where?" he asked. Patrick's patience was waning.

"The shoot is at a bridge today." She walked over to the guard. "Hi, Luke," she said.

"Hello, Ms. Cooper."

"Now, Luke," Merle mock scolded him. "How many times have I asked you to call me Merle?"

"Sorry, Ms. Coop... I mean, Merle. Is there something I can help you with?"

"My friend here would like to see Jean. Can you call Robbie over? Mr. Burnett said I could use him for transportation this morning."

"Just a second," Patrick spoke up. "Can I leave my bags here?"

"Sure, leave them here." Patrick gave them to him; he moved them inside his small security shelter. Once they were stowed away, he said, "I'll be right back." Luke left and went to Robbie. Patrick stood with her and waited. Robbie came running up, pulling a napkin out of his collar.

"I didn't mean to keep you waiting, Merle."

"That's all right, Robbie. But let's get going. I want to see

Jean's stunt today." He nodded and went to the car and held open the door for her. When he started to close it, she stopped him.

"He's coming also." She pointed to Patrick.

Robbie turned to the tall redheaded man. "Why?"

"Robbie," Merle said impatiently. "We want to get there on time, don't we?"

"Yes," he muttered and walked around to get in the driver's seat. Patrick had to jump into the vehicle as it took off.

"What was that about?" he asked.

Merle lowered her voice. "He has a crush on my sister."

"Hmm. Is it returned?"

She laughed loudly.

Robbie looked back at them. "What's so funny?"

"Nothing, Robbie. Nothing at all." That seemed to satisfy him, and they continued on their way. "The rain finally let up," Merle observed.

Robbie pulled into the small parking area. "We'd better hurry. It looks like they're about to start."

The trio got out and approached Mack, the director along with the cameraman, and a frowning Joe. Another man who appeared to be a train engineer was arguing with Mack.

"It's not safe for her to jump into the water," the engineer said. "The tide's too high today. We should wait for the waters to go down. The currents are too strong, and the water's already slamming into the trestles."

"No, no," Mack said, "this is perfect." He put up his hands to make a picture frame. "It'll be dramatic, and the audience will scream," he said, wrapped up in his vision.

Patrick stayed close. He wasn't sure how this worked in the movie business, but he was sure they'd only have one chance at this. He started to step forward, but Merle stopped him.

"Don't get involved."

He shot her a glance but did as she asked.

The engineer just shook his head. "I'll only do this if I can get the engine off the bridge as soon as possible."

"We'll make sure to give you a signal as soon as you're out of the shot," Mack promised. "Okay, everyone. We have one shot at this. We can't have anyone mess this up."

The engineer stalked off; Joe caught up with him and grabbed his arm. The engineer shook him off and walked to the engine. Jean waited for the engineer on the train and, when he climbed aboard, she asked, "Are we moving forward with the shot?"

"Yeah, against my better judgment," he muttered. He started to shovel coal into the fire box and, when it was hot enough, he squatted down to get out of the camera shot and Jean got the engine moving.

As they moved faster down the track, she could feel the engine beginning to shudder. "She's really shaking," she said and leaned out the window of the train so that she could be seen.

"Just keep her going; the sooner we can get off, the better," he said from his squatting position.

"We're on the bridge." The shaking had gotten worse. "I'm out now!" Jean tucked her hair behind her ear and jumped out of the door and down into rushing water. The water was moving much faster than she'd expected, it pulled at her skirts and dragged her under.

Jean struggled to the surface, but her heavy clothes kept pulling her deeper. *This is it. I'm going to die,* she thought.

"She isn't coming up!" Joe called.

"What do we do?" Merle yelled frantically.

Patrick didn't wait for an answer. He took off, throwing off his hat and jacket as he ran. Once at the bridge, he dove into the water. As soon as he dropped in, he felt himself being pulled down. He struggled to get to where Jean had gone in. He saw her head break the surface and fought against the rush of water to reach to her.

"Red! Are you getting this?" Mack yelled at the cameraman.

"I am!"

"Keep at it! This is great!"

Merle was beyond frantic. "You idiot!" she yelled, pounding

Mack with her purse. "She's going to die!" She started to rush to the bridge to help save Jean, but Joe grabbed her and held her back.

Patrick gripped Jean's skirt and pulled and yanked until he got her head back above water. He pushed hard against the furiously rushing waves and managed to get them to the bank.

Jean was turned over and spat out the water. She turned to the man she knew had saved her life. "Patrick?" She was confused. *I must be dead if I'm seeing Patrick.* Then reality set in. It really was him! "Patrick! You're here! Oh, God, it *is* you!"

She threw her arms around him and kissed him. He wrapped his arms around her and deepened the kiss. She broke the kiss and said, "Hold that thought. Gotta save the day." She jumped to her feet and ran to a station about thirty yards away at the top of the cliff. The engine was on a path to run headlong into another engine. Jean switched the rails and diverted the other train, ending the movie.

Patrick fell back on the bank, exhausted. "Where's Jean?" he asked, looking wildly around for her.

"I'm right here." He looked up at the soaking wet Jean.

"I..." he started.

She didn't let him finish; she just dropped down next to him. Her arms went around him in a fierce hug. "Thank you," she muttered into his neck. He crushed her to him.

Mack yelled out, "Keep shooting! That trestle looks like it's about to go!"

"Get that damn engine off that bridge!" Joe hollered. The engineer worked to get it off and, as the final wheel left the bridge, the water hit the trestle and toppled the bridge into the water and was washed downstream.

Patrick and Jean watched the bridge collapse. "What if the engine had been on it?" asked Patrick. Jean shook her head.

Jean looked up to where the engine now stood and waved to the engineer. He waved back energetically "That was too close; we don't normally cut it that close. We usually rehearse the stunts well in advance, and we aren't dependent on the weather or other external events."

"So, what was different about this stunt?" Patrick asked.

Joe walked down to the duo. He'd heard the question. "I was overridden by Mack. I won't let that happen again."

"You didn't agree with this stunt?" Jean asked her friend.

"No, I didn't," he said. "But I also never thought you were in any danger. You've proven you were a stronger swimmer."

"She almost wasn't strong enough for that undertow," groused Patrick.

"Well," said Jean, pulling herself up to her feet. "At least they can't say I didn't do the stunts myself."

Patrick stood up. "Is that what people are saying?"

"Yeah, a lot believe it's just a man in a wig."

"Look, I know it makes you nuts," Joe commiserated, "but don't go making foolish decisions just to prove yourself. Now, come on. Mack wants to talk to you."

Jean started to follow, then stopped. She held out her hand to Patrick. He took it and held it firmly. They got to the top of the cliff and Merle ran over and wrapped blankets around them.

"Oh, God, sis," Merle cried. "I thought you were dead."

"I woulda been if Patrick hadn't shown up out of nowhere."

Mack stomped over, followed by Patty and his assistant, Tom. He shook his hand at Patrick. "You there. You ruined my shot."

"Me?" Patrick asked.

"You did, but it turned out okay. In fact, I may have a job for you. Are you an actor with the studio?"

Jean laughed. "No, he isn't an actor. He's a policeman. This is Patrick Flannigan."

"A policeman, you say?" Mack tapped his finger to his cheek, thinking.

Tom spoke up. "We'll need someone of a similar build to him if we're going to keep the scene in the movie."

"Oh, we're keeping it," Mack stated firmly.

"What're you thinking?" Patty asked. As the star of the serial, any changes would affect her.

"That last scene was dramatic, and I think it will benefit the series."

"Hmm," she said studying Patrick, "what about Brandon?"

"That might work; he has the same build," Mack agreed. Jean and Patrick started to walk off, feeling they'd been dismissed. "Wait a minute there. I'm not done with you," he called to them.

"Is he talking to me?" Patrick lowered his head and whispered in her ear.

She shivered at the touch and stopped. "Sounds like. He's my boss, so please listen."

"Okay."

Mack walked over to the duo. "I want to see you back here in the morning," he said.

Patrick frowned heavily but didn't say anything. Jean, seeing his look, asked, "May I ask why?"

"Ah, I have something I need a police officer's input on."

"Is it something about this movie?" Patrick asked.

"As it happens, this affects many movies." Patrick waited for more information, but Mack turned and walked away.

Jean tugged at his shoulder. "We've been dismissed." They walked with Merle to the car lot, Patrick and Jean lagging behind. When he started to follow Merle to the car, Jean pulled him back.

"Aren't we all riding back together?" he asked, looking at Jean and then Merle.

Merle laughed loudly. "No, you're riding with Jean."

He turned to Jean. "You have your own vehicle?"

"If you can call it that," muttered Merle, looking at her sister.

"It's good transportation," Jean said defensively.

"Better him than me. I'll see you back at the studio." Merle walked to where Robbie held her door open for her.

"Hey, Jean," Robbie greeted her.

"Robbie." She nodded to him.

After Merle got in, Robbie stood waiting for Jean. "Robbie, let's go," Merle said.

"But..." he started and stomped off to crank the car. He got into the driver's seat and turned to Merle. "Isn't your man friend coming back with us?"

"He's not my man friend. He's Jean's." Merle had laid her head back and didn't notice Robbie clench his hands tightly on the steering wheel. "Let's get going. I'm tired," she murmured without opening her eyes.

"All right, we'll leave now." As Robbie pulled out, he watched Jean and that man.

* * *

"You mentioned a car?" Patrick asked.

"Nope."

He frowned, not understanding her. "Follow me," she said and turned to walk away from him. He followed her further into the parking lot, passing one car after another. Until she came to a stop.

"That's not a car," he observed, taking in the vehicle before him.

"No, but it rides beautifully," Jean said, touching the handlebars of the motorcycle.

"And just *who'll* be in the sidecar?" he asked with a sideways look. She didn't answer, just raised her eyebrows at him. "Me?"

"Well, it is my motorcycle." When he continued to frown, she asked, "Is it okay? I might be able to find you a ride with someone else."

He grinned suddenly. "Lottie has one and I ride with her all the time, just not in a sidecar."

"It isn't that bad. Merle used to ride in it all the time," she said defensively.

"Really?" He remembered her laughter. "What am I in for?"

She grinned back. "It's nice to have you here." As she moved to crank the engine, she noticed he was looking at her. "Goin' to get in?" she teased.

"I believe I am," he said, climbing into the sidecar. It was roomier than he'd expected.

"You're going to want to hang on," she said, climbing on and starting the engine

"It's a little loud," he called over the noise.

"Yeah!" she yelled back. She revved it one more time, and they took off. Patrick grabbed the sides and hung on. *Can't tell Lottie about this sidecar. She'll want one and Elise'll never forgive me.*

They quickly picked up speed, roaring past other cars on the road. Several people yelled at them as they passed. They pulled up to the gate studio in a cloud of dust. When Jean turned the motor off, he wiped the dirt off his face with his sleeve.

"Where've you left your bags?" she asked.

"They're here," Luke called, stepping out of his booth.

"Go get them and we can both shower and change," directed Jean.

He gave her a long look, then got out of the sidecar and walked to the guard's shack. "Thanks for keeping them for me."

"No problem. Are you really a copper?"

"I am."

He nodded. "I may have something to tell you later."

"Do you want to talk now?"

"No," Luke said, looking around, "not while I'm working." A car pulled up and he walked to it.

Patrick made a note to talk to him at a later date and walked over to Jean. He looked back at the guard.

"Is everything okay?" she asked

"I think so," he said, still looking at the guard. "I may have to follow up on something." He walked with her into the studio. They passed active sets with people running to and from them. "This is a busy place," he observed.

"It is."

"Is it everything you thought it'd be?"

She stopped suddenly and grinned widely. "It's everything."

He thought about her answer and said, "Look, Jean, I know we'd just met before and were just getting to know each other when you left. And now I show up unannounced. Jean, with all that's happening in your life, do you want me to leave?"

"No," she said, putting her hand to his cheek. "In fact, I think I'm still owed a date."

Patrick smiled. He now knew she was still interested in him after all this time. "You know what? I think you do." He leaned down and kissed her. Jean threw her arms around him and returned the kiss.

A few people whistled at them. She blushed, pulled back, and shook her head. "Want to get cleaned up?"

"After you." She led them toward a building that had a sign that said shower on the door. "Meet back here?"

"Yes."

Jean entered the shower; it was a simple place. Shower stalls, a toilet, and some towels piled on a stool in the corner. Jean quickly undressed and showered. Her hair was wet, and she brushed it quickly and fluffed it up. She finished drying off, dressed, and gathered her things to leave. She pushed the door open and found cleaned up Patrick already there. "Would you like to see how this place works?"

"I would."

"Let's take our things over to the costumer's building. They're friends of ours and we can leave our things without having to worry about them." She knocked on the door and waited. Sammy opened the door.

"We heard you got drenched. Did the clothes survive?"

"Thanks for thinking about me first," Jean grumbled at her friend. Sammy stuck her tongue out and Jean returned the gesture. "You think next time we can make them even lighter?" she asked, handing over the bag of clothes.

"The skirts were what pulled her under," Patrick commented.

Sammy started in surprise, then gave him a long look. "Well, hello. Aren't you a tall ginger?"

"Back off, he's taken," Jean said. "Where's Dorothy?"

"Touchy, aren't you? I was just looking," Sammy groused. "Ma! Company!"

"Who needs what?" Dorothy demanded and strode into the room. She stopped abruptly. "Well, well, someone new." She walked over to Patrick. "You're our next star?" she asked sweetly.

"He's taken, Ma," Sammy said.

"No, I'm not an actor," Patrick said.

"Even though he did just appear in my movie in a starring role," Jean commented. "Mack said he was a natural."

"Completely not planned, I assure you," Patrick said.

"Explain," demanded Dorothy.

"This is Patrick," Jean said simply.

Sammy said, "Oh, sorry about that."

"They know about me?" Patrick asked Jean.

"Well, I may have mentioned you once or twice."

"You're the copper," Sammy said.

"I am."

"But you were in a movie with Jean? How did that happen?"

"The stunt went wrong," Jean began. "After I jumped out of the engine, the water was going a little too fast. I was dragged under and couldn't pull myself up. Patrick dove in and pulled me out."

"Did Red get it on film?" Dorothy asked.

"I think so," said Jean.

"How did Mack react?" asked Sammy.

Jean laughed. "Like Mack. He was upset that the shot was ruined and then excited that the shot was ruined. He's looking for someone to take over Patrick's role."

"Good thing movies aren't in color," Sammy commented. "I don't know anyone on set who has your hair color. They'll have a hell of a time trying to match it."

"We're going to head out. I just wanted to drop off the costume from this morning."

"Where are you going?"

"I thought I'd take him around some of the sets to show him how the business works."

"Have fun," said Dorothy. "Sammy, back to work."

"Yes, Ma."

They exited and started toward an active set. "Stay with me. We'll go in behind the director." He nodded and followed her. They entered and stayed behind the camera. The director was yelling directions. The shot was a bank robbery. The girl saw the robbers, and they started to chase her around the room and up a staircase. "All right, cut. We got that one."

The director turned and saw Patrick standing behind him. "Hmmm. No, you're just too big. We'd have to put the camera across the street."

The assistant director looked at his clipboard. "I didn't call you for this job." He saw Jean standing nearby. "Oh, hello, Jean. Is he a new stuntman?"

"No, he's visiting me on set."

"Let's move, people," the director said. "The next scene will be set up in the shop." Everyone started exiting the set.

"Is that it?" Patrick asked.

"Just that part," Jean said. "They're going to another set to shoot the next scene."

"Hey, Jean," called a man's voice. She looked over and smiled. It was Paul. "Come on," she told Patrick. "I have some people I want you to meet." They went over to Paul, who was standing by a door at the back of the set.

"What're you doing here?" Jean asked.

"Shooting next door. Brought over some horses as background. Easy one today," he said.

"I know the one," she said. "*Back to Life.*"

"That's it. It involves a gambler and his sick wife. There're scenes in a saloon, the mountains, and inside homes."

"We're working together next week: horses and trains."

"I'm looking forward to it," he said. He looked at Patrick. "Who's this?"

"Paul, this is Patrick," Jean introduced them.

"Just visiting?" asked Paul.

"I was, but now I'm thinking of staying," Patrick replied.

Jean grinned but didn't say anything. She checked her watch. "I'm going to take him around to some more sets before heading home."

"Where are you staying, Patrick?" Paul asked.

"You know, I'm not sure. I just got here today." He laughed.

"We have an open room at the boarding house," Paul suggested.

"We stayed there when we first arrived," Jean said. "Do you want me to call over and see if there's a room for you?"

"Yes, please," Patrick said.

"Thanks, Paul. See you soon," Jean told her friend. She and Patrick left the set.

Charlie walked over. "What was that about?"

"Looks like Jean has a friend."

Charlie watched them leave, his hand clenching the paper he held.

* * *

"Want to check more sets?" Jean asked.

"You know what? I think I'd like to get settled first."

"Sure, I can run you over and help you get settled."

"Thanks." He frowned.

"What's the matter?"

"How are we going to get my bags to the boarding house?"

"Oh, that's easy. Just a second," she said and ran back to the set they'd just left. "Hey, Charlie." He didn't turn as she ran up. "Charlie." She reached out and touched his arm.

He looked down at her hand. "Yes?"

"Could you take Patrick's bags to the boarding house when you head home?"

He deliberately removed her hand. "Just leave them with Luke Garmon at the guard shack."

"Charlie, what's wrong?"

"Nothing's wrong. I have work to do."

"Okay, then. I can see I'm in the way," she said, backing away.

Paul called from the doorway, "Was that necessary?"

Charlie shrugged. "I'm not at her beck and call."

"Charlie, we're all friends here."

"Are we?" he said and walked away from him.

Chapter Thirty-Two

That night at Jean and Merle's home Jean and Merle sat staring at Patrick, waiting for answers to the questions they had been bombarding him with. He put down his fork and asked, "Would you mind if I finished my food first?"

Jean looked at Merle and, when she nodded, they picked up their forks and started to eat. Once they finished, Jean made coffee, and the trio moved to the living room.

"I'm tired of this," Merle said. "Tell us what's going on."

"You know you're no longer wanted for questioning," Patrick stated, sipping his coffee.

"Yes, but why?" Merle demanded, her impatience showing.

Patrick sat back in his chair. "Let me start with what happened that night and you can tell me what I've gotten wrong."

"Merle, sit and let the man talk," requested Jean.

"Okay," her sister said slowly and moved to sit next to Jean on the couch.

Patrick started. "You were hired by Bob Strathmore's father to break up his marriage. The car was your payment." Merle nodded and didn't volunteer any other information. "Things got involved and you had a relationship with both the husband and wife." She nodded again. "You blackmailed…"

"Those were gifts!" she interrupted loudly.

"Yes, that was confirmed by the family," he agreed. She opened her mouth and closed it without saying anything. Patrick waited to see if she'd comment, and when she didn't, he continued. "That night, Catherine caught you in bed with Bob, which was the job you were hired to do. But things went awry, and she shot him and then herself."

"Oh my," Jean said. "He knows everything."

"You know it all," Merle confirmed.

"That's good to know. Why did you run?"

Melse sat back and put her feet up on the table in front of her. "I'd been heavily involved in that mess, and it could've been argued that Catherine wouldn't have done what she did if I wasn't in the picture."

"Bob's parents didn't place any blame on you."

"Who told you about my arrangement?"

"Bob's father did, and they asked for the case to be closed."

Merle sighed and sat back in her chair. "So, it's over."

"You must have known that since you went back to using your real names."

"The newspaper articles had died down by then and, when we bought the house, we wanted it in our own names."

Jean nodded. "And after we did that, we decided to start using our real names at work."

"Didn't anyone think it was odd that your names changed?"

Jean and Merle laughed. Jean said, "No, everyone uses multiple names. If one doesn't work, they move to another."

"It's getting late," Merle pointed out, "and we have an early day tomorrow."

"I should get back to the boarding house," Patrick said.

"I'll take you," Jean volunteered.

"Why don't you take him in my car?" Merle said. "It's rather late to be driving the motorcycle."

"Good point," said Jean. "I'll get the crank and my jacket. Ready?" she asked Patrick from the doorway.

Merle called, "See you later."

He waved goodbye and followed Jean out to the car. "I'll crank it," he volunteered. Jean climbed behind the wheel and waited. Once it was running, Patrick got into the seat, and they headed out into the night.

Jean tapped the wheel with her hand and asked, "Patrick, how long are you staying?"

"I haven't decided yet," he said simply.

"You haven't?"

"No, I want to spend time with you and see where this goes."

She relaxed and sat further back. "I'm glad. Will you look for a job?"

"Since I'm not independently wealthy, yes," he said wryly.

"Will you work as a police officer?"

"I do have a name for the local department but, first, I want to find out what Mack has on his mind."

They continued to drive and let the silence settle around them. "You know, you still owe me a first date."

"Why do you think I came across the country?"

She reached out with her right hand to him. He took it and held it tightly.

Chapter Thirty-Three

The next morning Jean arrived to pick Patrick up at the boarding house. "How did last night go?" she asked after he got into the sidecar.

"Good. They're a nice group of people. They talked long into the night, and I learned a fair amount about the movie business."

"They're the reason we were able to get started in the business."

"Harry asked about Merle."

"They're friends," she confirmed. "She let him know that it wasn't more than that."

"I did receive some intense glares from Robbie."

"Yeah," she said, studying her hands.

"Should I look into him?"

"No, no. He'll get over it, just leave it alone."

He wondered about her intensity. "Okay, I will." She nodded. "Jean, if that changes, let me know."

"I will," she promised and revved the bike. He hung on as she swung them around and onto the dirt road.

He yelled over the engine, "Any idea why your director wanted to speak with me this morning?"

"None at all!" she yelled back.

"Have you met the head of the studio?"

"No!" She laughed. "He's not on my level."

He thought about that as she swung around a car and into the parking lot. The driver threw a few choice curses her way. She ignored him and pulled to a stop. "I'll leave you here," she said. "The main office is just inside on the right."

He climbed out and looked at her. "Where are you working today?"

"I'll be off set; we have a location rehearsal this week."

"What stunt are you rehearing?" he asked.

"Riding a motorcycle over a cliff. Got to go." She grabbed his shirt to pull him to her. They kissed and she turned the bike around and headed out of the parking lot.

"Driving a cycle off a cliff." He shook his head walked to security and saw Luke. Patrick said, "I'm on the list." The guard glanced down at the list and found his name. Patrick checked his watch. "I'm running a little late. Will you be here in about an hour?"

"I'll be here."

Patrick nodded and headed toward the building Jean had referenced. It was larger than those surrounding it. He knocked on the door and waited.

The door opened and a woman asked, "Yes?"

"I have an appointment with Mack."

"Let him in, Wilma. We're waiting for him," Patrick heard Mack call.

Wilma backed away to let Patrick into the room. "Through there," she said, walking back to her desk.

He walked to the room indicated. The double doors opened,

and Patrick could see that the room in front of him was large. At the far end of the room, he recognized Mack sitting in a chair facing the desk. "Patrick, join us," Burnett said, indicating the chair next to him. Patrick sat and turned his attention to the man behind the desk. "Patrick Flannigan, this is Carl Miller, head of the studio."

Patrick nodded at the man, and he returned the greeting.

"Mack, tell the man why he's here," Carl said.

Patrick turned to Burnett and waited. Mack pushed his hat back. "We have a situation that needs to be investigated. There've been several incidents over the past few months."

"What type?" asked Patrick.

"People have been hurt in stunts."

"Doesn't that happen occasionally?" He thought about the day before.

Mack had the grace to turn red from embarrassment and Carl said, "Yesterday's shouldn't have happened. We almost had to pay for a train."

"That wasn't deliberate," Burnett said, "and I take full responsibility. But it was an amazing new end to the movie."

"Tell him the rest," directed Carl.

"Stunts have been sabotaged: ropes cut though, grease on stairs, motorcycles brakes damaged. And others."

"Motorcycle brakes! When?" asked Patrick, thinking of Jean's stunt.

"None lately," Miller admitted. "And we've put extra safety reviews in place."

"Have these incidences stopped?"

"Just after we added safety reviews," Mack confirmed.

"Who'd benefit from the stunt people being hurt?"

Mack looked over at Carl and then back at him. "Jean."

"Jean!"

"Yes. The stuntwomen we hired for the new serial, each one was injured until we assigned Jean the role."

"But you don't think Jean..."

"No," interrupted Mack. "We don't. But someone is making these opportunities for her. "

"Do you have any suspects?"

"That's why we need your help. We want you to investigate."

"Who's the person in charge of the stunt people?"

"Joe Cummings," said Mack. "He assigns stunt people to the stunts."

"Can I confide in him?"

"Not for now," Carl said. "We need to learn who's responsible. We can't trust that Joe isn't involved."

"Mr. Miller, is this an actual position that's being offered to me?" Patrick asked.

"It is. But we need it to be kept quiet," said Carl.

"I'll need a reason to be on the set."

"You'll be listed as a consultant for now, assisting in the stunts."

"What if he's questioned?" asked Mack.

"Tell them to come see me," Miller said and that stopped the conversation. "Mack, don't you have a rehearsal to get to?"

"I do. Patrick, do you want to accompany me?" the director asked.

"I'd like to check in with the local precinct first."

"Good idea," said Carl. "We'll want to involve them as soon as we find anything out."

Mack said, "Join us onsite when you finish."

"I'll go now." Patrick stopped. "I forgot I don't have a car."

"You can ride over with me to the set," Mack said, "and my driver can take you into town."

"Thank you," Patrick said, relieved.

"Follow me." They walked out and Mack called, "Robbie!"

The young man ran up with a smile on his face. "Yes, sir."

"We're ready to go."

"We?" he stuttered as he noticed Patrick.

"Yes, after you drop me off on the set, you'll take Officer Flannigan where he needs to go."

Robbie swallowed. "Yes, sir." He turned on his heel and headed toward the parking lot.

The guard, Patrick thought. He looked at the gate and didn't see him. *I'll have to follow up with him later.*

Robbie held the door open for Mack and ignored Patrick as he moved to the driver's seat. Patrick shrugged and climbed in. Mack was already inside reading through a set of papers. He started, "Mack..."

Robbie interrupted. "Mr. Burnett doesn't like conversations in the car."

Mack grunted and Patrick sat back in the seat. The car came to a stop and Robbie jumped out and ran around to help Mack out. Mack said something to him in a low voice and Robbie nodded. He rejoined Patrick back in the car. "Where would you like to go?"

"The local police station, please."

Robbie swallowed. "The police station? Why?"

"I need to check in."

Robbie nodded and drove to the station. He got out and helped Patrick with the door. "You don't have to do that, Robbie," Patrick told him.

"Mr. Burnett says I do. He also says I have to wait for you."

"Thank you, Robbie."

"I'll be here."

Patrick looked at the tall building and walked up the stairs. He entered and found the clerk there.

"Yes?" the clerk asked.

"I need to check in with Captain Ackerman."

"Your name?"

"Patrick Flannigan, from New York."

The clerk called over to a young officer on his right. "Take this note to the captain." The officer took the note and headed into the area behind the desk. A few moments later, he was back. He handed the note back to the clerk. The clerk read quickly and said, "You can go back. He's waiting for you." The officer stood and Patrick followed him to the back.

Once they reached the captain's office, he left Patrick there. A voice called from inside, "Come in."

Patrick entered and saw a large man sitting in a large chair behind a desk. Ackerman sat back in his chair, the springs squeaking loudly. "I was expecting you yesterday."

"I went to the studio first."

"I understand there was some excitement about a train."

"There was."

"They've been having trouble on that production." Ackerman sat forward. "You want a job?"

"I do, but I also just took a job at the studio to investigate the trouble you mentioned."

The captain frowned. "That's where I want you. You can do both."

"Do I need to confirm that with the studio?"

"I'll work that out. Plan on reporting back to me."

They covered some additional information and Patrick headed out. Robbie stood at the car and opened the door for him. "Where to next?"

"Mack's set." *Time for me to start my new job.*

Chapter Thirty-Four

A*t the set rehearsal*

Jean revved the engine on the motorcycle, Joe standing next to her. "Now look, it's just a rehearsal, so try not to wreck the bike until we have to."

"I know, watch the budget."

"Exactly." He walked around the bike for a third time. "Check the brakes again."

"I've already tested them."

"Test them again."

Jean understood why it was important and tested them again. "They're good."

"Good. Go over the stunt with me again."

"I'm being chased by the bad guys in the car, and I drive to the cliff."

"You stop *before* the edge."

"Yeah, I know, before. Hey, Joe, are you worried about the bike or me?" She grinned at him.

"Both," he grumbled.

"Places!" Mack called. "We're starting the stunt rehearsal."

"Stop if you feel there's something wrong," Joe stated.

She nodded. "I will."

Joe moved out of the frame and watched the car get into place. They'd been given their instructions and knew not to overrun Jean.

A voice came from his left. "All safety checks completed?"

Joe whirled around, startled. "Patrick! Yes, everything's ready."

"Next time, I'd like to review the safety precautions with you."

Joe frowned at that. "And why should I do that? Aren't you just the boyfriend?"

"I've been hired as a consultant on the stunts."

"And who said that?" Joe demanded.

"Check with Mack."

"Oh, I will, after rehearsals," he promised.

"Tell me about this stunt," said Patrick.

Joe shrugged. "It's kind of an easy one. The bad guys in a car chase Jean on the bike. She'll stop at the edge of the cliff in rehearsal."

"What happens during the actual shoot?"

"She jumps off the bike and it keeps going over the cliff."

"How will she do that?"

"I'll be waiting when she tumbles off. We'll do it in one take."

"Why?"

"Wrecking bikes costs money." He saw the director wave. "Shut up now, we're starting."

They watched the car race by as they chased Jean. The car and the cycle stopped short close to the edge. "Perfect," Joe said. A break was called, and Joe took the opportunity and walked over to Mack. Patrick could see Joe was unhappy with the answers. His arms were waving and then he stopped abruptly. He started to walk toward Jean and waved for Patrick to follow.

Patrick ran over. "You work for me, I don't work for you," Joe said.

"Agreed," said Patrick.

That seemed to satisfy him, and they approached Jean together. "Joe," she started and stopped when she saw Patrick accompany him. She raised her eyebrows and Joe explained, "He's going to be a consultant on the serials for stunts."

She brightened. "I like that."

"How'd the rehearsal go?" Patrick asked.

"No problems; brakes were fine."

"What about when you have to go over the edge?" Patrick asked. "Is there a safe way to practice that?"

"Not without damaging the cycle," said Joe. Jean nodded in agreement.

Patrick walked over to the edge. "What if Jean used a bicycle instead of the motorcycle and a shorter drop? She could practice getting off safely."

Jean thought about that. "That might work." She turned to Joe. "What do you think?"

"We want to prevent injuries where we can. I think we can set up something for this afternoon. We don't plan to film until tomorrow. I'll get it in the works." He looked at Patrick. "That was a good suggestion," he said begrudgingly and walked off.

"Patrick," she said, "I'm so glad we get to work together."

"Me, too." He'd wait until after work to ask her about how she'd gotten the job on this film.

Joe came back. "Lunch and then back here. There's a small drop off and we have a bike we can practice on."

Patrick and Jean went to lunch and, when they returned to the rehearsals, using a bike proved to be beneficial. Jean realized she had to kick off the bike, but it needed to still fly forward. It took more than a few tries to get it right. At the end of the day, they were ready for the stunt to be filmed the next day.

* * *

That night at Jean and Merle's house

"Jean, are you aware of the injuries that happened to the other stunt women on your serial?" Patrick asked.

"Hmm?" Jean asked while stirring the soup.

"Injuries to the other stunt women."

"That's part and parcel of the business, unfortunately," Jean stated.

"Yeah," added Merle as she sat tearing leaves for their salad. "We couldn't get insurance for her on the set."

"What do you mean? What happens if you get injured?" he asked.

"Simple. I'm out of work until I can come back."

"She generally works through it," Merle said.

"You've been injured before?" he asked.

"Mainly bruises. Some scrapes. A burn or two."

"Don't forget that sprain," Merle brought up.

"That was nothing. I wrapped it firmly, and it was fine." Merle glared at her sister. "It was fine," Jean reiterated.

"Jean, what about the other stuntwomen who were injured on your serial before you?" Patrick asked. "I thought you were always the main stuntwoman."

"Yeah, me, too. I was contacted after my second stunt and told I'd be in the serial I was filming that starred Patty Dove."

"What happened?"

"Joe said that there were other stuntwomen who had been there longer. They went to Mack and said it wasn't fair, that I hadn't paid my dues."

"That was a depressing few weeks," Merle lamented.

"Yeah, I thought that was it, career over," Jean said.

"What did you do?"

"I worked with Paul and Harry providing horses and other animals to the sets."

"Did you suspect anything was happening to sabotage the other women?"

"Not really. Joe was in charge and I trust him."

"And after the third accident?"

"They came to me and basically said I was the only one left."

"Why so many questions?" Merle asked.

"I'm concerned about Jean's safety," he said. "Who inspected the ropes, lines, motorcycles, and other things before the stunt?"

"You saw it today. Joe does the initial review, but every stunt person knows it's their job to double check and make sure the stunt's safe."

"Tell me about rehearsals."

"We take our time working the stunts. Like the motorcycle one. Joe assigns the stunt person according to the script, in this case me. He also makes sure we have the proper equipment and that it's in good working order. We'll then work with the writer and director to develop the action in the story. Sometimes in the script, the stunt is very general, so we work together to see what's wanted and how to get it done. Next, we choreograph the stunt, usually walking through what's going to happen. We do that a few times and, if we have like a stunt with a horse or motorcycle, we'll start working with those to get the timing down. Once we have all of that, we start rehearsing on set or location to see how those places will factor into the stunt itself. Then, when that's finished and everyone has signed off on it, we do it for real and hope everything goes off according to plan."

Patrick looked thoughtful after Jean's explanation and started making plans in his head.

Chapter Thirty-Five

The day of the stunt

"We'll be shooting today, and we only want to do this once," Mack said.

Joe turned to Jean. "Are you ready?"

"I'm more ready with the additional rehearsals. I'm bruised from the repeated falls, but if those keep me from breaking a bone —or, you know, dying—it was worth it."

Patrick had gone through the safety checks on the bike; Joe had handled the ones on the car. The car had to stop before the edge. Patrick leaned toward her and said, "If anything's uncomfortable, stop the stunt."

"I will," she promised.

"Everyone, off the set!" Mack called.

Joe took Patrick's arm and moved him back. "She'll be fine. We did the stunt over a hundred times."

"I know," Patrick replied, though his eyes didn't leave Jean's form.

Jean started the motorcycle and zoomed off. The car with the "bad guys" started after her. Mack and Red were in the back of a truck pacing both vehicles, filming. According to the script, Jean looked behind her, saw the pursuers, and sped up. The car following did the same.

Jean could see the edge of the cliff approaching and prepared herself. She gave the bike a little more gas. She saw the "bad guys" swerve away out of the corner of her eye. She tucked her hair behind her ear, gave the motorcycle just a touch more gas, and then she and the motorcycle went over. The "bad guys" jumped from the car and ran to watch the bike crash in the ravine below.

"Cut and wrap!" Mack cried.

Patrick and Joe ran over to the edge. "Do you see her?" Joe asked.

Patrick searched frantically. "No." He started to look for a way to climb down when he was stopped by a voice to his left.

"Care to give a lady a hand?"

He ran over and saw Jean on a ledge just underneath the cliff top. When the bike started over, she had jumped off and landed on the ledge. Patrick laid on his stomach to reach her. She grabbed his arm with both hands and he pulled her up. "Are you hurt?" he asked, running his hands over her.

"Mmmm. Though I like the attention, maybe we finish the inspection later tonight." She giggled.

He stopped suddenly and laughed. "Wow. That was amazing."

"Yeah, it kind of was."

"Good job, Jean!" Joe congratulated her.

Mack and Patty ran over. "That went perfectly," the director exclaimed. "We'll have Patty climb up just like that." They'd added a male actor who resembled Patrick and could use him to lift her up.

Merle ran up to Jean. "Merle, what're you doing here?"

"The studio brought in a reporter from *The Motion Picture Story Magazine* and they said I have to talk to him."

"Merle, you're an up-and-coming actress and have been in a couple of movies," Jean reasoned. "Giving interviews is part of the business."

"I'm going to be in a magazine," she said, her tone wonderous.

"Remember when we used to read that back in New York?" Jean asked. "We used to dream about being in the movies."

"This will be fun." Merle grinned happily.

"Just don't forget that you're married when it comes up," Jean reminded her under her breath.

"Oh yeah, I forgot about that. Will you come with me?"

"Of course I will." The sisters started to walk off and Jean called back to Patrick, "Well, come on."

Chapter Thirty-Six

Sebastian and Margaret Strathmore's home

Sebastian Strathmore slammed the newspaper down on the table, causing the dishes to clatter.

"What's wrong with you?" Margaret complained. "I'm trying to eat breakfast."

"That woman," he snarled.

"What woman, Dad?" Stuart asked. "Got a piece on the side?" he snickered.

Strathmore ignored his son and slammed his fist again.

"At least tell us what's wrong," implored his wife.

"Merle Cooper is in the paper."

"Oh, did they finally find her?" Stuart asked as he picked up several rolls and started to juggle them.

Mrs. Strathmore frowned at her husband. "We told the police to stop the investigation. Why would they go against our wishes?"

Stuart dropped the rolls, stood, and walked over to pick up the crumpled paper. "The police didn't find her. Looks like Merle is a movie star. Apparently, the article was first published in *The Motion Picture Story Magazine* and, since she used to be a local girl, the newspaper republished it."

"Oh, is that all?" Margaret dismissed this news and settled back. "She can make trouble for other people. We're past caring about her."

Stuart kept reading and his eyes bugged out. "Oops." He turned to his father. "Do you think…"

"I'm almost sure," Strathmore said with a heavy frown. "The timing is suspicious."

"What're you two blabbering about?" Margaret asked, looking between the two.

Mr. Strathmore started to tell her, but Stuart interrupted him. "No, Dad, let me read it to her. Please?"

Strathmore laid his head on the back of the chair and waved for him to start.

Stuart started reading, a smirk on his face. "Merle Cooper has two new movies coming out in a few months, but the bigger news is Merle is married and will be starting a family soon."

"A family?" Margaret shouted. "What does that mean?"

"I think it means we have a grandchild on the way," Strathmore conceded.

"A grandchild? Do you really think so?" she asked, hope sounding in her voice.

"I do."

Margaret pounded her fist on the table. "Well, we're just going to have to get that baby from her. How do we find her?"

"That would be in Hollywood, Mom."

"Then that's where we'll go," Strathmore said.

Chapter Thirty-Seven

Jesse and Billie Harrison's kitchen

Jesse closed the magazine carefully and laid it on the plate in front of him. "Billie, I think it's time to move again."

"Where are you thinking?" she asked as she sat at the kitchen table. She handed him a platter of eggs and bacon. He took it and sat it down without taking anything.

"Hollywood."

She frowned. "Hollywood? Why there?"

"That's where my wife and baby are. I should probably join them."

She opened and closed her mouth several times before she got out, "You're what now?"

He handed her the magazine. The article he referenced was located on top.

"Merle? You and her..."

"Had relations? We did." Jesse's mind strayed to Merle most

days. He regretted letting her leave without knowing where he could find her.

"She says you're her husband."

"That's funny. I'm thinking we need to pay a visit to the little woman."

"Looks like you got yourself a movie star wife," Billie said as she studied the article.

"So, what do you think? On our way to California?"

"Well, hell. Why not." She stood and walked to the closet; the ever-present boxes were in place. She started filling them. "What about the business?" she asked.

"I'll see if I can sell it to someone around here. I do want to get our car shipped there."

"And us?"

"I'm thinking train. I'd like to get there as soon as possible and get some answers."

Chapter Thirty-Eight

Jean and Patrick at the studio

"Where are you working today?" Patrick asked Jean.

"I am doing some small stunts on a drama while our scripts are finished. What about you?" she asked.

"Inspecting more stunts and equipment. Joe wants me to help out on some other projects until the next serial is ready to start rehearsals."

"Found anything that needed to be fixed?"

"Just some small things."

She started to walk away and he grabbed her hand. "How about having lunch with me?"

"That's workable. Want to meet at the far end by the parking lot?"

"Sounds like a plan." She kissed him quickly and walked to her meeting.

He smiled and headed over to find Joe and to review the list of stunts for the day. He'd worked with Joe for a few weeks and felt the man wouldn't jeopardize his job by sabotage. He also seemed to genuinely like the stunt performers that worked for him.

Patrick had started a list of possible suspects. Initially, the list included Joe, Robbie, Charlie, and Paul. His suspects all had something in common; they were protective of Jean and wanted her to do well in the movies. Living at the boarding house had proved helpful; all but one of the suspects were there. He'd try to find quiet moments with each of them.

The morning stunts had gone well, and he was on his way to see Jean. He was close to the chosen meeting area and could see Jean walking toward him. She suddenly stopped.

"Patrick!" she screamed. He ran faster and found her standing over a body. He bent quickly and turned the man over.

"Is he dead?" she asked.

Patrick checked the man's vital signs. "He's dead," he confirmed. "Do you know him?"

"Yeah, he's a director, Zach Smith. What killed him?"

"Well, looks like a bullet in his gut." He opened the dead man's jacket.

Another man walked up. "Hey, what's going on? Is he dead?"

"We don't know. He was just lying there," Jean said.

A crowd started to form. "Isn't that the new guy, the one helping with stunts?" someone asked. "Did he do it?" The crowd started to move toward Patrick.

Patrick cussed under his breath and stood. The crowd pushed toward him with murder in their eyes. Jean yelled, "Patrick, tell them who you are!" He put his hand in his pocket.

"He has a gun!" someone screamed.

Patrick pulled out his badge and held it up. "Everyone, calm down. I'm a police officer." The crowd stopped and watched. "Jean, can you come over here?" He wanted her away from the volatile crowd.

A man at the front asked, "If you're an officer, why are you here?"

A woman pulled at the man's arm. "No, I heard he's a police officer from New York."

A tall, thin man ran over. "I'm Mr. Smith's assistant." He adjusted his glasses and looked at the body and said, "Or, I was."

Patrick looked around. "All right, we need to clear the area. If you saw Mr. Smith this morning, could you stay? I have some follow-up questions. Jean, go call the station for me. I need to get some people out here to control the scene."

She started off and turned back suddenly. "Who do I ask for?"

"Chief Ackerman."

"Got it," She turned and ran. "I'll go now."

The assistant spoke up. "Would you like some help?"

"I would. What's your name?"

"Phillip Hudson."

"Okay, Phillip, I need anyone who might have seen or heard anything to stay."

Phillip picked up a bullhorn and called, "If you were here or in the area and know anything, move to the right." Several broke away and moved to the area he directed. "The rest of you, back to work. I think some of you have active calls." That caused many to panic and they ran back to the sets. Others who had nowhere to be continued to stand there, looking at the body. Patrick started toward that group. Phillip stopped him and said, "I can handle them."

"People," Phillip started, "if you want to stay, I'll need each of your names so that we can remove you from your roles in the ongoing movies."

"You can't do that!" yelled one woman.

A man to her right muttered back, "Oh, yes he can."

"He can?" She looked at Phillip. He nodded and she said, "Fine, we'll go."

"Thanks for that," said Patrick.

"No problem. I have to herd them around on the set all the time. They're like little kids. They're generally trained to listen."

"Hmm," Patrick said noncommittedly.

"What about that group over there?" Phillip asked.

Patrick glanced their way. "We'll interview them when more officers arrive."

Jean ran back. "They're on the way."

"Good, this is a mess."

"What do you think happened?" she asked in a low voice.

"Right now, that's the question. He was shot." He looked at Jean and Phillip. "You said he's a director."

"Definitely. He has several movies ongoing," said Phillip.

"Anything you're in?" he asked Jean.

"Not right now. He's doing dramas. More serious stories," she answered.

"I work most movies with him," Phillip supplied.

"I informed Luke that the police would need to be let in," Jean told Patrick.

"Get a message to Mr. Miller, too," Patrick told her. "He'll need to be kept in the loop."

Trucks could be heard arriving. "Out of the way!" called several voices.

"You there, get the pictures." Captain Ackerman walked over to Patrick. "Tell me."

"I arrived at the parking lot to meet Ms. Cooper here and found her standing over the body."

"Was he dead when you arrived?"

"He was," said Patrick.

The chief turned to Jean. "And what about you? When you got here, was he alive?"

"No, he was just lying there. I'm the one that found him."

"What about those people?" Ackerman waved his hand to the small group.

"I had them wait. They may have seen or heard something," Patrick replied.

"Jonesy, over there please. Turner, join him. We need to start questioning these people." The officers walked to the group and started to question them.

"Do we know anything about the man?" Ackerman asked.

"Jean?" prompted Patrick.

"He's a director here, and ummmm... it's rumored that he's often involved with his leading ladies."

"Involved how?" Ackerman pressed.

"Romantically."

"Can you give me a name?"

"Patty Dove is the current one."

"Where's she now?"

She looked around and asked, "Where's Phillip?"

"Over there," someone pointed out. He'd moved to the accounting office steps.

Patrick waved him over. "Phillip, can you tell me about Ms. Dove and Mr. Smith's relationship?"

Phillip reddened a bit. "She and the director were living together."

"We'll need to speak with her," Ackerman said.

"Yes, I can take you to her. This way."

"We'll need somewhere private," Patrick said.

"We can use an empty office. There's one near the set. I'll drop you off on my way to get her."

Patrick looked over at Jean. "You know Patty. Can you come with us?"

"She won't like it," she muttered.

He frowned at that but didn't say anything to her. "Phillip, you were taking us to meet with Patty?"

"Yes, she's working on a drama with William Stone while we are on our break from the serial." They followed him and he indicated the office. "I'll bring her there." The three went in to wait. Phillip continued to the active set. The scene was underway.

Stone called out, "Patty, you've found out your lover is an adulterer. You read the note, and you start to wail. Tear it up." She followed his direction and tore up the letter and then there was a knock at the door. "Go answer it; pretend nothing is wrong." She ran down the stairs and opened the door, throwing her arms open wide to hug him. "Grab the vase," Stone directed. As he hugged her back, she reached behind her and used a vase to hit him over the head. Then she walked over and opened the closet and let out the wife. They left the house together. "Okay, that's a wrap. Patty, good job."

Phillip whispered in Stone's ear, "Patty, we need you over here."

She tossed her long, curly hair back and headed toward them. "What is it, Bill? I thought you were happy with the scene."

"Yeah, it isn't that. There are some men who need to talk to you."

"What's it about?" she asked loudly.

Stone lowered his voice and said kindly, "I think you might want to talk to them in private."

"I'll take her," Phillip said.

Stone frowned after them and called to his assistant. "Tom. We're done for the day. Tell everyone we'll start again tomorrow."

Patty and Phillip entered the office. "I'll leave you," Phillip said.

Her nerves showed as she reached out to him. "Stay, please. I'm getting scared." She took a deep breath and turned to Patrick. "Who are you and why do I need to meet with a stunt coordinator?"

Patrick stopped her and said, "I'm a police officer and this is Captain Ackerman from the local police department." She nodded, unsure of what to say. Patrick continued. "You have a relationship with Zach Smith."

Patty shot a look at Phillip. "Someone has been telling tales out of school."

"No tales," Patrick said, sitting on the edge of the desk. "You'll want to sit down for the next part."

"Why?" she demanded.

"Patty, just sit," said Phillip, pushing his hat back on his head. She flounced into the seat and waited. "So, talk."

"Patty, Zach is dead," Patrick said.

"Dead? What do you mean?" She whipped her head around from one to the other. "What do you mean!" She jumped up as if to go somewhere and stopped. She looked around the room and her gaze settled on Jean. She screamed wildly at her. "You! This was you! After all I've done for you! You bitch!"

Jean tilted her head. "Me? I didn't have anything to do with this."

Patty advanced toward her. "You injured him and left him by the side of the road." Jean remained silent and stared at her, not moving.

Patrick walked over and got between the two women. "We'll question her. For now, it's your turn."

Patty walked to a chair and sat down. "What do you want to know?"

"Where were you in the last hour?"

"On set, with Bill Stone."

"How long have you and Zach been together?"

"About six months."

"Do you know who might have a vendetta against him?"

"Yeah, her."

Jean snorted in response.

"No one else?"

She ignored the question. "I need to make arrangements. Who do I contact?"

"We'll let you know," Ackerman said.

The energy seemed to have drained from her, and she slumped in her chair. The captain walked to her. "Can I help you back to the set?" he asked.

"I have a dressing room. Could you help me there?"

"Of course," he said and offered her his hand. She took it and stood, walking with him to the door.

"I'd remind you, she's an actress," said Jean.

"What did she mean by that statement?"

"Which part?"

"All that she'd done for you. What's she done for you?"

Jean sighed. "When we first got here, I was in a few movies and then it looked like I was going to get the stunt work in her serial."

"You mentioned that it didn't work out."

"Patty saw me perform a stunt and went to Mr. Miller to request me. Then the stunt women found out about it and pushed back, and I was out."

"Until the injuries started."

"Yeah, until the injuries started."

"Have you and Patty always gotten along together on the set?"

"Yeah, until a few weeks ago."

"What happened?"

"Zach asked me to ride with him for a morning meeting. Robbie was driving us."

Patrick wiped his hand on his face. "Go on."

"We were discussing a movie for me, and the next thing I knew, one hand was down my blouse and the other was up my skirt. I screamed and kicked, but I couldn't get him off of me. Suddenly, the car door flew open, and Robbie pulled him off me. I couldn't see what he did, but the next second, we were driving away quickly."

"I'll have to thank that boy. Did Patty know any of this?"

"No, I wasn't aware she knew what happened with Zach."

A knock sounded on the door and Tom poked his head in. "Jean, you're wanted on the set to review the next chapter in the serial," he said.

"Oh, okay. Is Patty there?"

"She is."

"On my way." She followed him out.

Patrick's voice stopped her. "Jean, you won't run this time."

She turned back. "No, this time I have you looking out for me."

"Yeah, you do," he agreed.

Chapter Thirty-Nine

At home that evening Patrick followed Jean into the house. "I didn't see her on the set. Maybe she's already home." He closed the front door, and she called, "Merle! Are you here?"

"In here," her sister called. Jean followed her voice and found her in the bedroom. Merle was packing. It felt very familiar.

"What're you doing?" Jean asked calmly.

"We need to get out of here."

"Merle." Jean walked over and took her by the shoulders. "We don't need to run. This is our home, and we have people to help us."

"You do," Patrick said from the door. "I'm on your side, Merle; nothing will happen to Jean."

Merle took a deep breath, tears started to stream down her face, and she collapsed on the bed. "We don't have to run?"

Jean sat next to her and took her sister's hands. "We have a home here. We haven't done anything wrong."

Merle sniffed and said, "I'm so tired."

"Lie down. Patrick and I will make dinner." She helped Merle get into bed and covered her up. She kissed her on the head and walked out to join Patrick in the hallway. Jean waved toward the living room. They both sat on the couch

Patrick asked, "It wasn't your idea to run?"

"Back in New York? No." Jean sighed. "Merle reacts to situations like this by running. When our parents died, her response was to leave immediately, and then in that mess in New York."

"Will she stay here?"

"I think so. With the baby coming, we need a stable home. We have that here. Patrick, what's going to happen next on the case?"

"Right now, we're just figuring out the players."

"And it looks like it's someone connected to me."

"Both the suspected sabotage of the stunts and Smith's murder seem to be connected," he confirmed. "Who wanted you on that movie?"

"Patty, Joe, Mack, Paul, and Charlie."

"Who had grudges against the director?"

"Other than me, I'm not sure. I didn't know much about him and, from what I understand, he just showed up out of nowhere and became a director a few years ago."

"Sound like a lot of stories around here," he said, raising his eyebrows to her.

"I guess it does."

Chapter Forty

A *week later*

Joe was reviewing the final information before the shoot. "Jean, the stunt's been set up. Patty will be riding the motorcycle and then you take over." They'd rehearsed over several days and this was just a reminder.

The director's assistant ran over. "Patty's in place."

"Got it," Jean said. He walked off and she turned to her sister. "Merle, you don't have to be here for every stunt."

"Until we have some answers about who killed Zach, I want to be with you," Merle said, crossing her arms over her chest.

"Aren't you needed in the writer's room?"

"I have my scripts with me," she assured Jean. She tapped her arm. "You know, I have this job because you were watching out for me on the set of that car movie."

"They had no business expecting you to do stunt work without safety training." Merle had been loaned out by Selig to the Balboa Studio. The movie she was involved in had her driving a car backward down an incline at twenty-five miles an hour. Jean protested and loudly suggested they didn't need an actress but a trained stunt person. Merle told Selig not to loan her out to Balboa, she would not work for them again, and Jean agreed with her.

"You stepped in and told them it wasn't safe for me." She took Jean's hand. "I want to be that person for you."

Jean squeezed her hand. "We've rehearsed this stunt numerous times. It's safe."

"Then I'll be here to watch the fun," Merle said, not moving.

Joe called, "Jean, we're ready. Patty's finished her scene, so be ready when the train moves."

Jean waved to him and went to the bike. "I will be," she said, pulling on a long dark wig and goggles. She got onto the bike and started it. The train started to move, everyone cleared out, and the director yelled, "Action!"

She tucked her hair behind her ear, revved the engine, and headed toward the side of the train. The bike started pulling toward the wheels of the train. It was accelerating, and she couldn't slow the bike down. And when it started to slide down and under the train, it pulled her with it. She saw the train wheels were too close and would crush her. She jumped off, trying to clear the wheels, and landed on her face and chest. The grinding gears ate the bike and drowned out all other sounds. When it finally stopped, the screams reached her.

The first person to her side was Joe. She felt herself being turned over. He shouted two inches from her face. "Jean! Jean!"

The breath had been knocked out of her. When she could, she took a breath and opened her eyes. She gasped, "I'm okay. I just needed to get my breath back."

"Can you stand?"

She held out her hand and he pulled her up. "What's that noise?"

"It's Merle. She's tearing the hide off of the mechanic."

"We need to help her," Jean said, taking deep breaths.

"Don't worry, she has company," Joe said, still holding her arm.

Her vision cleared and she saw that it wasn't just her sister yelling. It was also Mack and Patty. Jean shook off Joe's hand and ran over. As she got close, she could hear what everyone was shouting.

"It was your job to inspect the bike!" Merle yelled.

"I did and it was fine," the man said defensively. He pointed at Jean. "It was her; she just can't drive!"

"You're a pig," Merle said, ready to punch him. She wouldn't let him level any insults at her sister.

"And you're a—" he started.

"You stop right there," Jean snarled at him. "Let's all try to calm down."

The mechanic wasn't finished with her. "You! This is all your fault."

Another voice broke in. "I told you that I experienced the same thing with the bike." They all quieted and looked at Patty. No one was going to question their lead actress.

Mack pointed to the mechanic. "You're out!"

"But it wasn't my fault. It was hers," he whined. "I need the job."

Mack waved over to his hired guards. "Get him off my set."

The mechanic started to run. The guards chased him and tackled him in the grass. He must have gotten a mouthful of it because he was spitting it out as they pulled him away.

Merle linked her arm with Jean's and watched him being dragged past them. "I'll get you!" he screamed and shook his fist at the sisters.

"Drive him far out of town before you let him go!" Mack shouted. The guards nodded and pulled the man towards a dark car.

"Jeez, we need a new bike," Mack grumbled, rubbing his face with his hands.

"I can get another one in about thirty minutes," Joe told him.

"Everyone back here in thirty minutes," Mack said and walked off.

Merle turned Jean to her. "Tell the truth now. Are you up for this again? Were you hurt?"

"Thankfully, I wasn't," she said. "I got through it. Just some bumps and bruises and I want to do the stunt."

"All right."

"Will you stay?" Jean asked.

"Of course. I'll be right here," Merle promised. They stayed together and watched the train being pulled back into position.

The assistant came over. "Joe's back and has the new bike."

"I'll head over now." Jean started toward Joe and didn't try to stop Merle from coming with her.

Joe was bent down and looking over the bike. Jean knelt next to him and together they went over each part to make sure it was working properly. When they finished, Jean started to climb on it, but Joe stopped her. "No, I'll test it first. All stunts are my responsibility."

Jean nodded and stepped back, watching as Joe climbed on. He rode it up and down and near the now stopped train. When he finished the test, he stopped the bike in front of her. "You next. It rides well and I don't see any problems."

She climbed on the bike and performed a similar test. "It's not pulling like the other one. I'm okay with it."

"Get with Patty and review the bike with her," Joe directed. "I'll let Mack know we almost ready."

As he walked away, Merle said, "I'll find a seat."

Jean nodded and walked over to Patty. She was sitting in her chair with her assistant fanning her. They hadn't talked since Zach had been murdered. "Patty, the new bike's here."

"Is it safe?" she asked shortly.

"Joe and I tested it," Jean confirmed. "This bike is working properly."

Patty said something to her assistant. The assistant looked at Jean. "She'll be ready when Mack calls."

Jean nodded and walked off. She felt like she'd lost a friend.

The scene with Patty started again and she finished her part with no problems. Joe ran over to check to on her. They talked for a moment and Joe called out, "We're good for the next scene."

Jean grabbed her wig and goggles and walked over to the bike. Patty didn't wait to talk to her but walked back to her chair.

"Move the bike back to the starting point," Joe told Jean.

She moved the bike into position and, at her signal, Mack called, "Action!"

Jean revved the motorcycle and drove it by the now moving train. It operated properly and she moved into position. A stuntman was dressed as a prisoner and her job was to climb on the train and fight him. As she got closer, she tucked her hair behind her ear, reached for the handle on the train, and turned the bike handlebars away from the train. She swung herself up on the train and walked towards the "prisoner". They fought for a couple of minutes and then he broke away and ran off to the passenger cars. She chased him through the car; then they exited and climbed onto the top. They struggled together and she dropped him off the side of the train. There was a car with a mattress on the other side for him to fall onto. The shot was completed, and the train slowed to a stop.

"We got it!" Mack called.

"That's great," Jean said, suddenly worn out, and laid down on the train roof.

"That's a wrap for today," called Mack.

"Jean!" Merle called her. "You can come down now."

Jean got up and started to move down the side of the train. The aches and pains that she'd said didn't exist were suddenly showing up in full force. She moved slower than normal and limped a bit. Most of the crew had started to clear out of the area.

Merle watched her inching along. "Jean, are you okay?" she asked, concerned.

"Yep. Just peachy," Jean said firmly. "Some little bumps and bruises, nothing a hot bath can't fix."

"You're sure?" her sister asked, watching her closely.

"Sure, I'm sure."

Merle grabbed Jean's arm and put it over her shoulder.

"Ah, ah. Careful. Still a little sore."

"Oh, sorry. Well, lean on me anyway."

"I do that and we'll both tip over," Jean teased.

"My balance is fine."

"How's the baby today?"

"She's moving a lot," Merle admitted.

"Sure it's a girl?"

"Yeah, I think she's widening my hips; like I needed that," she said wryly.

"Well, you look wonderful," commented Jean.

"Thank you." They walked slowly to the car. "I'm driving," Merle said.

"You know, I'm good with that," Jean admitted. "Though I'll crank for you." Wincing against the pain, she turned the crank and the engine started. They moved from the crowded areas onto the roads toward home. It was a longish drive, but it was long enough to shake off the day.

"You need to mention the mechanic to Patrick. He'll need to be added to the list. He threatened you," Merle said.

"I'd planned to," Jean said thoughtfully.

"Good." Merle was tapping the steering wheel. "Jean, I have an idea for some stunts."

"You do?" Jean asked, surprised. "You've been writing dramas."

"Now, I think I have an idea for your serial and maybe another serial idea for later."

Jean looked over at her and said, "That's wonderful. Would you like to write some things out this weekend?"

"I would."

"We're always looking for original ideas. Can you give me an idea of the stunts?"

"Well, I was thinking of hanging you off a bridge trellis and then dropping you onto a moving train to get the bad guys."

"Oh my God," Jean said.

"What, too much?"

"That sounds so awesome! I can't wait to do it." Jean laughed. "And here I thought your ideas would be too safe."

"Really? You like it?" Merle started to think about her other ideas. "We'll work on some of them this weekend and pitch them to Mack on Monday." Merle pulled them into their driveway. "I think Patrick beat us here."

Jean nodded and saw Patrick was already holding the door for her. She got out of the car slowly.

"Are you hurt?" he asked, concerned.

"Just the normal bumps and bruises."

"Let me help you in." The trio made their way into the house. Once they were inside, Jean said, "I need a hot bath before dinner."

"Can you make it on your own?" Merle asked.

"I can. I'll be down in a few minutes." She left them and walked slowly toward the back of the house.

Once she was out of sight, Patrick looked at Merle. "You going to tell me what happened today?"

"The stunt went wrong and nearly killed Jean."

He frowned and asked, "Was Joe there?"

"He was. It looks like it was the mechanic's fault."

"And where is he now?"

"Mack fired him and had him thrown off the set." She looked at him and asked, "Do you think this is tied in with Zach's murder or the sabotage?"

"It doesn't fit," he muttered.

"Why not?"

"The theory is that the sabotaged stunts were to help Jean and even Zach's murder supported that conclusion. This one, though, this one seemed to be directed at hurting Jean."

They both mulled that over as Merle pulled out the items to start dinner. She handed him the knife and carrots. "Cut."

Chapter Forty-One

The stunt that Merle and Jean put together was accepted into the next movie. Joe walked it out and muttered, "The distance between the station and the train's been measured."

"And I've practiced the jump several times when the train was standing still," Jean reminded him.

"So, we're ready."

"We're ready," she confirmed.

They moved off the train and Joe said, "They'll move the train back to position and we'll start the stunt in about thirty minutes."

Jean glanced around the set. "Is Patty here today?"

"No, she won't be in this scene. Why?"

"No reason. I just thought I saw her here earlier."

"Hmmm. We'll meet back here when we're done."

"Okay."

"Clear the set!" Mack called. "Tell Jean to get ready and get the train moving."

They could see Jean on the bridge. She tested the rope, tucked her hair behind her ear, and climbed over the railing. She lowered herself until she was dangling under the bridge. As the train got closer, Jean felt the rope give a little bit. She looked up and could see it starting to come apart. *Oh, that's not good*, she thought. She looked down and saw the train approaching. She looked back up and could see the rope coming apart faster. She looked back and forth between the rope and train, wondering if the train was going to pass under her before the rope fully came apart.

And then, the rope did break, and Jean dropped toward the speeding train. *This is gonna hurt.* She landed on the top of the train and was knocked off her feet. *Shit*, she thought as she was dragged to the end of the train. She could feel her legs dangling over the edge. She knew if she went over, she'd be dead. Jean saw a safety line attached to the top of the train and wildly grabbed for it. Jean barely managed to grab hold of it, wrenching her arms in the process. She grasped harder on the cable and managed to pull herself up.

"Oh, shit!" Joe cursed.

"That wasn't what we planned," Merle said. "Do you think Jean changed it?"

"No, the rope must have broken. You see it flying out behind her?"

"Should we stop the scene?"

"No, she looks like she's all right now."

They watched as Jean stood and moved down to catch the bad guys.

"Cut! Wrap! Joe, tell Jean good job and I like that last change she added," Mack called.

"Was that a change or a problem?" Merle asked Joe.

"Jean wouldn't have changed the stunt like that without talking to me first. We'd rehearsed it too many times. I'll need to check that rope," he said, striding toward the slowing train and jumping on. He climbed to the top and found Jean holding the piece rope. She threw it at him.

He picked it up and saw the cut. "Sabotage."

"Yeah," she said, glaring at him.

"Why are you looking at me like that?" he demanded, dropping the rope.

"Oh, I don't know, Joe, why don't you tell me?"

"Are you accusing me of cutting this?"

"Do I need a reason to?"

"Joe, I need you to follow me for some questions," Patrick said from the ladder.

"I didn't do it! I wouldn't ever hurt Jean!" Joe hung his head and walked toward the ladder. Jean picked up the rope and the three made their way down. Tom ran up to Jean.

"What's going on? Where's Joe going?"

"Patrick has some questions about the stunt."

"Oh, okay. Mack said to tell you the stunt was great and he liked the last-minute change."

"Thanks, that wasn't my idea."

"Whose was it?" She held up the rope. "That looks like it was cut," he said tentatively. "Is it supposed to look like that?"

"Nope."

Chapter Forty-Two

Joe's interview

At the precinct, Joe and Patrick entered an interview room. "Sit," Patrick ordered. The door opened and the captain entered.

"I'd like to sit in on the interview."

Patrick nodded and opened his notebook.

"I didn't do it!" Joe exclaimed.

Patrick ignored the statement and asked, "Joe, what did you do before this?"

"Carnival performer, boxer," he muttered.

"How long have you been a stunt coordinator?"

"Two years."

"You were on each set when the sabotage occurred?"

"I was but..."

"You inspected each stunt before it was performed."

"Yes, that's my job."

"So, you had the opportunity?"

"I didn't do it!"

"Do you carry a knife?"

"Well, yeah," Joe said and reached for it. He found an empty sheath. "It isn't here. I must have misplaced it."

"You initially fought to have Jean as the stunt person on this serial?"

"It wasn't just me! Mack and Patty wanted her, too. She's the best I've seen."

"And yet, she wasn't chosen until the other stunt women who were picked started having accidents."

"I wouldn't hurt anyone, ever. And especially Jean. If I fought to have her on here, why would I try to kill her now?"

"That's the question," muttered Patrick.

Chapter Forty-Three

Jesse and Billie, back at the Selig Studio

"Do you have an appointment?" Luke asked Jesse and Billie.

Jesse smirked and said, "No, I don't have an appointment. I'd like to see my wife."

"And who would that be?"

"Merle Cooper Harrison."

Luke's eyes opened wide, and he stepped back to let him in. Jesse strolled through the gate. Billie cleared her throat and tapped her foot. "Oh, yeah. Her, too," he said. "She's my sister."

Luke looked at the duo, a wide smile on his face. "I'm sure Merle will real be happy to have you here."

"Oh, I'm sure she will," Jesse said cryptically.

Luke called out to a man walking by. "Hey, Oscar, come here. I need you to walk these two over to the writer's room."

Oscar walked over. "Sure, I'm going to a set nearby."

Billie turned to Jesse. "Writer's room?" she asked in a low voice. "I thought she was an actress?"

Luke overheard her and said, "Oh, she was, but I think the car incident at Balboa Studio scared her, so she moved over here to start writing. They've already produced two of her scripts. It's very exciting stuff."

Oscar waved at them to follow. Billie and Jesse were silent as they looked around at the very busy area. People in different types of dress ran past them. Oscar called out to one of the women. "You're late!"

"Sorry, boss," she said, trying to pin up her hair as she ran.

"Do you make the movies here?" Jesse asked.

"Some of them," Oscar replied. "The serials require things like trains, cars, horses, so they have to go out on location." He stopped them in front of a small building, "I'll drop you off here." The sign on the door said, "Writer's room".

"Well, what're you waiting for?" Billie asked her brother.

Jesse shook himself and said, "Nothing." He walked up to the door, knocked, and waited. The door was pulled open by a short, round man, his hair standing on end.

"WHAT?" he demanded.

"I'm, umm, I'm looking for Merle."

The man called over his shoulder. "Merle, you got someone here. Don't stay out too long."

"Who is it, Ed?" her voice floated over. "Is it Jean? She's early."

Ed scratched his head. "Don't look like Jean to me." He eyed Jesse suspiciously, then Billie.

"I'll be right out," she called back. She carried her pencil and pad and was jotting notes when she stepped out on the porch.

"Get back in here as soon as you can," Ed said, returning to the room.

"I will," Merle promised and looked up to see who was visiting her. Her pencil and paper fell to the ground. "Wha... Jesse! What... What... are you doing here?"

"Your hair's back to blonde," he noticed.

"Yeah," she said, touching it. "I feel more like me now."

"I like it." He stuck his hands in his pockets and asked, "Can we talk?" Billie picked up her pencil and pad and handed it to her.

Merle took the items back absently and smiled at the woman. "Hi, Billie." A loud voice called from behind her; she looked back and then at them. "I have to work; we're on a deadline."

"I get that. Can we meet tonight? I think we need to talk." Jesse looked pointedly at her belly. She bit her lip and forced herself not to put her hands over her bump.

"Please," he pleaded.

"Okay," she said. "We can do that."

"Where?"

"Jean and I have a home; you can come there." She wrote quickly on the pad. She tore it out and handed it to him. "I'll be there after five."

He took the paper and read it. "Okay, we'll see you then." He and Billie started to walk away.

"Wait," Merle called after them. "Do you have someplace to stay?"

"Not yet, we just go into town."

And you came here first, she thought. She smiled and said, "A friend of ours has a boarding house." She jotted down the address and walked over to them. "This is her address. She helped me and Jean out when we first got here." Jesse and Billie walked off toward the gate.

A few hours later, Jean walked quickly from the other direction and ran up the stairs. Jean knocked on the door and it opened quickly.

"*What!*"

Jean grinned. Ed was in the same mood as always. "Is Merle ready?"

"Yeah, yeah, come in. Merle, another visitor."

Another visitor? Jean thought with a frown. Merle stood and began packing her things into a large tote. "Need any help?" Jean asked.

"No, I'm good," she answered and pulled the bag straps onto

her shoulder. "Ed, I'll work on that outline tonight. I have some ideas for that stunt."

"Just don't use that one we got in the mail," Ed replied gruffly.

"Which stunt?" Jean asked. Hearing about new stunts always interested her.

"It involved a horse jumping over a train," Merle said.

"Hmm, that sounds..." Jean started.

"Don't even think about it," her sister admonished. "It's way too dangerous, even for you. And especially the horses."

"True, true." Jean decided she would ask Ed to show her the letter later.

"Be here early tomorrow," Ed told Merle.

"Aren't I always?" she teased.

"Oh," he said absently, "there was an envelope dropped off for you." He pulled it out of his desk. She put it in her bag without looking at it.

"I let Patrick take the bike," Jean said as they walked to the parking lot.

"Good. I need to talk to you and a car is better."

"Long day?" Jean asked.

"You could say that." At the car, they put their bags into the back and Merle sat in the driver's seat while Jean cranked the car. Once it caught, Merle moved across to the passenger seat. She sat back with her eyes closed. "Not too fast, please," she said.

"Not too fast, right," confirmed Jean. She liked speed and enjoyed how the wind felt in her hair. But she looked at her sister. "Did you work too much today? Maybe you should go part-time?"

"No, no. It isn't that." Merle opened her eyes and sat up. "Jean, could you pull over for a second?"

"Are you going to be sick?"

"No, I just need you to pull over, please."

Traffic wasn't too bad, so Jean moved to the side of the road and stopped. "I think we're okay here. What's up? Did something happen at work?"

"Not like you think," Merle muttered.

"What is it then?"

"Jesse showed up today." Jean sucked in some air and choked. "Breathe," Merle said, popping her sister on the back.

Jean gasped. "I'm okay. What did he want?"

"I don't know."

"How did he know you were here?"

"Probably from that article that came out."

"I wonder who else has seen it," Jean pondered.

Merle groaned. "I don't want to think about that."

"So, did you talk about anything?"

"The baby, you mean?"

"Yes."

"I was at work; I just didn't have the time or energy to deal with them. So, I asked them to come by the house tonight."

"Them?"

"Billie was with him."

"She was nice enough."

"She was."

"So, they could be at the house now?"

"They might be. I also gave them the address to the boarding house. They needed a place to stay."

"Are you okay with going straight home?" *Is this going to set Merle off in a spiral and make her want to run away again?* Jean thought.

"Let's go home," Merle said firmly.

"I guess this meeting needs to happen, get everything out in the open," Jean said as she got the car moving again. After a few minutes, she said, "I never asked. Why did you pick Jesse to be the fake husband?"

"I don't know. His was the first name that came to me."

She reached over to take Merle's hand. "You know I'm here for you, no matter what."

Merle squeezed her hand. "I know, and I appreciate that." They reached the house and Merle said, relief evident in her voice, "They're not here."

"What time did you tell them?"

"After five."

"It's just that now," Jean said and turned off the car. "Let's go in." They got out and Jean grabbed their bags. "I have them. Let's go in. You need something to eat."

"I could use something," Merle admitted, rubbing her stomach. They went into the house and Merle smiled; the house always made her feel settled. This was theirs, bought and paid for. Many weekends had been spent fixing up the outside to match the inside.

"Go sit and I'll start dinner."

"You're sure?" Merle asked, eyeing the couch.

"Yes, go lie down. I'll call you when it's ready."

"Just something simple, please."

"There's ham and potatoes left over from yesterday."

"And a salad?"

"I think we can manage that."

Jean got to work and, when dinner was ready, she went into the living room to get Merle. Her sister was fast asleep. Jean hated to wake her, but she didn't need to go without a meal. "Merle, wake up. Dinner's ready."

She yawned and stretched. "Already?"

"Yes. Come on now." Jean gave her a hand up and they walked into the dining room.

"It smells good." Merle was already picking up her fork and eating. They finished quickly and were moving the plates to the kitchen when a knock sounded at the door. Merle glanced at it and then at Jean.

"We have to answer it," Jean said.

"I guess I did invite them."

"You did. Want me to get it?"

"Please. "

Jean squeezed her arm and went to the door. She pulled it open and saw Jesse and Billie there.

"Hello, Jean," Jesse said awkwardly.

"Hello," she said, her voice dry.

"Merle here?"

"Maybe."

"Jean, stop teasing the man and let them in," Merle called. Jean stepped back and let them into the house.

Jesse looked around. "Nice place."

"We were able to get it from someone who had to move out quickly," Merle told him.

"That sounds familiar." He grinned.

"It does, doesn't it?" She grinned back.

"You both seemed to land on your feet," observed Billie.

"We were lucky," Jean admitted.

Jesse kept staring at Merle.

Finally, Billie said, "Jesse, why don't you and Merle go out on the porch?"

"Yes," said Jean. "It's nice tonight."

Merle looked a little panicked and her hand shook. She shoved it into her dress pocket.

"Merle, would you like to go outside?" Jesse asked.

She took a deep breath. "I think I would." He opened the door, and she followed him out.

Billie looked at Jean. "Got anything strong to drink?"

Jean glanced toward the door. "You know, I think I do. Come into the kitchen." Billie followed her.

* * *

"Why don't we sit?" Jesse asked. Merle sat on the porch swing, and he sat next to her. "Am I going to be a father, Merle?" She started to cry. "No, no, don't do that. I didn't mean to make you cry." He pulled her to him.

She pushed back and looked at him. "Jesse, I'm not sure

whose baby this is. There was another person I was involved with in fast succession. And I just can't be sure." She could feel his chest shaking and sat back, indignant. "Are you laughing at me?"

"No, hun, we're just so similar. This has to be fate. I know that we just had that one night together and we hardly know each other, but I haven't stopped thinking of you since then." Jesse stood up, took a box out of this pocket, and sat next to her again. "Merle, I'd like you to marry me and give the baby a name."

* * *

"What do you think's happening out there?" Jean asked Billie.

"Well, knowing my brother, he's probably proposing. He got our mom's ring out this morning."

"Hmm, that could work," Jean said.

"Looks like we're going to be sisters," said Billie, holding up her glass.

Jean clinked her glass to Billie's and laughed. "Looks like."

* * *

"Marry you?" Merle asked. She stood and walked over to look off the front porch.

"Well, yeah, you already call yourself by my name so why not?" he reasoned.

"Why not indeed?" she asked and crossed her arms, still not turning to him.

He slapped his leg. "I got this all wrong, didn't I?" She didn't comment; she waited to see what he'd say. "Merle, I didn't come here just because of the baby."

She turned around. "You didn't?"

"No, I had plans to find you as soon as I got established."

She bit her lip. "I'd hoped that was the case."

"I haven't been with anyone else. I waited for you," he admitted.

She started to cry again and turned to him. "So did I."

"Is this going to be a permanent thing, all these waterworks?" he asked, handing her his handkerchief.

"I think it's the baby," she said, patting her eyes. She held out her left hand to him.

"Does this mean what I think it does?"

"Ring, please," she teased.

He quickly opened the box and took out the ring. He placed it on her finger before she could change her mind.

"It's lovely," she said, looking at it.

"It was my mother's."

"Thank you, that means a lot to me."

"Will you say it?"

She smiled. "Yes, Jesse, I will marry you."

"Whoo-hoo!" he yelled, grabbing her and swinging her around.

"Stop!" she said desperately.

"Why?" he asked as he put her down. Her face had a green tinge. He turned her quickly and bent her over the edge of the porch. She stayed that way for a long moment.

"I think I'm okay."

"I guess I need to be gentler," he said, rubbing her back.

"For a little while longer. The morning sickness is really an all-day thing."

"Are you able to work? Do you want to stay home?"

"No, I love working. And writing every day is wonderful."

They walked back to the seat. "When?" he asked.

"When?" she asked, laying her head on his shoulder.

"Yes, when can we be married?"

"Hmm. Well, I guess we do need to get that taken care of."

"We do," he said and put his hand on her belly.

Merle bit her lip. "Jesse, you don't think this is too fast?"

He tightened his hold on her. "No, I think we're just at the right speed."

"Then maybe we wait a week, get the license, and find a nice quiet place to get married."

"That sounds like a plan."

* * *

Inside, Jean opened the envelope that was sticking out of Merle's bag. She had a glass of water in one hand and the envelope in the other. Her face drained of color and the glass fell to the floor with a crash.

"Goodness, nerves getting to you?" Billie said. "I think they'll be fine."

"It isn't that," Jean said.

"What is it?" Jean didn't say anything as she passed the letter over to Billie. Billie read through it quickly. "I don't understand. What does this mean?"

"It means that the marriage better happen and soon!" She grabbed the papers and ran out onto the porch. Jesse and Merle were kissing. "I hate to break things up..." Jean started.

Merle held out her hand to show her the ring. "We're getting married."

"Good, we should find somewhere to make that happen tonight."

"We were thinking," Merle said tentatively, "about the weekend or next weekend."

"No, it has to be tonight."

"Why the rush?" asked Jesse.

"Jesse, you better listen to her," Billie said from the doorway.

"Merle, you need to read this." Jean thrust the papers at the couple.

Merle frowned and started to read, Jesse studying over her shoulder. "What does this mean? They want my baby?" Merle put her hand protectively over her belly. "But it's not born yet."

"I think they want the baby after it's born," Jesse said. He kept reading. "This is threatening to expose your lascivious behavior and declare you an unfit mother."

"Why? Why would they do that?" Merle asked.

"Their son is dead, and I guess they think this will replace him," Jean reasoned.

Jesse folded the paper. "Jean's right. We need to be married tonight. Any baby born in the marriage will be mine."

Merle put her head on his shoulders; her hands were shaking.

"Do you know anyone who could help with a hurried marriage?" Billie asked.

Jean looked at Merle. "Dorothy," they said at the same time.

"How do we contact this person?" Jesse asked.

"That's easier than you think. Wait here," Jean said and ran down the stairs. She raced to Dorothy's house and knocked on the door. Sammy answered. "Hey, Jean, what's up?"

"Dorothy here?"

"Sure, come on in. Ma, Jean needs you." They moved inside and met Dorothy in the living room.

"What's wrong," she asked. "Is it the baby?"

"No, well, kind of."

They looked at her. "What do you mean, kind of?" Dorothy asked, worried.

"We have a situation where Merle needs to get married as soon as possible. Tonight, if we can manage it."

"Why the rush?"

"And do you have a husband for her, or do we need to supply that also?" Sammy asked drolly.

"No, we have one of those. Jesse Harrison."

"You mean there's a real man with that name?" Dorothy was surprised.

"There is. Merle chose someone she knew."

"And now he's here? This is a little fast, isn't it?"

"It is, but there are complications I can't get into right now. Do you have someone we can use?"

Dorothy looked at Sammy and back to Jean. "I do, just a minute," she said and walked to the telephone.

"Who's she calling?"

"My father," Sammy said simply.

"Your father? I thought he wasn't in the picture," Jean said, trying to remember past conversations with the mother and daughter.

"My parents couldn't get along, but things are better now. He's a judge. And he can marry Merle and Jesse quickly."

They were silent as they listened to Dorothy's side of the phone call. "We have an issue... Personal... some friends need to be married... No, it's not Sammy... No, it needs to be tonight... I can't help I'm interfering with your damn dinner party... We can be there in an hour." She looked over at Jean for confirmation. Jean nodded. "Yes, will meet you there... Yes, goodbye. And, Gary, thank you." She hung up the phone and looked at Jean. "He's willing. Go get Merle and Jesse organized. We'll need to leave in the next fifteen minutes."

"Where're we going?"

"We're going to gate crash a party at my ex-husband's."

"We'll meet you back over here." Jean ran back to where everyone waited for her on the porch. "We need to get organized, quick. We have someone who will marry you tonight, but we have to go now."

Billie clapped her hands. "This is going to be good."

Merle looked at Jesse. "It's a bit of a rush."

"Yes, but this is what we want," he said and squeezed the hand he held.

"It is," she said. She looked over at Jean. "Can I take a minute to change?"

She checked her watch. "Yes, but hurry."

Merle started in and looked at Jean. "Can you change, too?"

"Really?" She and Merle looked down at her pants. "Fine," she said and followed her in.

Billie walked over and straightened her brother's tie. "Big day," she commented.

"The biggest," he said. "I'm getting married."

"And a father-to-be."

"I know. I love her, Billie."

"This isn't just an attraction?"

"No, I don't think it was ever just that."

The sisters came back out in dresses with hair brushed and makeup touched up. "Okay, let's go," Jean said. They headed to Merle's car.

"There'd be enough room to have everyone in the same car," Merle brought up.

Suddenly, headlights brightened the yard as a motorcycle pulled up. Merle grabbed Jesse. "It can't be them already."

He frowned. "If it is, I'll handle it." He started walking toward the light when a voice rang out.

"Hey, where are you going? I thought we were hanging out tonight."

"Patrick!" Jean said.

"Oops, got distracted, did you?" Merle asked.

"Yeah, and I almost left again without telling him," Jean muttered. "Give me a minute." A honking from down the street reminded her that people were waiting for them. She ran over to him and said, "Patrick, would you like to go to a wedding?"

"Depends," he teased, "is it ours?"

She grinned. "Not yet."

"I'd love to go."

She called over to her sister. "Follow Dorothy and we'll follow you."

"Who's going to be in the sidecar?" Patrick asked.

She grinned. "I will." The other cars started out and Jean and Patrick fell in line.

"So, who's getting married?"

"Merle and Jesse."

"Wasn't she already married to someone named Jesse?"

"Well, to stave off unwanted attention from her pregnancy, we thought the best way to protect Merle was to tell everyone she was already married," she explained.

"Makes sense." In New York, he saw all kinds of couples and boundary pushing, but outside of New York, there were still people who would've judged her for having a baby outside of wedlock.

"You never asked about it," Jean observed.

"Not my business."

They drove for about thirty minutes and finally pulled up to a large stone home surrounded by cars. "This a party?" he asked.

"Yeah, the man who lives here is a judge and he's going to work us in." He nodded but didn't ask any further questions. Everyone walked to the house and knocked on the door.

It was a motley crew that the butler found standing there. "Yes?" he asked. These people were clearly not invited to the party.

Dorothy started to talk and was interrupted by a deep voice in the foyer. "Carson, send them to my study."

"Yes, sir." Carson turned back to them and saw the judge's daughter. "Miss Samantha, welcome. Follow me." They followed him through the foyer, past a well-dressed group in the room across from the study.

When the doors closed, a gentleman in a suit came over to them. "Dorothy," he said in a low, gravelly voice.

"Dad!" said Sammy and ran over to him.

He hugged her tightly. "Sammy how are you?"

"Good, I'll be here this weekend."

"I'm looking forward to it." He kept his arm on her shoulder and turned to the group. "Now, who do we have here?" He saw Patrick. "Patrick," he said, walking over to him. "I didn't know this was your wedding."

Patrick shook his hand. "No, sir, I'm just a witness today."

Jesse stepped forward and stuck out his hand. "It's my wedding, sir. I'm Jesse Harrison." They shook and he said, "This is my bride, Merle, and my sister, Billie, and my sister-in-law, Jean."

"Merle Cooper, it's nice to finally meet you. Sammy has told me all about you and Jean." The sisters greeted him. "I'm Judge Huntington, so why don't we get to it?"

Coats were removed. Jesse and Merle clasped their hands and stood in front of the judge. The witnesses stood on each side of the bride and groom. "Before we start," Huntington began, "I want to ask, is everyone here of their own free will?"

He's noticed the bump, thought Merle.

"Yes," Jesse said.

"I am," Merle said.

"Very well, that's all I needed," the judge said and started the ceremony. When he got to the part about the rings, Merle frowned. She didn't have one for Jesse.

"Ring? Wait, I got this," Jean said. She dug into her pocket and held the object up. It was a black metal ring from a piece of equipment. "It's been good luck for me."

"Thank you," Merle said. She took it and slipped it on Jesse's finger. He'd removed her engagement ring and slid it onto her finger again.

"This time, I want it to stay where it is."

"It will," she said softly.

"I now pronounce you man and wife. You may kiss the bride."

"And that should do it," Jean muttered, relieved.

"You're going to have to explain that," said Patrick in the same tone.

"Later," she murmured.

"Now, here's your license," Huntington said. "Sign here." The bride and groom moved to the desk and signed. "Now, the witnesses." They moved to the desk to sign.

With the paperwork completed, the judge said, "I'll have this processed in the morning."

"Thank you," Merle said.

"You know, I wanted to meet you after I saw your movies. You were excellent in those."

She turned red. "You liked them?" she asked.

"I did and I hope to see more from you."

"Maybe at a later date. I'm writing movies now."

"I look forward to it."

"Thank you, sir." Jesse shook the judge's hand.

"Yeah, thanks, Dad." Sammy moved to his side and kissed him.

Dorothy nodded. "All right, people, we need to let the man get back to his party."

The group followed her direction and went to the foyer and outside to the waiting cars. The judge came out carrying a box. "Dorothy!"

Dorothy walked back up and took the box from him.

"You'll let me know what this was all about?" Huntington asked her.

"I will as soon as I find out myself." She kissed his cheek and walked out of the door.

"Everyone meet at our house?" Jean called out.

"Yeah!" the group called back.

Jean got into the sidecar while Patrick drove the bike. He called out over the engine. "You know, for a minute there, I thought you were leaving again."

"I wouldn't do that, Patrick. I told you, I want to be with you."

"I guess we need more time to trust each other." She nodded. "Can you tell me why Merle and Jesse had to get married tonight? Something's happened," he guessed.

"Yeah. Something came up with the Strathmores."

He frowned. "The Strathmores?"

"Yeah. They found us."

"Why would they try to find you? They asked for the investigation to be dropped."

"They want Merle's baby."

"The baby? Oh, I get it. They think it's their grandchild."

"Yeah, and the only way to protect Merle was for her to marry Jesse."

"But why Jesse?"

"Well, that's a longer story. On the way here, I told you we sold the car to get the money for our new life."

"Go on."

"Well, Merle sold the car to Jesse."

"And?"

"And during the negotiation, they got to know each other."

"Enough so that she thinks it might be his?" he guessed.

"You got it. Merle and Jesse seem to have found something in each other."

"Hmm. Where will they live?"

She jumped at that question. "I hadn't thought of that," she admitted. "I guess with me."

"It'll be a little crowded."

"It'll be fine." *At least I hope so*, she thought.

They pulled in behind Jesse's car. They held hands and followed the others inside.

"Too bad we don't have cake," Merle said, disappointed.

"Hey, Ma," called Sammy, "they want cake."

"Well then, I think I have something they'll like," Dorothy said, opening the box she'd carried into the house. It was a cake!

"It's from Dad," Sammy explained. "He thought you might like this to celebrate."

"That was very nice of him," Merle said, starting to cry.

"Jeez, here we go again." Jesse handed over his handkerchief with a smile. "You might as well keep it."

"Thank you."

"We need to lift a glass and toast the couple," Billie said. They lifted their glasses with a cheer and drank. Introductions were made to those who didn't know each other and the cake was cut.

"I hate to break things up," said Billie, "but where's everyone staying tonight?"

LIGHTS, CAMERA, MURDER!!!

Merle's face reddened. "I hadn't thought of that."

"Me either," said Jesse. "I should probably give you some time to get to know me. Billie and I can stay at the boarding house."

"That's not a good idea," Jean said.

"I agree," said Patrick. "Can I see those papers?" He read through them quickly. "They're going to be watching you, and probably already are."

"You think so?" Merle asked. Jean went to look out the front window.

"I do. And I think, Jesse, you should stay here. You need the appearance of a real marriage."

Jean nodded. "He's right. This is now about protecting that baby and Merle."

"So, I stay here," Jesse said.

"I'd like that," Merle said softly, looking him in the eyes.

"Patrick, I think I see something," said Jean, looking out the window.

"Back away from the window and pretend you're having a good time. I'll go out and around to the front."

"I'll come with you," Jesse volunteered.

"Let's go. Follow me." The two men exited.

"What do we do?" Merle asked.

"We continue to act like we're having fun," said Dorothy. They did that, and the front door suddenly swung open with a bang. The two men came in, dragging a young man with them.

Merle was the first to recognize him. "Stewie? What're you doing here?"

"Hey, Merle." Stuart raised his hand in greeting.

"Merle, who is this?" Jesse asked, shaking the boy.

"Jesse, this is Stuart, the Strathmore's son."

Patrick took over. "What're you doing here?"

Stuart turned his head toward Patrick. "Hey, I know you. You're one of the officer's who came to the house after Bob and Catherine died."

"That's right. Why are you here skulking in the bushes?"

"I wasn't skulking. I just wanted to make sure I was in the right place." He looked at Merle. "Mom and Dad are here, and they want your baby."

"We know, Stewie," she said quietly. She held out her hand to Jesse. He dropped the boy's arm and moved to her side. "We're married. The baby is Jesse's."

Stuart stared at her for a few minutes and then he started to laugh until it bent him over. "You beat them! Finally!" Everyone frowned at him. "Whoa, whoa, I'm on your side. Merle was nice to me. We were friends."

"Now that you know," Merle said, "what're you going to do?"

"I think I'll let it remain a surprise. I should get back. Can anyone give me a ride to the hotel?"

Patrick sighed. "Jean, can I borrow your motorcycle?"

"Sure, pick me up in the morning."

He turned to Stuart. "Go outside and wait for me by the cycle."

"The one with the sidecar? Cool!" Stuart left the house at a run, the door slamming behind him.

"What're you looking at, Sammy?" Dorothy asked her daughter.

"Me? Just a cute guy."

"Well, stop it."

"It's time for me to head out. I'll stay at the boarding house," Billie volunteered. "That will give you some space here. Jesse, I'll need you in the morning. We need to find some space to set up the business."

"What kind of business?" Patrick asked suspiciously. He didn't want Jean and Merle involved in anything illegal.

Jesse saw the look in Patrick's eyes and laughed. "Easy there, copper. We buy, repair, and sell cars. Legally."

Merle looked surprised. She hadn't asked for details given her prior life.

Billie explained. "We were able to use the profits from selling

Merle's car to kickstart our business. We have several locations across the Midwest. We're hoping to start another here."

Jesse said in Merle's ear, "We won't cause any trouble."

"Neither will I," she promised. They'd both decided to move forward and leave their past behind.

Patrick looked out the window to Stuart and said abruptly, "I have an update on the incident today."

"With all of the excitement," Jean said, "I forgot. Was it Joe?" She hoped not; she counted on him daily in her job.

"Incidents?" Jesse asked. "Has someone been hurting you, Jean?"

"Some of my stunts have been interfered with and Patrick is investigating them. He interviewed the stunt coordinator today."

"We released Joe," Patrick explained. "He had the means and the opportunity but no motive."

"What about the murder?" asked Merle. "Do you think it's related to the stunt incidents?"

"Murder! Who was murdered?" Jesse demanded.

"One of the directors was shot," Merle told him.

"Who shot him?" Billie asked.

"Well," Jean spoke up, "initially, they thought it was me."

"Not me," Patrick said.

"No," she said softly, "you didn't."

"It appears we have two goals here: one, keep Jean safe and two, keep Merle and her baby safe," said Patrick.

"My baby also," Jesse said.

"Yes, your baby," said Merle, taking his hand in hers.

"You know, we're good with these types of threats," Billie said, referencing the paper. Their business activities had led them to work with people who had questionable backgrounds.

Jesse said, "She's right. Let us handle this part."

Patrick looked at Merle. "If Merle is okay with that."

"I am," said Merle. "I can give you all the information I have on them."

"I do have an idea that might help," said Patrick. "I'll let you know."

"Thank you," Jesse told him. "People like this think they can get what they want because they have money."

"There's something you don't know," Patrick said. "They're scared of the publicity. They don't want how their son and daughter-in-law died made public."

"Hmm, that might be important later," said Jesse.

"So, that just leaves the saboteur and the murder," Jean brought up.

"Yes, we assume they're related because of the connection with you."

"How's Jean connected to the murder?" asked Jesse.

"She's the one who found the body," Merle said.

"Merle doesn't know?" Patrick asked Jean in a low voice.

"No, she doesn't," she said shortly. Jean looked at Merle. "Merle, Zach Smith attacked me in his car a few months ago and Robbie saved me from getting raped."

Merle stuttered, "You didn't tell me!"

"I wasn't hurt, and I didn't want to upset you."

"Upset? UPSET! You didn't want me to get upset? Well, now I'm upset." Merle stood and advanced on her sister.

"Merle, babe. She did what she thought was right," Jesse said, holding her back.

Merle took a deep breath and calmed down. "You're right. I'm sorry, Jean."

"That's okay."

"I'll have to do something special for Robbie," Merle said.

"You know," said Patrick, "there's someone else who's related to both sets of events."

"Patty," said Merle and Jean together. "Patty was living with the director."

"I don't see how that works, though," Dorothy said. "She got what she wanted initially with getting Jean the job, but she seemed to have been genuinely upset when Zach was killed."

"I still have things to go over," Patrick said. "In the meantime, everyone be careful."

Billie walked over to Merle and kissed her cheek. "Welcome to the family, Merle."

"Thank you," murmured Merle.

"Need your keys," Billie said to Jesse, holding out her hand.

"Oh yeah, here," he said, offering them to her. "We'll probably need to get a second car."

"Among other things. I'll meet you here in the morning."

Jesse rubbed his chin. "Why don't we meet at the studio? I'd like to go in with Merle in the morning."

"That works. I'll get your things and pay off the room."

"Do you have things for tonight?" Merle asked him.

He smiled. "Well, I didn't want to presume, but I did bring a few things."

"Just in case?" she teased.

"Yeah, just in case," he said softly. "Let me go out and get my bag." He kissed Merle and followed Billie out.

Patrick turned to Jean. "I'll be going also. I'll see you here tomorrow morning."

"I'll be here."

"Can you walk me out?" he asked.

"I can," she said and walked over to Merle. "Still mad at me?"

"No, I understand."

"This was a fast night. Are you okay?"

"I'm married," she said, sounding dazed.

"Yeah, and having a baby."

"I am."

"I'm going to walk Patrick out now."

Merle shook herself. "Oh sure. Patrick? Thanks for joining us."

"Thanks for inviting me. Congratulations, Merle."

"Thank you." She sat on the couch, staring at nothing.

"Will she be okay?" Patrick asked Jean.

She looked over at her sister. "I think she just got what she wanted all at once and I think she just needs to take it all in."

They walked out onto the porch. They could hear Billie and Jesse laughing at their car.

"I may have to get with Billie about a car," he commented. They walked toward the motorcycle. "Your house is going to be a little full."

"Just one more person and we have three bedrooms," she reasoned. "We've lived in one room before."

"Yes, but they're a family now."

"Yeah, that's something we'll have to think about." He kissed her and looked over at the cycle. Stuart was already in the sidecar. Patrick cranked the bike and got on. "See you in the morning," Jean told him.

* * *

Patrick dropped off Stuart and made his way back to the boarding house. He walked in and Hannah called, "You missed dinner. You can go make yourself a sandwich."

"Thanks, I think I will," said Patrick. The cake hadn't gone far, and he was hungry.

Hannah followed him and found Billie in the kitchen. "Where's your brother?" she asked.

"He's going to stay with his wife."

"His wife!" repeated Hannah.

"Yes. We've been away on business, and she'd moved. So, we took the rooms just in case we had trouble locating her."

"Does that mean you're moving out?" Hannah asked, calculating the room cost.

"No, not me, anyway. I'll pay for my brother's room. He probably won't be back."

"Who's he married to?" Hannah asked as Robbie walked into the room.

"Merle Cooper," Billie answered.

Hannah's hands shook for a moment. "You know Jean and Merle?" Robbie asked. "I drive for Merle occasionally." Patrick had his head stuck in the refrigerator and Robbie didn't see him. "Did Jean get married?" Robbie stuttered.

"No, she's talking about Merle," Patrick said as he revealed himself and carried the food to the table.

"Oh, it's you," Robbie said, dismayed.

"It's me."

"Ma, I have to go to bed, early morning."

"Wait," Patrick said. He walked over to the younger man. Robbie took a step back and hit the wall.

"What do you want?" he asked, squirming.

Patrick held out his hand. "I want to thank you for helping Jean get away from Zach Smith."

Robbie slowly reached out his hand and shook with Patrick. Robbie dropped his hand and scooted past him and out the door.

"He drives for the important directors," Hannah said. She waited a beat, then said, "I'm glad Merle worked it out."

"Worked out what?"

"Having a baby without help is the hardest thing in the world," she said. Billie nodded in agreement. "Oh well, I'm off to bed as well. The whole household gets up early. Breakfast is at seven sharp."

"Good night," called Patrick and Billie. The two made their sandwiches and ate. While they were cleaning up, Billie looked at Patrick.

"Should we worry about those two?"

"Jean doesn't think so. They're just trying to get by."

"What about that statement about raising a baby alone?"

"I think it was about her and Robbie," explained Patrick.

"Oh." Billie thought about the conversation as she walked upstairs to her room. She'd keep an eye out here just in case.

* * *

Merle and Jesse back at the house

When Jesse walked back inside, Jean stayed outside on the porch.

"Got my bag," he said, holding it up.

"Want me to show you... our room?" Merle asked.

"Our room," he murmured. "Yes, please."

They passed a closed door, and he asked, "What's that room?"

"It's storage currently, but it'll be the nursery." She laughed lightly. The nerves that had flooded her seemed to dissipate now they were alone. "This one is ours." She indicated to the left.

He ran his hands on the molding as they entered the room. "The details on the house are amazing."

"We were lucky to find it." He walked around the room, looking at the pictures and other knickknacks.

"So, do you want to get ready for bed?" she asked tentatively.

He could see the day's stress reflected on her face. "Merle, we don't have to have sex tonight."

She turned to him and smiled suddenly. "I thought that was a perk of marriage." She sauntered toward him and said, "I'd hoped what I heard was true."

"Well, if you feel that way," he murmured, lowering his face to hers for a long kiss.

She pushed back and said, "I'd like to clean up first."

"Me, too."

She retrieved her nightgown from the dresser. "I'll be back."

"I'll be here waiting my turn."

She hurried and returned to the room, then she laid on the bed and waited for him. When he returned, she held out her arms to him and he joined her on the bed.

Chapter Forty-Four

Later that night Jean heard something in the kitchen. She pulled herself up and checked the time. It was 2 am. She laid there but, when she heard another thump, she sighed and stood up. She walked into the kitchen and saw Jesse at the table. He'd dug out some leftover ham and bread.

He saw her at the doorway and said, "Sorry, did I wake you?"

"Yes, but that's fine. Hungry?"

"Yeah, in all of the excitement, I forgot to eat."

"It was rather exciting." She sat at the table and laid her head on her folded hands. "Jesse, will you be a good husband?" she asked.

He took the question seriously and replied, "I plan to do my best."

She asked the hard question. "Do you think the baby is yours?"

"The baby *is* mine," he said firmly. "There's no question."

That's exactly what she wanted to hear. "I guess we'll be roommates for a while then."

"Yeah, I don't want to move Merle from a place where she's comfortable. Anything we do will happen well after the baby is here."

"I'm glad. We have plenty of room and I want to be here to help Merle and the baby."

"Just let me know if I get in your way."

"Oh, I will." She pushed her chair back. "Back to bed, early morning stunt tomorrow."

"Thanks, Jean."

She yawned and waved as she made her way back to bed.

Chapter Forty-Five

P*atrick and Jean at the rail station*

"Who are we picking up?" Jean asked Patrick. The last two weeks had been relatively quiet. They weren't shooting the next serial until the next week.

"It's a surprise."

"For me?"

"Mmmm, more for Merle than you."

"Hmm." They pulled into the parking lot of the train station. Patrick had gotten a car from Billie and Jesse's business. It rattled a bit and would need some work, but Jesse said he'd help him with that. "You've mentioned your meeting with Captain Ackerman."

"We went over the suspects."

"We don't have many left," she reminded him.

"No, we don't. Joe's out as a suspect. Paul, Robbie, and Charlie were on jobs during your last two stunts. Patty's still a maybe."

"I don't see her climbing up on trains to cut my ropes," said Jean. "Is there anyone else?"

"Not at this time." *I still need to talk to that guard. He hasn't been around lately.*

"Do you think we should set a trap?"

"I don't want you to get hurt."

"I think Joe and I can work it out. Would you mind if I talked to him about it?"

"I don't mind, but keep me in the loop."

"Patrick!" They heard a female voice call. He got out of the car and waved to Lottie. She ran over to him with her bags.

"I've missed you so much, big brother!"

"I missed you, too," he said and hugged her tight.

Jean had gotten out of the car and approached them. Lottie grinned at him and turned to Jean. She held out her hand. "It's good to see you again. I've been enjoying your serial."

Jean shook her hand firmly. "I'm glad you're here. Patrick told me you were a surprise for Merle."

They released hands and Lottie said, "She's going up against a powerful family and we want to stop this from ever going to court."

"That's what we hope," Jean said.

They climbed into Patrick's car and waited for him to crank it. He walked back to the driver's seat, and they were on their way.

"Where am I staying?" Lottie asked.

"You'll like it. It'll be just like old times," he commented. When she looked at him in puzzlement, he laughed. "We're back in a boarding house."

"Then the food should be good," she commented and pulled out a notebook.

"You remind me of Aunt Emma when you do that," said Patrick.

"Not a bad person to take after." Jean looked between them but didn't ask any questions. "Do we have a copy of the marriage license?" she asked.

"We do. Jesse and Merle have it at the house," Jean told her.

"I'll take custody of it until we go to arbitration."

"Arbitration?"

"We'll meet with the Strathmores in the company of a judge."

"A judge?" Jean said faintly. "Do we have to go that far? Can't we just send them a copy of the marriage license, or have you written a letter?"

"I'm afraid that this has already been scheduled. The Strathmores using their money and connections to push things forward."

"How do you know?" Patrick asked.

"After you called me, I contacted Judge Huntington to find any information about this case."

"Sammy's dad," commented Patrick.

Jean nodded. "What do we need to do?"

"We show a solid marriage with Merle and Jesse. Are they living together?"

"They are, at our house," Jean confirmed. "Jesse moved in the night they got married."

"I'll need to meet them as soon as possible."

"They're at the house now."

"Good. Got anything to eat there? It was a long trip."

"I think we can find you something," Jean told her. "Thank you for coming all this way to help us."

"Patrick asked," Lottie said simply.

At the house, Lottie took a big bite of her sandwich and drank some beer. "The court will want to make sure that this is your baby," she said to Jesse.

"It is," he said firmly.

"The date on the license coincides with the letter received from the Strathmores," she observed.

"That's just a coincidence," he replied. "Merle and I agreed that I'd come here when I got my businesses organized. That's why she started using my name before the actual marriage."

"That's good," said Lottie. "That works." She put down her

papers, "This should be cut and dry. The baby will be legitimate and you're the father." They nodded; Merle gripped Jesse's hand.

"So, we go to court?" Merle asked, grasping Jesse's hand tighter.

"It's just in the judge's chamber for the arbitration, so there won't be an actual trial. Have you received any other type of communication from the Strathmores?"

Merle shook her head. "Do you expect something else?"

"I'm expecting them to make a monetary offer."

"You think they'll try to bribe her?"

"Oh, I know they will, and if it happens the way I think it will, it'll be before the arbitration. They have to know they don't have a winning case, but again, they'll try to use their money as an influence to get what they want. The arbitration's scheduled for next Wednesday, so let me know when you receive the next communication."

A few days later, after work, Jesse and Merle sat talking in the living room. Patrick and Lottie were with Jean in the kitchen, trying a German pastry recipe. "Are you sure it's supposed to be shaped like that?" Jean asked, holding up the misshapen treat.

"Doesn't look like one that Mama would make." Lottie smirked.

"Hey, give me a chance, I'm trying," said Patrick. "Besides, Mama's not here." Lottie stuck her tongue out at him.

"There's a delivery at the door," called Jesse.

"This might be it," Lottie said.

The three joined Merle in the living room. Jesse walked back in with a letter. He hadn't opened it. Lottie put out her hand.

"Let me see that." He handed it over. She opened it quickly and read through it. "They want to meet tomorrow."

"The day before the arbitration?" asked Merle.

"Is it money?" asked Jesse.

"Yes, what we were expecting," Lottie replied.

"They say no lawyers," Patrick said, reading through the paper.

"Yeah, that's not going to happen. I can guarantee that theirs will be present."

"What do we do?" Merle asked Lottie.

"We go. You two stay quiet and let me do all the talking."

They nodded.

Chapter Forty-Six

The day of the meeting, they arrived at the hotel arranged for them. It was grand and expensive, exactly as Lottie had expected. She went to the front desk, and they were directed to the Strathmore's room. Lottie was accompanied by Merle and Jesse. Jean had been upset at not being included, but Lottie had pointed out she was there to protect her sister and brother-in-law. Jesse knocked firmly on the door. The door opened and they saw Stuart standing there.

"Hey, Merle."

"Hi, Stewie," Merle said. She looked at Lottie. "This is their younger son. He used to come to the parties."

"I do miss them," Stuart said. "It's rather boring now."

"Bring them in!" roared Mr. Strathmore from inside the room.

"Oh, goody, Mr. Strathmore's here," muttered Merle.

"Come on in, and good luck," Stuart said as he grabbed his hat and coat.

"You're not staying?" she asked.

"Oh, no. I don't want to be involved in this. I thought I'd check out the movie business."

"Stewie, wait." She took out a pad and paper. "Check in with

Sammy Huntington in the costume department. She can show you around the studio that I work at."

"Thanks, Merle." He leaned over and kissed her cheek. "You were always a nice girl."

"What was that all about?" Jesse asked. "Should I be jealous?"

"Oh, he's a good kid. He just lacks guidance," said Merle. "An example of their parenting."

"Okay, folks, the talking stops here. Got it?" Lottie said.

"Yes," Jesse replied and kept hold of Merle's hand.

They went into the large room and found two men sitting at the table. They walked over to them and Lottie spoke, "Lottie Flannigan for Mr. and Mrs. Harrison."

"I thought we said no lawyers," Strathmore grumbled.

The man next to him stood. "Troy Shay, attorney for Mr. and Mrs. Strathmore."

"I thought you said no lawyers," Lottie said sarcastically, taking a seat across from them. She waved Jesse and Merle to the seats next to her.

"Well, we decided it might be a good idea to have a cool head in the room," Shay replied.

"My thoughts exactly," Lottie said. "Mr. Shay..." she began.

"Troy, please," he interrupted.

"Then Lottie, please."

Shay inclined his head in agreement. "We asked to meet before the arbitration to offer your clients an incentive to turn over custody of the baby after it's born."

Jesse's arm jerked. Merle gripped it and stared at Mr. Strathmore.

Lottie ignored the response and asked, "What type of compensation are you considering?"

Troy pushed a paper toward her, and she picked it up to review. It was a long few moments, and then Lottie ripped the paper into many pieces. "That's what we think of your offer to buy my client's child."

"What about a counteroffer?" Troy offered.

Strathmore ignored his lawyer and pointed at Merle. "You! I want you to talk. I dealt with you before. You're nothing but trash and you're all about the money. How much will it take to get my grandchild?"

Jesse's arm tightened; Merle glanced over at Lottie. She nodded.

"You're right, Mr. Strathmore, that's who I used to be. I'm no longer that person and this baby belongs to me and my husband. No amount of money will make me hand over this baby to you."

Strathmore turned purple and started to swing wildly at Merle. Troy grabbed him by the arm to hold him back. Jesse, Merle, and Lottie moved away from the table. "Mr. Strathmore! You can't do this! Stop or I'll leave."

Strathmore shook the lawyer off. "Bah, get out. You're useless anyway." He shook his hand at Merle and Jesse moved in front of her. "This isn't over."

Lottie shook her head. "No, sir, I believe it is."

"Lottie, Mr. and Mrs. Harrison, I'll accompany you out."

"Thank you, Troy."

Once they were in the elevator, Lottie asked, "Troy, did you just lose a client?"

He pulled at his tie. "Thankfully, yes. The man's a jackass and his wife is worse. I never wanted to broker the sale of a baby." Once the elevator got to the bottom floor, he said, "You might want this." He handed her an envelope. "I suggest you go to the arbitration; he'll lose." He left them there.

She put the envelope in her bag; she had an idea of what it was.

"Is that it? Is it over?" asked Jesse.

"Not quite. We follow his advice and go to the arbitration."

* * *

The next day, at the judge's chambers

. . .

"They're late," Jesse commented. The three were alone in the outer office.

"We wait," said Lottie.

A half-hour later, the judge's clerk opened the door and looked at them. "Please, come in," he said. The judge smiled broadly when he saw Lottie.

"Lottie, I'd hoped to see you in California when I saw Patrick working here."

"Hello, Judge Huntington. It's nice to see you also. I understand you know Mr. and Mrs. Harrison."

He turned to the couple. "I happen to have married them. How are you both?"

"We're good," Jesse said. He was a little surprised by this turn of events. Merle wiped a tear from her cheek.

"Now, now, none of that, my dear!" the judge said and pulled out his handkerchief for her. She took it and sniffed. "I have news for you to make those tears dry up."

"You do?"

"The case isn't going forward. It should never have reached this stage in the first place. That baby will be born as part of a legal marriage and belongs to both of you. They have no claim."

Merle cried harder and leaned on Jesse. "It's the baby," he said and had to wipe his tears away.

Lottie said, "Let's get you both home."

"Lottie, we'd love to have you and Patrick over for dinner," Huntington told her. "We can discuss future work together here and in New York."

"I'll call your office to confirm."

"I'm looking forward to it."

Later, they pulled up to the house. Lottie had driven them home. "Looks like everyone's waiting to hear," she said, pointing to the cars parked in the driveway. Lottie got out and said, "I'll leave you to talk. See you inside."

Merle sighed. "It's over. The baby's safe." Jesse worried about the threat that Strathmore had made on the way out. "Lottie said we have nothing to worry about."

"I'm happy that you and the baby are with me."

"I wouldn't be anywhere else."

They went inside and a cheer went up. It was a joyous evening. Lottie got into her cups and started telling stories about Patrick when he was little. Patrick had to escape and grabbed Jean's hand to take her out to the porch.

"Hey, I was getting some good information there," she complained good naturedly.

"I have more stories on her than she does on me," he assured her.

Jean dropped down on the swing. "I did want to talk to you. We're ready for the next stunt."

"Already?"

"The studio wants the serial to go into the can for a few months."

"What'll you do then?"

"Other movies or I might start helping coordinate stunts."

"I'll be there tomorrow."

* * *

Patrick at the studio the same day

Patrick walked up to the guard shack. "I'm looking for Luke Garmon. He mentioned he wanted to talk to me. I promised him a while back that I would follow up."

The guard shook his head. "His wife isn't doing great. He's with her."

"What happened? An accident?"

The man looked around and said in a low voice, "Someone beat her into a coma and raped her. She's been in the hospital for a few months."

"Which one?" Patrick asked. His gut was telling him this was related to his investigations.

"Southern California Hospital."

Patrick nodded and headed back to the parking lot. He cranked his car and drove to the hospital. Once inside, he went to the counter. "I'm looking for Luke Garmon."

"He's over there in the garden area," the nurse said, inclining her head to the left.

Patrick nodded. He went to the doors and out into the garden. The man sat with his head in his hands. Patrick went up to him. "Hi, Luke."

Luke looked up and saw who it was. "You're here!"

"I am." Patrick sat next to him. "You wanted to talk to me."

"I did," he said. "The hospital has taken up all of my time. They said I had to be here, that something was happening to Sandy."

"I'm sorry. Do you want me to leave?"

"No, I need to tell you why Sandy's here. It was Zach Smith; he attacked her and left her for dead."

"How do you know it was him?"

"I didn't at first, but every time he saw me, he smirked. I just knew."

Patrick had the man's history, but he needed more evidence. "Was there anything else?"

"Yes, he'd attacked Sammy Huntington a few months later. She made it out alive and identified him."

"Were there charges filed?"

"No, Patty Dove said Zach was with her and the cops didn't believe Sammy."

"Mr. Garmon, we need you to come back," called the nurse from the door.

"I need to go," he said, standing quickly.

"Luke, did you kill Zach Smith?"

"No, but I wish I would've," he said and left to follow the nurse.

Sammy, thought Patrick. He got in his car and headed to the studio. Once it was parked, he walked to the costumer's building. He knocked and Dorothy opened the door. She smiled at him.

"Patrick, come in. Sammy, Patrick's here."

Patrick didn't say anything. Sammy walked over and asked, "Is something wrong?"

"Is there anyone here else here besides the two of you?"

Dorothy looked at his sober demeanor and said, "No, but I'll make sure no one bothers us." She moved to the door and locked it. "Go ahead, say what you came to say."

"I need to confirm your locations on the day of Zach Smith's murder."

Sammy sucked in her breath and looked at her mom. Dorothy sat down heavily. "I'm guessing you know about what happened to Sammy." It wasn't a question.

"I do." Patrick turned toward Sammy. "I'm sorry that happened to you."

"Me, too," Sammy said, and she started to cry. "I'm not sorry the man is dead." Dorothy started to interrupt, but Sammy stopped her. "We didn't kill him; we were in the middle of a large movie fitting. More than fifty people can vouch for us."

Patrick sighed in relief. "I'm glad. The more I find out about that man, the more I wish I'd killed him myself."

They heard a banging at the door. The three jumped and Patrick said, "You can answer it."

Dorothy nodded and stood to answer it. She opened the door and Adam, one of the security guards, was there. "What is it?"

"It's Sandy Garmon. She woke up!"

"Oh, thank God," Dorothy exclaimed.

Patrick looked up and said a silent "Thank you."

Chapter Forty-Seven

Patrick and Billie at the boarding house the next morning

Paul looked at Patrick. "Can you give us an update on who murdered Zach Smith?"

"We're getting close," Patrick said.

Robbie's fork clattered onto his plate. "Ma, I can't do this anymore."

Hannah grabbed his hand. "Don't say anything."

"What can't you do anymore, Robbie?" Patrick asked.

"*Robbie!* Don't!" Hannah implored.

He pulled his hand out of hers. "Patrick, I have something I need to tell you."

"Okay, Robbie, we can do it here." He turned to Billie. "Can you act as a witness?"

"I can," she said.

"I'm coming with you," Hannah said, standing abruptly, her chair falling behind her.

"Of course." Patrick looked around and walked to the study, the others following behind.

The four stood silently. Patrick leaned back on the desk, the largest piece of furniture in the room. "You have something to tell me, Robbie?"

"I killed Zach Smith," he admitted.

Hannah shouted out, "He was... he was Robbie's father!"

"Were you married?" asked Patrick.

"No, he attacked me. Raped me. Robbie came later."

"That man, my *father*, was a horrible person. He hurt so many people," said Robbie.

"He held a gun on Robbie," Hannah blurted out.

Patrick looked at Robbie. "Is that true?"

He nodded. "He was angry that I'd interrupted him when tried to rape Jean. He said I had to pay."

"What did you do?"

"I ran at him. I didn't want to die. We both... We both had a hand on the gun, and... It went off. I thought I was dead, but then he fell to the ground."

Patrick stood up. "Where's the gun?"

"Here," Hannah said. She walked over to the bookshelf and pulled out a small book; behind it was the gun.

"It was there all the time," Patrick said.

Chapter Forty-Eight

Jean at the ranch set

The stunt was set up. Jean was to be shot, then she was to fall between the horses and get pulled away. She and Joe had checked the gun and bullets, taking the bullets out and checking each one before checking on the horses. The straps were double-checked so that she had a secure hold when she was between them. Joe called, "Break for twenty minutes, then we're back here for the shoot."

The workers scattered and the area emptied out. Joe and Jean walked off, talking about the stunt.

A figure watched them and stealthily approached the table where the gun was located. The person picked up the gun, emptied it, and replaced the bullets. It was laid carefully back in the same spot. Next, the figure moved to the horses, pulled a knife, and started to cut the supports for the saddles.

"You can stop there," a man's voice said. She turned to him with the knife still in her hand.

"Step away from the horses," Patrick said.

"Why, Patty?" Jean asked from behind him. She moved so she could be seen. "I thought we were friends."

"Why?" Patty asked, waving the knife in the air. "You killed Zach after I helped you get this job."

"What help did you provide?" Jean asked.

"I just made it possible for you to have the opportunity."

"How?" Jean demanded.

"Fine, I set up the stunts so that the stuntwomen couldn't do the job."

"You hurt them."

"Oh, grow up. Stunt people get hurt every day. It's their job," Patty said flippantly. Then her tone hardened. "Then you killed Zach. He was everything to me."

Patrick interrupted. "Patty, we found out what happened that morning, and Jean wasn't involved."

She frowned and the hand holding the knife sagged. "She wasn't? You're wrong. She had to be."

"Drop the knife, Patty."

Patty dropped the knife and fell face down on the ground, crying.

Chapter Forty-Nine

The dinner table that night: Jean, Patrick, and Merle

"All in one day," said Jean. "You caught a murderer and a saboteur. You're quite the detective, Officer Flannigan."

"Well, it wasn't just me. I had help. And poor Robbie, he was just ready to confess."

"What'll happen to him?" Merle asked.

"I asked Lottie to stay and represent him. She agreed that it would probably be ruled an accident. We were able to confirm the gun belonged to Zach. Patty identified it for us."

"Where is he now?" Robbie didn't do well away from Hannah.

"He's at the station. Lottie's down there, too. She should be able to get him released to Hannah."

"Good," Jean said. "I can testify for him about the car incident."

"Be sure to let Lottie know."

She nodded.

"What about Patty?" asked Merle. "What happens to her?"

"She did hurt five people and could've killed Jean. It'll be up to the courts," Patrick replied.

Chapter Fifty

That night at the house Jean and Patrick sat on the porch swing, her head on his chest and his arms around her.

"Billie and Jesse have set up their business near the studio. They already have contracts to provide cars."

"I'm glad. Merle needs stability," Patrick said. "What about you? Is your serial over now that Patty's been fired?"

"Funny you should say that. Mack asked me to stop by tomorrow."

"Any idea why?"

"Rumor is that I'm to take over the main role."

"Actress and stuntwoman?"

"Looks like."

"So, about that first date," he said.

She started to laugh and turned her head up to him. "Tomorrow night too soon?"

"Sounds like a plan," he said and lowered his head to hers for a

KIMBERLY MULLISN

long kiss.

Historical Notes for Lights, Camera, Murder!!!

The Strathmore case in the book was loosely based on the 1913 Edey Case. Jealously and betrayal can lead to violence. Henry Edey, a wealthy businessman, and his wife, Katherine, were involved in a scandalous love triangle with another couple. The arrangement, which was supposedly consensual, turned deadly when emotions ran high. Unfortunately, the outcome was similar to that of the Strathmores, Henry Edey shot is wife Katherine, then himself.

Whenever I mention my book involves a stuntwoman in 1913, California, I always get—Did you make this up? No, I loosely based the character of Jean on Helen Gibson and her work in "The Hazards of Helen". She was amazing and performed all of her stunts, including jumping from moving trains, climbing and hanging from moving vehicles, and high falls. Insurance was not available for those brave women.

Silent films-Were there scripts? Or did the actors just follow the director's instructions. The actors did not rely on visual clues but there is evidence that the scripts existed and were used during the entire production. Interestingly lip reading experiments have shown that the lines the actors spoke corresponded to the cards displayed during the film.

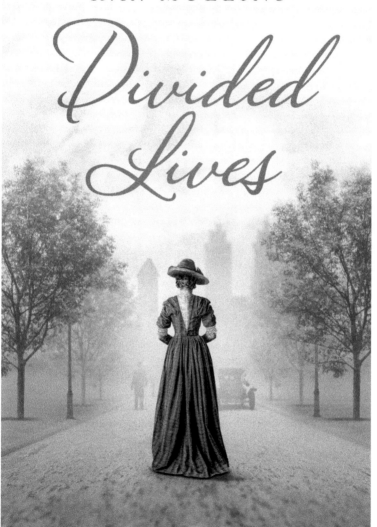

About the Author

Kimberly Mullins is the author of series of books titled "Notebook Mysteries", "1897 A Mark Sutherland Adventure", and a book called "Divided Lives". Her stories are based on historical events occurring in the 1880s to 1913. She holds a BS in Biology and a MBA in Business. She lives in Texas with her husband and son. When she is not writing she is working as a Process Safety Engineer at a large chemical company. You can connect with her on her website www.kimberlymullinsauthor.com.

Photo Credit: Blessings of Faith Photography

 x.com/kremullins_kim

Milton Keynes UK
Ingram Content Group UK Ltd.
UKHW022201111124
451073UK00017B/369/J